at Midnight

Lisa Marie Wilkinson

Medallion Press, Inc.
Printed in USA

DEDICATION:

This book is dedicated to family:

To John Wilkinson, who never failed to believe in what he could not see.

To Clyde Stock: I wish I had known you sooner and longer.

To my mom, Maxine: Thank you for being absolutely certain, always.

To my sister, Chris, for too many reasons to state here. You're the best.

To Dante: Thank you for the dragonflies.

Published 2009 by Medallion Press, Inc.

The MEDALLION PRESS LOGO
is a registered trademark of Medallion Press, Inc.

Typeset in Adobe Garamond Pro
Printed in the United States of America

ISBN:9781933836546

10 9 8 7 6 5 4 3 2 1
First Edition

ACKNOWLEDGMENTS:

To Jackie Flick and Felicia Case, for the nurturing friendship that has greatly enriched my life.

To fellow authors Stacey Kayne, Christine Wells, Michele Ann Young, Jenna Kernan, Ann Macela, Kimberly Killion, and Christie Craig: Thank you for your support and generosity.

Thank you, Helen A. Rosburg.

Chapter One

I am sane."

The sound of her own voice anchored her. It kept her from going mad. "I am eight and ten. I am called Rachael Penrose. I have been here nine days. My brother was called James—" She stifled a sob. "My brother *is* called James." Even the tinctures they fed her did not dull the pain of not knowing the fate of her baby brother.

She froze when she heard the scratch of claws on stone. A rat, attracted by crumbs of moldy bread, began a stealthy approach. She shared her meager rations with the rats because they displayed less interest in her when their bellies were full.

There had been no hearing and no formal declaration of insanity. An exchange of gold from one greedy hand to another had sealed her in this place. With no blanket, she shivered in the bitter cold. Beneath the thin shift she wore, faint and fresh bruises mottled her skin. Her stomach rumbled, the sound loud in the quiet of the small chamber.

She tensed as metal creaked. The door to her cell swung open. Freezing air rushed in, and she trembled as the strong scent of citrus cologne, a harbinger of her uncle, mingled with the foul, musty odor of the cell.

Victor Brightmore handed a gold coin to the guard accompanying him. "Her doctor and I require privacy." Victor lifted the hem of his cloak to prevent it from sweeping the floor of the filthy cell as he entered.

The attendant checked the chain securing her right leg to the straw-filled pallet upon which she lay. He tested the iron ring riveted around her neck and the circular iron waist bar holding her arms pinioned to her sides. She suppressed a shudder when his hands lingered over her breasts and followed the double link to its point of origin at the wall. Powerless against the intimacy, she gritted her teeth and stared at the gray stone ceiling above her. Apparently satisfied with the security of her restraints, the attendant withdrew, leaving Victor and the doctor alone with her.

Rachael remained silent while Victor angled the shaft of the candle he held until the flickering yellow light illuminated her face then leaned toward her, his blue-gray eyes glittering with malice. She looked into the face of pure evil. Tall, with burnished gold hair and even features, his pleasing exterior concealed his twisted nature. As he watched her, shadows played over the upward cast of his lips.

"You cling to life with such tenacity, Rachael."

He moved the flame along the length of her jaw inch by agonizing inch, stopping near her eye. The light from the candle was painfully bright, and her breath quickened as she struggled to hide her terror.

Oh, God, is he going to blind me? Gasping, she shrank from him, but the linkage of chain held fast. She was at the mercy of a man who had none. How she despised him!

"Victor!" The candle wobbled on its perch as his companion jerked it away from her face. "How would I account for burns on her body?"

"Her eyes mock me, Elliot." He peered down at her, scowling.

"She is feverish," Elliot said. "She is in the grip of the drug. We can speak freely."

"It appears I have need of your help once again, good doctor. Keeping my niece isolated is not the permanent solution I seek."

It did not bode well that he spoke so openly in front of her. With both her parents dead, once Victor succeeded in his plan to dispose of her, there would be no one left to protect James. Victor was desperate to inherit, but he was also crafty and cautious. He would not risk the hangman.

Elliot peered down at her. "Perhaps her food might

be—"

"The attendant told me she tests her food on the rats. Besides, we dare not risk poison now."

"I can keep her indefinitely," Elliot said. "Her whereabouts are unknown. No one here will believe anything she says."

"Tarry Morgan knows the truth." Victor searched within the folds of his cloak. His hand shook as he withdrew a letter. The edges of the parchment gaped where the wax seal had been broken.

Her heart sank at the sight, and she felt light-headed with despair.

"This letter details her discovery of my plan to poison James. She sent it to Morgan, one of the few allies she has left. She must have dashed it off before we brought her here." Victor glowered in Rachael's direction. "The fact that James must die before I will inherit is clear motive to anyone who would investigate."

"So, is Morgan dead?"

Rachael stopped breathing while she waited for Victor's response.

"No. His servants were rousing; I barely escaped with the letter. I was only able to wound him."

"Can you buy his silence?"

"Morgan cannot be bought." Victor crumpled the letter in his hand and began to pace the floor. "He is her loyal little lapdog. He remains silent because I have taken the proof and threatened Rachael's life. He has delusions he will rescue her, but he won't remain silent for long. We must dispose of them both."

The weight of her terror squeezed the air from Rachael's lungs. She would never forgive herself if she brought harm to her childhood friend.

"And what about her brother?"

"My nephew is sickly," Victor said. "His nanny has often commented on his frailty. With your help, I'll be rich. When I am rich, I will be generous."

"Monster!" Rachael sobbed. She screamed in outrage and struggled against the restraints. The tortured souls in the adjacent cells heard her and added their voices to hers. Hearing them, she fell silent. *Screams of torment are routine in this place. I'm just another Bess O' Bedlam. No help will come.*

Victor spun to face Elliot. "'Senseless,' you promised. 'Incoherent.' 'Her mind will be incapable of coping with her surroundings.'"

"Having her wits about her in this place is an added torment, not an advantage," Elliot said. "We will dose her with laudanum to keep her quiet, and she will be released into your custody."

"Released? You seem a likely candidate for a straitwaistcoat yourself."

"Victor," Elliot said patiently, "we must remove Rachael from Bedlam. Morgan is searching for her, and he has the resources to find her. I will have her transferred to Bethnal Green."

"She will be no less dangerous to me in a private asylum."

"She will never *reach* Bethnal Green," Elliot said. "You, of course, must appear distraught over your loss."

Rachael locked gazes with Victor, who nodded vigorously. His smile told her time was running out.

"Doctor, I believe you have arrangements to make on my behalf." He leaned down to Rachael and added, "While I joyously prepare to grieve."

Rachael lay still. The doctor had left the cell, but she sensed Victor's malevolent presence and steeled herself at the sound of his approach. Her nerve endings drew taut with anxiety.

Without warning, he seized her jaw in a brutal grip with one hand while, with the thumb and forefinger of the other, he pinched her nose, blocking the flow of air through her nostrils. When she opened her mouth to gasp for air, cold fluid slid over her tongue and down her throat. Choking on the bitter stuff, she swallowed convulsively.

"Good girl," Victor intoned, patting her head. "I didn't dilute the drug with water; you'll soon be *dead* to the world." His fingers gathered in the locks of her hair, smoothing them, and she jerked at his touch. Rachael opened her mouth and spit out what little of the fluid she had not managed to swallow, and the irons tinkled faintly.

"What a selfish chit you are, Rachael. I had no wish to harm Tarry, but your letter has left me with no choice. James's death must appear a common cot death. I cannot leave anyone alive who will claim otherwise."

Rachael looked up at him, willing him to see hatred on her face instead of fear. She would not give him the satisfaction of seeing she was afraid.

"Oh, still hoping for rescue?" he taunted. "Pining for the fresh air and blue skies of Cornwall, are we?" His eyes held no warmth, but his mouth formed a languid smile. "It will be easier if you accept your fate. A far worse one awaits you outside these walls. I've spread the rumor among your neighbors that you are the Customs informer who exposed their smuggling operations. You cannot go home."

Rachael's breathing slowed, and she blinked, fighting the effects of the drug. Her ears rang, and a foul taste coated her tongue. Had he deliberately given her enough of the drug to kill her? The thought brought suffocating terror as she struggled to focus on his words. If she died, she would fail James. Victor would win.

He inspected the ornate signet ring he wore. "The informer also caused the ship and goods of Sebastién Falconer, a French smuggler, to be seized by Customs. Meeting up with him in his present mood would result in a worse fate than even I could arrange for you."

"—James?" Her own voice sounded far away. Her

mouth felt as if it had been filled with wool.

"Have no fear; your brother will join you in heaven soon enough."

She mumbled, and when he leaned down to hear her words, she spat on him, the stream of saliva hitting him squarely in the face. Victor stepped back with an oath, shaking with rage.

"I will allow you that," Victor ground out as he mopped his face with a silk handkerchief. "I have the intense satisfaction of knowing you will soon be dead." He yelled and pounded on the cell door, and the face of an attendant immediately appeared. "Where is the usual turnkey?" Victor demanded.

"He's well into his cups by now," the young man replied in a bored tone. "I can turn a key same as any man."

When the attendant stepped back, Victor brushed past him. The staccato rap of boots filled her ears, then faded. The attendant had not moved to follow Victor out of the cell. *Why?* Rachael tensed, her heart pounding.

Groaning, she felt the urge to retch as her stomach suddenly rebelled against the strong drug. The need to purge the contents was bad enough; now she had the added worry of why the attendant had remained.

"Rachael Penrose?"

He stepped forward with a rusty ring of keys in his hand. Placing a lantern on the stone floor, he hastily unlocked the fetters holding her.

"I'm a friend of Tarry's," he said as he eased her into a sitting position. "My name is John Wyatt. We've not long before the rightful owner of these keys comes looking for them. I have a carriage waiting at Bedlam Gate."

The shackles fell away. Rachael winced, rubbing where the irons had chafed and bruised her flesh.

"Come, we must get you out of this place," John urged.

A wave of dizziness swept over Rachael, and she swayed. She could not lift her head without feeling as if she were under water. Shadows in the room shifted like specters; the floor seemed to be moving as well.

"You're strong, Miss Penrose, or you would not have survived this hellish place." Rachael felt his arm around her waist, felt him lift her to her feet.

The door to her narrow cell seemed miles away and Bedlam Gate even farther. But for the first time in days hope had eclipsed endless terror.

Warn Tarry. Save James.

The welcome lights of a coaching inn limned the black horizon. John urged the horses forward, desperate to elude the men following. He'd been a fool to believe he'd whisk Rachael through the gates of Bedlam without being observed by one of Brightmore's minions. The evidence of his folly took the form of the two riders who trailed them on the deserted road. Inside the carriage, Rachael huddled in a corner, unresponsive.

John was the stable master's son on the Morgan estate. He had witnessed Victor's attack on Tarry and the theft of the letter. Morgan had asked him to follow his assailant, hoping the man might lead him to Rachael. The thought of his own young wife or sister in Rachael's predicament was enough to spur him into action.

The inn was all that stood between them and an encounter with assassins. Located on the main road to London, the busy inn saw the bulk of travelers going to and from the city. At least a dozen carriages were being attended, even at such a late hour.

He guided the horses into the midst of a throng of conveyances, jumped to the ground, and opened the carriage door.

Rachael jolted awake with an inarticulate cry, wide, glassy eyes holding no hint of recognition. She shrank against the wall of the coach and looked around in confusion.

"What have I gotten myself into, Tarry?" John muttered.

At the mention of Tarry's name, Rachael stirred. "Tarry?"

Pity washed over John. Tarry had described Rachael as a striking beauty, but he might not recognize her now.

Starvation and maltreatment had etched the delicate bones of her face in sharp relief, her blue eyes were haunted, and her porcelain complexion had a bluish translucency. Dirt and clinging bits of straw matted her long, sun-gold tresses. Her petite form, slender to the point of thinness, gave her an ethereal appearance.

With a sinking heart, he realized he could not hide Rachael inside a public inn. Not in her condition. He doubted she could manage to walk even a short distance.

"Do you remember me?" he asked. "Tarry sent me."

She shivered and closed her eyes. "I had a bad dream."

"That's two of us," John mumbled as he doffed his cloak and spread it over her, gently tucking it under her chin.

When he leaned out the carriage window to view the roadway, he saw one of their pursuers dismount and enter the inn. The other man had already begun searching for the carriage among the vehicles assembled outside. John snatched the carriage curtains closed.

"They don't dare attack us while there are witnesses about," he said with a bravado he did not feel. The men had only to wait until he became desperate enough to risk the open highway, or until no witnesses remained in the yard.

John leaned across Rachael and swept the curtain on the opposite window aside to view the surrounding carriages, now fewer in number. One fine, lacquered specimen sat parallel to theirs, separated by a few yards.

He threw open the compartment door and hopped down. As he approached the handsome vehicle, he had a brief glimpse of the man and woman inside before the driver slammed the door shut. The woman adjusted the velvet draperies to afford them more privacy.

John removed his tricorne and rapped sharply on the polished surface of the door panel. He waited, and when there was no response, freed the latch and yanked open the door.

With stunning speed, he found himself spun around and pinned with his back against the coach door. He stood face-to-face with a tall, dark-haired stranger whose wide-set, deep green eyes seemed to miss nothing.

John twisted to look at the woman peering at him from inside the carriage. Her complexion was unnaturally white, with smears of carmine at her cheeks. She eyed him with amusement as he stared in fascination at her heavily drawn eyes and bold red mouth.

"Relax, luv, he's barely more than a lad," she said.

His assailant suddenly released him, and John stumbled. The man muttered something in French as he entered the carriage again, and the woman laughed. John thrust his hat against the door latch to prevent it from closing.

"Wait!"

The door exploded outward, and he backed away as

the man sprang from the coach, wearing an expression as menacing as the stiletto he held. He thrust the blade outward, forcing John to retreat.

John held up his hands to show he was unarmed and was dismayed to see that they shook. "I meant no offense. I am in need of assistance."

The man spoke to his companion, and she extended a gloved hand toward John. He smiled wanly and shook his head at the gold coin she offered. The man raised one black brow in inquiry, a look of annoyance crossing his face.

"My sister and I were attacked by highwaymen," John said. "Our coach was stolen. She is frail, and the experience has taxed her to her limit. We must get to Newbury. We have a friend there, Tarry Morgan."

"Hire a coach," the Frenchman snapped. His eyes narrowed when John appeared surprised he spoke English.

"I thought you might allow us to share yours."

"*Non.*" The response was quick and definite. "I'm on my way north."

"All the vehicles have been reserved. A coachman allowed my sister to rest in his empty carriage but only temporarily. She is in no condition to sit a horse." He cleared his throat to squelch the note of desperation in his voice. "I can pay you."

"How do you know I won't take your money and slit your throat?"

"You look trustworthy enough."

A loud cough covered the woman's amused laugh. The Frenchman pursed his lips as his eyes made a slow arc across the starlit sky.

"The lady offered me charity a moment ago, at your behest, I believe. That is not the action of a killer," John pointed out. "After our recent experience, I would feel safer if we were not forced to travel alone."

He could not think of a more suitable guardian for Rachael than the man standing before him. The foreigner had demonstrated wit, quick reflexes, and a charitable nature, no matter that the last quality had been grudgingly revealed.

The Frenchman whispered to his companion, his gaze still on John's face.

"I say 'tis a guileless face he has," the woman replied. "They'll not be sending one Englishman to do what the Court of the Exchequer could not."

"Anna!" The Frenchman spoke to her again, this time in a language John did not recognize. He slashed his finger across his throat in a brutal pantomime demanding silence.

"Right you are, luv," she said. "We haven't seen proof the girl exists yet." She chuckled when her refusal to speak in any tongue other than English brought a glare from the Frenchman.

"Let me see this sister of yours," the man demanded.

"Of course. Follow me."

Chapter Two

John opened the door and lifted Rachael out of the vehicle, taking care to conceal her filthy, ragged clothing and bruised limbs with his cloak. She stirred and moaned.

The Frenchman sheathed his dagger in a single fluid movement, his face inscrutable as he beheld the slender form in John's arms. A slight elevation of his brows and faint pursing of his lips were his only outward reactions.

John was anxious to conceal Rachael within the Frenchman's carriage and stepped forward impulsively to press Rachael into the man's arms. The Frenchman accepted the burden in a move that was nothing more than reflex. The muscle in his angular, shadowed jaw tightened.

"My sister, sir."

The Frenchman drew breath noisily between clenched white teeth. His eyes blazed, and for a moment, John feared the man would fling Rachael to the ground.

Instead, he crossed the distance to his own carriage, booted the gaping door open the rest of the way, and deposited her onto the seat opposite his companion, muttering to himself the entire time.

The Frenchman slammed the door panel shut and rejoined John. "I will take you only as far as Newbury," he said. "Make no mistake, if you cause me any trouble, I *will* leave you both along the roadside."

John nodded. "I must express my thanks to the coachman who allowed my sister to rest in his carriage." *If I put my own coach up for hire, they might follow the decoy.*

"Two minutes." The Frenchman braced a well-shod foot against the carriage board, folded his arms across his chest, and scanned the surrounding area while he waited.

John rounded the corner in search of the coach master and almost collided with one of Victor's men. The man shouted to his accomplice, quashing John's hope he had not been recognized, and he sprinted away from them, reckless with terror. He would have to act as the decoy. There was no other choice.

John climbed onto the coach box and urged the horses forward with a yell, attracting the Frenchman's attention. The man's relaxed posture became ramrod-stiff with suspicion as John gave every indication of preparing to flee.

"*Où allez-vous?*" the Frenchman shouted. "Where are you going?"

John pulled the coach alongside the Frenchman. "Take her to Newbury, and ask for Tarry Morgan. Tell him John Wyatt sent you. You will be paid." He shook the reins free of the Frenchman's attempt to snatch them and urged the team forward.

Sebastién Falconer entered the carriage, meeting Anna's bewildered look with a scowl. Drawing aside the velvet curtain, he glimpsed a rider falling out of the shadows in furious pursuit of the coach driven by Wyatt.

He dropped the curtain back into place before turning his attention to the girl asleep on the seat opposite him and sat brooding for a moment before calling the destination of Newbury to his driver.

"Something is wrong," he said. "I'd leave her with the innkeeper, but this is not the opportune time or place to call attention to myself. We will be paid to take her to Newbury."

Anna uttered an unladylike grunt. "That's a comfort, right, luv? With you bein' so *needy*." She leaned in his direction and slid her hand over the taut muscles of his forearm, but he shifted on the seat and brushed her

17

hand away.

The coach lurched forward, and Sebastién scrambled to catch the girl before she slid to the carriage floor. He moved to the opposite seat, braced himself against the sidewall of the coach, and with an inaudible oath drew the slumbering girl into his lap, enfolding her in his arms in an effort to hold her steady on the seat.

His nose wrinkled in distaste. She was filthy, and if he'd had a bottle of cologne in his possession, he would have doused her with it. He scowled and squirmed beneath the dead weight of the sleeping girl while his companion fanned the air and laughed at the pained expression on his face.

She shifted without awakening and nestled her head against his shoulder, half-burying her face in the soft fabric of his coat. Sebastién lifted his head and turned his face away.

"I should have left her with the innkeeper."

"Afraid you'll ruin your reputation?" Anna chided softly. "Pirate turned nursemaid?"

"Privateer," he amended curtly. "Pirates are criminals. A pirate would not be chivalrous, nor would he find himself in such a ridiculous situation."

He stared down at the blond head pressed into the crook of his shoulder. What had happened to the young man and his sister on the roadway? Why were they being followed? By whom? The girl was not merely traumatized and covered with road grime; she was either ill or drugged, or both. She bore no odor of alcohol.

Annoyed that he had been moved to pity, Sebastién reminded himself that a young female informant like the girl he now coddled in his lap had already cost him a great deal and might yet cost him his life. Rumor had it Rachael Penrose was somewhere in London, and he intended to flush the fox out of her hiding place. It was the reason he was on the coaching road to London in the middle of the night instead of crossing the channel to safety in France.

"How far is Newbury?" he asked.

"Why? Have you more urgent business than putting Land's End behind you?"

"*Oui*," he replied stiffly. "My ship and cargo are forfeit; my men are dead or jailed. I shall not leave England until I have had my revenge upon Rachael Penrose, the English bitch responsible."

"If her ladyship is wise, she'll have gone into hiding, Sebastién."

"No matter. She cannot hide from me." To remain in England was the same as thumbing his nose at the hangman, but finding the woman responsible for the misfortune of so many had become an obsession.

The girl moaned and huddled closer against him, one hand clutching his collar in a death grip. Distracted from his thoughts, he smoothed the hair back from her brow, and frowned when his fingers touched moist, heated skin. If his luck held true, she probably carried the plague.

He lowered his arm and leaned his head against the upholstery. "I should have left her with the innkeeper," he said again.

"Aye, you should be safely in France by now, instead of tending some English girl."

His hand closed over the girl's small, fragile hand and tugged, but he could not dislodge her grip from his collar.

"Ah, the English," Sebastién muttered under his breath. "Damn them all."

Tarry Morgan responded to the pounding on his front door by grabbing a lamp from the desktop in his study and dashing down the stairs. Startled servants scurried out of his path.

"John!" he exclaimed as he threw open the front door. "I've been expecting—"

He froze. It was not John Wyatt at his door, but a tall, scowling, dark-haired stranger. The stranger's gaze lingered on the blood-soaked bandage wound around Tarry's forearm. Tarry silently noted the expensive cut of his visitor's clothing and the handsome coach resting in the oval driveway.

"*Monsieur* Morgan?" the man inquired. His fingers

rested on the hilt of the dagger strapped to his thigh.

"So, Victor found a French assassin to do his killing for him."

The man's eyes narrowed to slits. "If I had made the journey to kill you, you would be dead." He indicated Tarry's bloodied arm with a slight inclination of his head. "If you wish to see more of your blood spilled, I can oblige."

Tarry winced as he shifted his injured arm and cradled it against his chest. "If bloodshed is not your intention . . . what, then?"

"To discharge my duty and be on my way."

"Your duty?"

"*Oui*," the Frenchman said. "A delivery." He turned and moved in the direction of the coach.

Curious and cautious, Tarry trailed the tall foreigner, hanging back when the man opened the door and leaned into the carriage. Tarry shouted in surprise when he glimpsed the occupant then ran forward and roughly elbowed the Frenchman aside.

Entering the coach, Tarry used his good arm to gently ease Rachael upright against the upholstered seat. Her head lolled, giving her the look of a broken doll. He pressed her cheek to his own, rocking her and smoothing his hand over her hair, struggling not to weep in the presence of the impassive stranger.

"So you do know her." The Frenchman nodded, his expression guarded. "*Bon*."

Tarry lifted his head and peered beyond Rachael into the dim interior of the coach, where he spied a woman whose face glowed eerily white with paint. The luminous effect of the cosmetic transformed her skin into a shining beacon that glowed with reflected light. When she bobbed her head to acknowledge him, the sight was unsettling.

"Where is John?" Tarry asked Rachael. "What became of John?"

Rachael closed her eyes and moaned, as if in pain. "Victor has James." Her teeth chattered.

"There is little we can do about that at the moment, sweetheart," he said. "What of Wyatt? Did John escape?"

His words propelled the Frenchman in his direction, and Tarry stole an uneasy glance at the man when the Frenchman's hand drifted toward his weapon.

"Did the girl's husband not precede us here?" the Frenchman asked.

Tarry avoided his gaze. What story had John told in his desperation to see Rachael to safety?

"Answer me!" the Frenchman demanded.

"Perhaps he was delayed," Tarry suggested.

His answer did not have the calming effect he had expected. The Frenchman drew himself to his considerable height, stance rigid, eyes gleaming with anger.

"The man claimed to be her *brother*, not her *husband*," he informed Tarry. "But you are agreeable to any tale, *n'est ce pas?*"

He drew his weapon in a flash of steel and motioned Tarry out of the vehicle then crooked his head at the carriage behind him.

"Shall I guess, *monsieur*? I would say the young *mademoiselle* has implicated me in her escape from Newgate."

"Newgate?" Tarry said, his own anger rising. "Your suggestion is offensive, sir."

"I have spent several hours closeted in my carriage with her. Do you think I am blind to her condition? She has the appearance of one who has been incarcerated."

"She is no criminal," Tarry insisted. "Her rescue has been brought about for a just cause. That is all I can tell you."

"Escape is a just cause to anyone awaiting the gallows."

"That is not the case." He would not trust this arrogant Frenchman any more than he would Victor Brightmore. "I regret you were involved, of course—"

"*Bien sûr!*" The Frenchman spat the words back at him. "You have only begun to regret it."

Sebastién hesitated, glaring at Tarry before he opened the carriage door and vaulted inside. Tarry had one more glimpse of Rachael before the compartment door swung shut with finality. She had appeared to be either blissfully asleep or unconscious.

Tarry ran to the carriage and tried to pry open the

door, but the Frenchman's knife at his throat stilled his hand. "What do you mean to do?" he cried in alarm, voice breaking.

"You have involved me in some sort of mischief. I already have difficulties of my own with the English authorities. I require some form of insurance. I will not share her punishment if you have made me party to a crime. I shall return her to you when you have told me the truth." He thought for a moment. "And have compensated me for my inconvenience."

"You mean to ransom her?" Tarry was shocked and indignant.

"*Non*," he said mildly. "If she is a criminal, I will hand her over to the authorities in exchange for leniency in my own case. If you can prove she is not, I require only the cost of her upkeep from now until the day I release her to you."

"The day you . . . Free her now, and I shall tell you everything!"

The Frenchman's face was resolute; there was undeniable ruthlessness in the man's expression. "*Non, enfant*, you had your chance. I do not abide lies, and I would not believe you now. You will gather proof of your story, present it to me, and I shall return her to you unmolested."

Was it his imagination, or had the man placed deliberate emphasis on the word *unmolested*?

"*Proof*? How will I obtain proof?"

"You would know that better than I."

The Frenchman withdrew inside the coach and thumped against the side wall. The carriage slowly pulled out and Tarry stumbled after it.

"How am I to contact you?" he shouted. "I don't even know who you are." He added a curse, but it was lost when he ran to keep pace with the carriage.

"Make inquiries and you'll find someone who can lead you to me," the voice drifted back to him. "Ask for Sebastién Falconer."

The name hit Tarry like a brick in the chest. His legs suddenly buckled under him and he pitched forward onto his knees. He looked on in horror as the carriage disappeared from sight.

The white cottage surrounded by thorny brambles and scattered primroses crowned a high hill. The dwelling was inaccessible but for a haphazard, snaking path that coiled around the moors. Sebastién relished the irony of a French smuggler owning property on the Cornish coast, although the cottage had been purchased in the name of a local parish priest, preventing ownership from being traced to him.

A light drizzle dampened the southern coast of Cornwall. Opaque mist drifted inland in patches, enveloping the modest cottage of coarse, lichened stone until the white exterior appeared a dour gray.

The journey to Sebastién's secluded property had been arduous. He was numb with fatigue, and his "guest" was feverish and incoherent. He would have ordinarily roused his housekeeper and placed the responsibility of the girl's care in Mrs. Faraday's capable hands, but he decided to keep this vigil himself.

He would be there the moment the girl's delirium lifted. He would pry the truth from her before she could apply defense or deceit, before she was able to discern whether he was friend or foe. Even her incoherent ramblings might prove useful, so he slid his chair closer and inclined his head toward the girl lying on the bed.

Sebastién considered the delicate, heart-shaped face captured by the glow of a single candle. Her breathing was shallow and ragged. Her fair hair clung to her damp face. *What mischief have you and your young friends been up to?*

Banishing the pinprick that might escalate into pity if he allowed it, Sebastién withdrew the silk handkerchief from his vest pocket and dabbed at the girl's moist brow then tucked the covers more closely around her. She moaned and curled into a tight ball, writhing as if to escape demons as the fever fanned over her fragile body.

His plan for a ruthless interrogation evaporated into self-loathing. Was he so much like his grandfather he would browbeat a sick young girl when there might be others who could yield the answers he sought?

A low moan drew his attention back to the girl, who dozed fitfully. She had kicked away the covers, and he looked on with a bemused frown as her fingers plucked at the drab gown she wore.

Sebastién leaned in to still her restless limbs and grunted in surprise when she struck him squarely on the nose, bringing blood. He muttered in florid French and raised his handkerchief to staunch the flow of blood.

Snatching her arm and pushing it back under the covers, he seized the other as well, pinning her arms to her sides and holding them there against her feeble efforts at resistance. Her skin was hot, burning, and he was disconcerted by the frailty of the limbs he stilled so effortlessly.

He could hardly solicit the services of a physician without inviting questions he was ill prepared to answer. With a determined twist to his mouth, he left the room and returned moments later, carrying a basin of cold water, a large, soft sponge, and a neat stack of snowy linens.

Sebastién placed the basin atop the bedside commode and rolled up his sleeves as though he was a surgeon about to embark upon a delicate procedure.

The woolen garment she wore was heavy and saturated with moisture. It clung to her, refusing to be pulled free with a single tug, and Sebastién had to grimace at the irony—he usually found the fair sex to be cooperative when he was attempting to remove their clothing.

He managed to ease the sodden fabric up the length

of her slender frame by pressing her tightly to him with one arm, while his other arm worked the heavy fabric free, then he guided the gown up and over her head and tossed it blindly. The garment hit the floor a few feet away, and the stench of unwashed female wafted from the gown like a noxious cloud. How long had it been since she had bathed?

Naked beneath the shift, the girl lay fully exposed to Sebastién's gaze as he swept the cool, wet sponge over her pale, glistening skin. She was slender, not the gangly child he had expected, but a petite woman with rounded, rose-tipped breasts, a narrow waist, and slim hips that tapered into shapely legs.

Sebastién's hand wavered as his gaze traveled over the girl's form. Her bare skin was like a firebrand to the touch when he grasped her shoulders to ease her back against the thick bank of pillows. Suddenly, he froze, his sharp intake of breath loud in the small room. Her eyes were open and fixed upon his face.

The blue of her eyes was startling. He had never seen eyes that shade, like the depths of a calm sea. Her lashes were long and spiked with moisture from her fever. She murmured something in a low, musical voice. Sebastién canted his head, still lost within the depths of her eyes.

"Only a laudanum dream," she repeated breathlessly.

Very young for an opium fiend. He looked down at her in pity. He had not considered that possibility.

Her circumstances must have been worse than he had thought.

Rachael floated on a haze of opiate. The phantom whose face hovered near hers was a narcotic vision of erotic promise. His eyes were gold-flecked, vivid green, and ringed with dark lashes, lips sensuously full beneath a black mustache, chiseled, masculine face inscrutable and mysterious. Men like that existed only in dreams.

The hallucination was so vivid she imagined his warm breath on her cheek and his cool, strong hands on her body. The image of the saturnine stranger did not waver, however, nor did it fade to shadow as she had heard was usually the case with such dreams.

She was drawn to him, compelled by his heat and potency, but secure in the certainty he was a specter conjured by the laudanum. The sense of being held in an embrace, poised for a kiss, filled her clouded mind, and Rachael abandoned herself to the fantasy, summoning boldness as she lifted her head and tangled her fingers in his thick black hair, urging his head down until his cool mouth met her fevered one.

She felt him stiffen in surprise before she drifted back into oblivion without fully savoring her phantom's kiss.

Stunned, Sebastién relinquished his grip on the girl, and she fell back against the pillows, lips forming the faint arc of a smile. He touched his fingers to his mouth, recalling with acute clarity the warmth of her lips, the faint, bitter taste of laudanum, and the feel of her fingers tangled in his hair.

Sebastién reached into the basin and groped for the sponge, ignoring the dull patter of water hitting the floor as he stared at the girl. Her skin shimmered like satin in the faint light, the fever giving her flesh a rosy hue.

She lacked the emaciated look of long-term addiction; perhaps the drug was a new vice? Her arms and legs were mottled with bruises. Some of the abrasions looked suspiciously like the marks made by shackles. To judge by her physical condition, she had endured hell, and he braced himself against the sudden rush of pity. No Englishwoman deserved his compassion.

He would never forget the moment she had opened her eyes and her bright azure gaze had held him transfixed. If she had been a snake, he would be stretched on the floor now, his body filled with venom.

Sebastién dwelled on every sensation stirred by the brief kiss, and damn if his body did not quicken at the memory, heating his skin and producing an uncomfortable heaviness in his groin. He finished bathing her with quick, impersonal hands, remembering his promise to Morgan that he would return the girl unmolested. A threat without substance, glibly implied at the time. A promise he might come to regret.

Flinging a cover over the girl, Sebastién sank into the chair beside the bed. She became restless again, mumbling and moaning as she thrashed about. The bath had not calmed her. Well, it certainly had not had a calming effect upon him, either.

He knew no more about her now than he had back at the coaching inn. His purpose in bringing her here had been to get at the truth. If the authorities sought her, it was in his best interest to know it, since he had been made party to her escape.

Sebastién frowned and slid farther down in the chair, pressing his back against the hard wood as he stretched his legs out before him. His gaze remained on the girl, but when watching over her continued to provoke memories of the unbidden kiss, he rose to his feet, deciding to lay his burden in the lap of the Almighty for a few hours. He was exhausted, and the ache in his loins showed no sign of abating.

The girl shifted again and sighed with such anguish that the expulsion of air sounded like a low, plaintive moan. He heard the desolate sound and paused at the door.

Turning to look at her over his shoulder, Sebastién frowned when she began to mumble, her breath coming in gasps. She appeared to be deep in the grasp of a nightmare and was speaking aloud, reciting words as if by rote. He crossed back to the bed and peered at her while she plucked at the covers, as if trying to be free of their weight. When he reached down and pinned her wrists, the action seemed to heighten some element of her nightmare, and she grew more agitated.

"I am sane," she said. "I am eight and ten." Her soft voice faltered, and Sebastién leaned downward. "I am called Rachael Penrose."

Chapter Three

Sebastién stared down at the girl in dumb amazement, and a few seconds passed before he remembered to breathe. He walked the floor with the aimlessness of a sleepwalker, propelled by disbelief.

He had boasted he would wreak vengeance upon Rachael Penrose, whom he had pictured as a plain, plump, spoiled member of the English aristocracy. He had vowed he would punish her. Not this slender, pale, shivering, drug-addled waif.

Rage followed astonishment as Sebastién drew back his hand and punched the wall. Despite his stinging, abraded knuckles, he felt a savage satisfaction as plaster and paint drifted in a cloud to the floor. He raised a booted foot and kicked the chair beside him, and it skittered across the floor, hit the wall, and toppled over.

Just how clever was Rachael Penrose? Had some betrayal resulted in her being there, or had she schemed to be delivered into his hands in such a pitiful condition? His vow of vengeance was known up and down the English coast. When word had drifted back to him that she had disappeared, he had assumed she had gone into hiding.

The memory of the kiss suddenly infuriated him. Had her eyes conveyed awareness? She was isolated, vulnerable, and at his mercy. He could simply open a window and expose the feverish, fragile girl to a chill and his revenge would be complete. But it would be an empty victory visited upon a hapless victim. The idea was repugnant. He did not want to kill her; he wanted to savor meting out her punishment.

He drew back the coverlet, exposing her naked body to his steely gaze and studied her slender form, jaw so tense it ached. Sweeping his hand over her ribs and across her stomach, Sebastién felt the fire of her fevered flesh when he touched her.

She shifted to avoid his probing hand, moaning and tossing as if aware of his touch, and he drew the blanket over her again, brushing his hand against her cheek, fingers splayed at the base of her throat.

"*Oui,*" he said in a low voice, "your sleep should be restless, *jeune fille.* Young lady. I have you now."

"Mr. Falconer!"

He heard the rustle of skirts when his housekeeper

entered the room. She stopped in mid-stride when she saw the girl on the bed.

"Your pardon, sir." She noted the overturned chair, the damaged wall, and looked again at the girl. "I heard noises coming from this room. I was not aware of your return."

Mrs. Faraday was a study in calm. Under different circumstances, he might have found her composure amusing.

"Information denied you by the depth of your slumber," he irritably replied.

"It appears I have intruded," she said, turning to leave.

"*Non*." He beckoned her closer with an impatient sweep of his hand. "You will remain and care for my . . . guest. As you can see, she is ill. Use the salve from the apothecary for the bruises on her wrists and ankles."

"She was bound?"

Sebastién scowled at her horrified expression. "*Mon Dieu*, how debauched do you think I am, woman? I found her in this condition. The damage to her skin is consistent with shackles." He paused. "She is not to leave this house."

Mrs. Faraday's jaw dropped. "Mr. Falconer, how can I possibly—?"

"Lock her in her room!" he exploded. "Confine her to a closet! Barricade her in the basement! Just see to it that she remains inside!"

"Is she your guest or your prisoner, then?"

He was silent for a moment. "She is Rachael Penrose."

Mrs. Faraday's eyes widened and she cast a furtive glance at the girl on the bed.

"I see," she said slowly.

He moved to the window and stood watching the rain as it spattered against the pane.

"I will not be able to convince her to stay once she recovers and learns she is your . . . houseguest."

Sebastién turned back to face her.

"You will tell *Mademoiselle* Penrose she is a guest in the home of a friend. The name is John Wyatt. Tell her she has been sent here for protection. She knows of the danger she faces; you have only to hint at it."

"And if she wishes to leave?"

Sebastién shrugged and turned again to look out the window. "I will return before she is well enough to leave."

"And what will happen to her then?"

The rain pelted the window's glass in a fresh assault, completely obscuring his view, but Sebastiéen kept his back turned to the housekeeper. "She will be held accountable for her actions."

Returning to Nag's Head Inn was something like

visiting a landmark in the aftermath of its destruction, although it was he who had nearly been destroyed, not the old inn.

Sebastién had come with one objective in mind: to learn as much as possible about the woman who believed herself a guest in his home, unaware she was, in fact, a prisoner awaiting his judgment.

Why had she risked her life to ruin one Frenchman and a gang comprised of her own kinsmen? Even if she opposed smuggling on principle, her actions would not impede the commerce of the fairtraders who operated up and down England's coast; there were too many involved in the trade.

How had Morgan received his injury? What had happened to the man called Wyatt, who had placed Rachael in his care? Were these simple acts of reprisal by the kin of the men she had betrayed, or was there more to it?

The inn was as spare and silent as morning. Rough plank tables and sturdy oak chairs littered the floor of the common room. Funnel-shaped wall sconces diverted light from musty corners, and the air was acrid with the smoke from tallow candles.

The public house was the greatest underground dispatch in all of England, as well as the premier meeting place for smugglers wanting to arrange for the profitable distribution of goods. He chose a table in a corner and sat down to wait.

After several minutes, a blond, giant of a man with

a pitted face and rheumy blue eyes approached him. Grasping a chair with one huge hand, he heaved a muscular leg over the seat, straddling it.

"Falconer," the man boomed in a thunderous voice.

The snaggletoothed vipers etched in red and blue-black ink upon his muscular forearms rippled when the giant gripped Sebastién's hand and shoulder. Distinguished by his impressive size, his Nordic pallor, and the striking artwork a Chinaman had skillfully wrought on his skin, he was known by all as simply "The Dane."

He folded his arms across his massive chest. "We do not proceed until I see the mark."

Sebastién exhaled in a noisy hiss as he divested himself of his coat and vest, his hands swift with impatience. He jerked the sleeves of his shirt down over his arms, tearing the fine lawn garment as he bared his upper torso.

"I have only to witness your temper to be certain of your identity," The Dane chuckled.

He seized Sebastién's right arm and raised it high, revealing a small, well-executed *fleur-de-lis* in permanent blue-black marking on the underside of Sebastién's upper arm. The same mark was found on the arm of every man who belonged to Sebastién's group of fairtraders.

Satisfied the artwork was not recent, The Dane nodded and released his arm. "We agreed no information would be given to a man who could not reveal the mark. I am only following your rule," he scolded.

"Why cling to formalities? It seems a poor joke

when our compatriots languish in the gaol or hang from gibbets along the highway," Sebastién said bitterly as he pulled on his shirt.

"You still have enemies. You must be on your guard."

Sebastién nodded and shrugged. "Has anyone made inquiries about me?"

The Dane pushed back his shock of bright hair, revealing his face, which was swollen and mottled with livid bruises.

"What happened?"

"Your brother sought information of your whereabouts. I would not provide it."

"I am sorry, *mon ami*."

"The men sent by your brother look far worse than I," The Dane said. "It was no more than exercise to me."

"And my brother calls *me* criminal," Sebastién grated.

"There are those who believe you spy for the Crown," The Dane said carefully. "Some are curious to know why you do not keep your men company in the common cell, or join them on the roadside gibbets."

"These English are never satisfied! My English brother is obsessed with gathering evidence to hang me, while my French grandfather wields his influence to protect me from my brother. I am caught in the middle and condemned by both sides!"

"I've never known brothers who owe their allegiance to different countries."

"I do not claim Jacques as my brother," Sebastién replied. "He is an Englishman, and as such, he is my enemy."

Sebastién and his brother had been estranged for as long as he could remember. Their mother had escaped to England twenty-five years earlier with only Jacques, leaving Sebastién behind in France. Sebastién had been raised with an iron hand by his grandfather Hugh, who had schooled his grandson in the Falconer traditions, a hatred of the English among them.

Sebastién had taken over the Falconer merchant and shipping business at his grandfather's insistence. When France and England once again began to view each other through hostile eyes and the talk of war escalated, he had obtained a Letter of Marque and Reprisal from King Louis XIV and hoisted the flag of privateer above his ships.

He had then proceeded to organize and lead a band of fairtraders on English soil, only to discover his brother held a position of high rank within the English Customs House. His relationship with his brother was a simple one: Jacques enforced English Customs laws, and Sebastién broke them.

"Beyond the stranger born brother to me, who else searches for me?"

"Your grandfather's solicitor has been sent to urge you to return home."

Sebastién rolled his eyes at that news. "Who else?"

He expected a description of Tarry Morgan to follow,

but the man The Dane described was not familiar. He frowned. Morgan should have begun making inquiries about him by now.

"The man I expect to try to contact me may not know how to go about it. Perhaps I should visit him," Sebastién said.

"Describe the man, and I will find him for you."

"I know where he lives. I prefer that he find me."

"Is he dangerous?"

"*Non*, a puppy. He owes me a debt. I withheld his property as security."

Sebastién rose and donned his coat. "You will overlook my temper," he instructed. It was as close as he would come to an apology, and both men knew it.

The Dane grinned. "As always," he replied.

Tarry Morgan sat upon the frigid ground with his knees drawn to his chin and stared at his father's house. It had been reduced to a blackened skeleton of charred beams and glowing embers.

He watched the clouds of sticky black smoke dissipate, a brown blur across the overcast sky. His eyes stung, and he closed them. The smoke burned his throat and made drawing breath painful. He rested the palms of his hands flat against the ground to steady the trembling of his body.

As a result of his home having been deliberately razed, Tarry was now certain Victor Brightmore had no knowledge of Rachael's whereabouts. It was ironic Falconer had probably saved Rachael's life by abducting her.

Whatever the Frenchman had intended, Tarry doubted rescuing Rachael from an act of arson had been a part of it. Tarry at least knew where Rachael was *not*, and that gave him an advantage over her scheming uncle.

He was hesitant to make inquiries to locate the Frenchman, fearing Victor would learn of it. He did not want to provide Victor with clues concerning Rachael's whereabouts. But now, he had no choice. Victor was desperate to silence Rachael. Tarry would have to find her first.

Tarry rose to his feet, dusting off his breeches while his father sped toward him. Phillip Morgan was an officer in Queen Anne's army, and had served as ambassador to France. Away on a diplomatic mission, his father had not been at either of his residences recently.

Another rider trailed at a distance behind Phillip, and for a moment, Tarry thought the two traveled together until the other man abruptly turned down a neighboring lane.

Phillip Morgan was a seasoned version of his son, with the same warm brown eyes and urchin features. Phillip slid from the horse's broad back and stared at the ruin of his once grand home. He reached out and placed his hand against the shoulder of the horse to steady himself.

"No one was hurt," Tarry said. "None is without shelter. The servants have been placed among our neighbors."

Phillip drew a deep breath and poked at the rubble with his walking stick, as if too stunned to consider the soot threatening to spoil the hem of his gray silk long coat. Yards away, a timber fell, raining a shower of sparks, like hundreds of tiny red sprites. He tugged at the white neck cloth around his neck.

"What happened?"

"If I told you a maid was careless with a candle . . ."

"I would wonder what would give you cause to lie to me." Tarry bowed his head at the sharp rebuke. Phillip sighed. "It appears one of us has made an enemy." He continued to survey the area where the house had stood. He shook his head and wiped away the tears brimming in his eyes.

"I will rebuild," Tarry asserted.

"No. You will provide names, and I will see that the culprits are apprehended and punished."

He knew what his father would do if he told him he suspected Victor was responsible. He would demand to know what motive Brightmore could possibly have, and Tarry would be forced to reveal what had transpired.

Tarry had attempted to bribe a nursery maid in Brightmore's household to gain access to James, only to learn Rachael's brother had been moved to another location undisclosed to his staff.

If his father organized a search for Rachael while she was still in Falconer's custody, there was no telling what the Frenchman might do. He didn't want to force Falconer into a desperate action. If anything happened to Rachael, it would seal her brother's fate as well. No, he had to use discretion, or he would endanger them both. He had to do this alone.

"I do not know the identity of the central villain," Tarry lied. "I have only suspicions about the identities of those who aid him. I need time to make sense of all this. 'Twould accomplish nothing to pull the weeds and leave the root intact."

"Once you are certain of their identities, I will be the one to purge the garden of its weeds." Phillip's soft tone was encased in steel.

"Yes, of course, Father."

"You shall have one week to conduct your investigation. Then you will reveal your conclusions to me and retire to a safe location while I . . . tidy the garden."

With a nod and a murmur of thanks, Tarry excused himself to arrange for a horse from a neighboring stable. He glanced back at the charcoal rubble that had once been his home and saw his father stiffly mount his horse and slowly ride away, looking older than Tarry had ever seen him. A lump rose in his throat. He had never lied to his father before.

Before the fire struck, Tarry had asked a scullery

maid if she knew how one might contact Sebastién Falconer. She had appeared shocked by the inquiry, but had nevertheless been accommodating. Tarry was on his way to Nag's Head Inn in Holborn to arrange a meeting with a fairtrader known only as "The Dane."

A cloaked, hooded Sebastién Falconer emerged from behind a nearby cottage and turned down the alley, facing the ruins of the once impressive Morgan home. He surveyed the destruction, squinting against the residual heat of the blaze and the scattering of ash. Morgan had an enemy, that much was obvious, but did this have anything to do with Rachael Penrose?

He had been about to confront Tarry when the elder Morgan had arrived to join his son. From the brief conversation he had overheard, Sebastién guessed the younger Morgan entertained the foolhardy notion of rescuing Rachael alone.

With a shout, he urged his horse into a gallop, consumed by the thrill of speed and the rush of cold air coaxing the heat from his face as he raced to return home in advance of Morgan's arrival.

Chapter Four

Convalescence was a journey over unsteady terrain for Rachael. Mrs. Faraday was kind, but their conversation was stilted and limited to pleasantries. Not wishing to jeopardize her own safety or the safety of her absent host, Rachael avoided revealing any personal information.

She spent most of her time gazing out the upstairs bedroom window at the hills carpeted in brown heather that curved below the cottage. From this vantage point, she could see all the way to the sea. Although the panorama was breathtaking, the long idle days had left her feeling isolated and wretchedly alone.

Her recollection of her escape from Bedlam remained hazy. The man who had freed her from Bedlam and deposited her here had been lost to her in all manner of detail. The only enduring memory she had was from a fever dream. She was haunted by the image of a man whose masculine beauty was offset by the coldness in his brittle, gold-flecked eyes. It was not the face of anyone she knew; in fact, she was certain he did not exist.

Sebastién paused at the bottom of the steep ascent. He felt his horse surge toward the familiar path, sweat from the vigorous ride rising from its flanks in a vapor.

Rider and mount sprang into fluid motion, the beast's hooves churning up clods of damp earth as the horse propelled them toward his hideaway. He was pleased that he could disappear at will into the wilds of the rocky Cornish coast. The remote location suited his need for discretion and seclusion.

He lifted his head and glanced toward the tall, narrow cottage, his thoughts centered on the girl he harbored within. A movement at the window on the upper level caught his eye and he slowed the horse.

A striking young woman with flaxen hair and huge eyes set against a fair, delicately formed face sat watching him. The layer of sea salt rimming the outermost edges of the window added a wraithlike quality to her appearance.

Rachael Penrose, on display in the window. If he had instructed she not be allowed outdoors, did it not also follow that she be kept away from the damned windows?

A moment later, he stormed into the cottage, slamming doors and mouthing curses as he sought out Mrs. Faraday. When he failed to find his housekeeper, he opted to deal with the matter himself. He found the room the girl occupied, grasped the latch handle firmly, and burst inside.

"Do not stand in front of the window!" Too late, he realized he had shouted, his displeasure no doubt evident in his tone and expression.

"I did not hear you knock, sir." The soft, mellifluous voice carried a hint of rebuke.

Rachael stared at the intruder, finding him remarkable. It was just as well she'd spoken before getting a better look at him. All coherent thought had fled the moment she looked into his darkly lashed green eyes. They were an arresting contradiction of ice and the candle-spark of a strong will.

His long glossy hair, black as a raven's wing, was tied in a queue at the nape of his neck. A mustache framed his upper lip. Without it, he would look younger, yet the hard glint in his eyes belied youth. His face conveyed wariness and keen intelligence. A strong, square jaw framed his generous lower lip. He did not smile or attempt to ease the severity of his expression.

He stood tall, with broad shoulders, narrow hips, and an impression of compelling strength. *He looks like a warlord from an antique painting.* Rachael drew a shallow, hitched breath as recognition dawned. This man was the sensual phantom from her fever dream. Had she actually kissed him? Her heart skipped a beat and hastened its pace at the thought. Warmth flooded her cheeks as mortification set in. She wasn't certain which was worse: the possibility she *had* kissed him, or the fact she could not remember it in greater detail.

"I am not accustomed to knocking in my own home," he finally replied to her mild reproach.

His voice stunned her. It was deep, resonant, and unexpectedly harsh. A tremor of confusion passed through her as she registered the accented tones of his speech. Surely her host was English?

"This is your home?"

He nodded, dark brows vivid slashes above his wide-set eyes. Unsmiling, he continued to study her.

Rachael took a hesitant step in her host's direction, smiling as she extended one elegant hand. "You must be John Wyatt. I am delighted to make your acquaintance, sir." Her slim fingers gently pressed his hand. "I can never fully repay my debt to you."

Sebastién shrugged, using the slight movement to shake off her hand. He could not help but gawk at her.

49

The purplish craters beneath her eyes had disappeared, and her skin was exquisite in its fairness, framed by a glorious mane of golden hair that tumbled over her shoulders and cascaded down her back.

She looks like a porcelain doll, like she would crush easily. He frowned, ill at ease with his own musings.

Rachael remained standing where she was, wide blue eyes fixed upon him, and he found he needed a moment to frame a reply to her remark.

"You owe me nothing," he said finally. Goaded by an irrational urge to flee the room, he crossed to the door then paused to recover himself before turning back to her. Sebastién smiled slightly, the affectation making his jaw flex. "Except, perhaps, your companionship this evening."

He reached the foot of the stairs just as Mrs. Faraday entered the house. She glanced down at the parcel she carried before greeting him.

"It pleases me to see you have returned," she said.

"Why, when you are free to disregard my instructions in my absence?"

"What do you mean?"

"You left my 'guest' unattended."

"I saw no harm in it. She knows she must not leave

the house."

"With no one around to convince her otherwise, she is likely to stray outdoors."

"I must go to market if we're to eat."

"*Touché*," he conceded. "She has fared well enough in your care."

"You've seen her, then?" Her mouth faded into a white line.

"*Oui.*" He saw her swift, apprehensive glance at the staircase and grunted. "She was alive when I left her. Be wary of her," he warned. "You do not know the depth of her villainy."

"She's no more than a child. What if you take revenge upon an innocent girl? You do not seem a man without a conscience." She flinched. "Your pardon, sir, it was not my place to comment on your character."

"What have you told her?" he asked.

"That she is staying at the home of a friend."

"What has she told you?"

"Nothing. She seems reluctant to speak about herself."

"A reticence she will soon shed," he predicted ominously. He noticed the parcel she held. "What have you there?"

Mrs. Faraday hesitated. "It was bought with my own wages."

He frowned. "I asked you what you have there, not how you paid for it."

"I fancied a new gown." She turned to go. "With your leave—"

"*Non.*" He pivoted, catching her arm as she moved to sweep past him. "You will show me your new gown. Perhaps I will make you a gift of it."

"That is not necessary," she assured him, visibly flustered when he reached out and snatched the parcel.

Her words of protest trailed away as he unwrapped the package and withdrew a richly tailored mantua of patterned silk. The gown spilled over his arms in a waterfall of muted blue fabric.

"A costly bit of fluff," he remarked. He held it out, pausing to look askance at her. "Have current fashions changed so much during my absence?"

"What do you mean, sir?" she asked in a tiny voice.

"This gown will fall no lower than . . ." he lifted one booted foot to illustrate, "here," he concluded, pointing to mid-calf. "Not that I object to the sight of a shapely leg . . ."

She reached for the gown, but he dodged her, holding the dress aloft. "I am afraid the seamstress has made other miscalculations as well," he observed. "The gown will suit a woman of a more petite stature, *non*?"

"Perhaps someone of Rachael's size?" she suggested, a little too hastily.

"The gown is your property, do with it as you wish," Sebastién said. Tiring of the game, he handed the gown back to her. "Take the cost from the household account."

"It should look quite lovely on her. This shade of blue will enhance the unusual color of her eyes—"

"I have said you may do with it as you wish!" he snapped. Sebastién waited until she had reached the top of the landing before he called out to her, "Did you think I would not have the decency to clothe her?"

Mrs. Faraday stepped back from the railing as if to avoid his gaze. "Do you want the truth?" she asked.

"If you are capable of it."

"I feared the only garment you would purchase for her would be a shroud."

Rachael felt her composure waver as she sat with her striking host in the modest parlor. While she shared the sordid account of her incarceration at Bedlam, she occupied her hands with smoothing the skirt of the beautiful gown Mrs. Faraday had given her.

She shuddered as she recounted the chain of events that had begun with her discovery of Victor's plan to introduce poison into her infant brother's formula in trace amounts.

Her hastily scrawled letter to Tarry Morgan had kept Victor from killing her outright, but he had viciously attacked her. The arrival of Dr. Elliot Macaulay had stopped her uncle's assault, but the doctor had drugged her, and when she had awakened sometime later, it had been to the horror of Bedlam.

Now that she had escaped from Bedlam, she speculated to Mr. Wyatt that Victor would be forced to move with caution. He would not dare harm James until he had determined what fate had befallen her.

The expression on Wyatt's face gave away nothing of his thoughts as she related her misadventure. To make matters worse, she was plagued by the haunting recollection of their shared kiss. The warmth of a telltale blush crept up her neck and over her cheeks at the thought, and his proximity made her think of the kiss much too often.

Was it a memory or just a dream? The fact that he did not mention it made it easier to believe it had never happened. His decorous conduct did not stray beyond basic propriety. If anything, his manner was almost surly. He was preoccupied with his wine, turning his glass this way and that, holding the vessel up to the light, inhaling the bouquet, but rarely taking a sip.

Rachael concluded her story and fidgeted in the chair, waiting for some comment from him. The delightful evening of repartee she had anticipated had instead been an awkward, one-sided conversation. She felt foolish for having been so concerned with her appearance. Why had it seemed so important to look nice this evening? Certainly not for him. She hardly knew him.

He had abandoned his interest in his wine and sat staring at her with an intensity Rachael found unnerving.

She felt like a small bird under the rapt scrutiny of a cat with a voracious appetite.

"A curious predicament," Sebastién commented finally.

Her imagination has not been idle during my absence. Yet there was the niggling doubt certain details invited, such as the fading abrasions on her limbs that told of iron restraints, the injury Morgan had received, and the destruction of the Morgan estate. Someone had abused her before she fell into his hands, but an informer would incur the wrath of many. It did not necessarily follow that her story was the truth.

Sebastién kept his plan of interrogation uppermost in his mind. No doubt this hoyden made deliberate use of her physical allure. She had taken pains with her appearance. She was a beautiful woman made more so by the gossamer haze of candlelight. He was not about to become a besotted fool and allow her to emerge victorious in their match of wits, no matter how damned attractive he found her.

"You must be disappointed that Tarry has not visited," he said.

"It is safer for us all if he keeps his distance. Victor is likely to have him followed. The longer I remain here, the greater the risk that Victor will find me."

Was she about to broach the subject of her departure? He was just as determined to deflect any discussion on the topic.

"My friend Tarry would never forgive me if I allowed you to risk your safety," he said.

"How did you and Tarry become acquainted? I wasn't aware that he had any friends from across the Channel."

"Are you acquainted with *all* his friends, then?" he asked. He did not allow his faint smile to lessen the challenge in his tone. It was better to keep her on the defensive; it increased the likelihood that she would trip herself up.

"Tarry has friends at court I have never met," she replied. "He may have mentioned you by name, but I would not have expected a Frenchman. Is it John, or Jean?"

"Call me whatever you like," he responded in a dry tone. "I am actually part English, but schooled in France." That much of the truth suited him. He marveled at her skillful attempt to draw information out of him. "Penrose is a common name in Cornwall, is it not?"

"Yes. I am a Cornish Penrose." She lifted her brow at the question.

"Then why not remain here? You are safer here than you would be in your own village."

"If I remain here, my presence will endanger you, and my brother will not be safe. I am fortunate that Tarry has a gallant, courageous friend who was willing to come to my aid, but I've already imposed upon you enough."

"You give me too much credit, *mademoiselle*," he said with a dismissive wave. "The Cornish coast is no place for a young woman to travel alone without benefit of a guardian."

"I grew up here. This place holds no danger for me."

"Have you no fear of the fairtraders who roam the coast?" He watched her face for a reaction. Surely she knew she was a pariah among her own kinsmen? Her ingenuous manner was disturbing.

"I have no fear of fairtraders. Fairtrading is a way of life on the coast. Why shouldn't a Bodmin shopkeeper be able to afford tea when a Customs official drinks it with every meal simply because his purse is better suited to pay the duty? I don't view the fairtrade as a criminal enterprise. I know many who participate in the trade."

"Such knowledge would make you popular with Customs." He resisted the urge to frame it as an accusation.

"The fairtraders are my friends and neighbors. I would never inform on them."

"What happens to those who turn informant?"

"I shouldn't like to think about it—a wise informer would never return to the coast."

Her complexion had pinkened; she either felt guilty

or passionate about the subject. She frowned at him as if perplexed by the turn their conversation had taken.

"It seems the risk would far outweigh the gain."

Rachael nodded. "You need have no fear on my behalf with regard to fairtraders. It is unlikely I would be mistaken for a Customs agent." She smiled at him as if the thought amused her.

Was the woman composed of stone? She did not seek to avoid his steady gaze. There was no detectable tic or tremor in her face or hands. She breathed easily. No sheen of perspiration marred the fair, smooth skin of her brow. She remained calm, even smiling while he hinted at the truth. He felt his frustration grow with each verbal parry.

Perhaps she already knew who he was and was enjoying watching him stalk the perimeter of his verbal cage. He was tempted to reveal his identity to her, if only to see her reaction. She was wily, infuriating, and intriguing, and Sebastién was actually enjoying their little game of cat and mouse.

How could he prevent her departure without making a prisoner of her? He noted the high color at her cheeks and the limpid blue pools of her eyes. The fact that she did not seem to find him unattractive was an advantage he might put to good use. After all, this was war and he had to use whatever weapons were available to him.

"Your presence here makes me realize how empty

my home will be after you have gone," he said, shifting strategy. "I will regret the departure of such a lovely guest."

Rachael blushed as if she had no experience with flattery. Could a woman fake a blush as a stratagem? He had not seen that done before. Still, she was in an elite league among liars, so anything was possible.

"I only hope you have felt safe in my home, and that you feel I can be trusted."

"Of course."

Her politic response sent a prickle of exasperation through him. It was clear she did not trust him enough to opt for honesty.

"I fear Tarry will view it as a lapse on my part when he arrives and finds you gone."

"You expect Tarry soon?" Her expression brightened and she flashed a winsome smile.

"*Oui*. At any moment." He had been expecting Morgan to charge through the door and attempt to rescue her for the last several hours. He should have sent the young fool directions to the cottage via courier.

"Perhaps I *should* wait for Tarry to arrive."

"It would mean a great deal to me to witness your reunion," he said, meaning it.

If she agreed to stay until Morgan arrived, he would have additional time to wear down her reserve. Failing that, they would have it out when Morgan attempted to rescue her.

He rose from his chair and moved to look out through the salt-framed windowpane. Bright moonlight dispelled the darkness outside, bathing the distant shoreline in a shimmering silver glow.

"What a magnificent view of the sea," she remarked. He was unaware that she had followed him, and she took a step back when he whirled around to her in surprise. "Can this cottage be seen from the beach?"

"Why do you ask?"

He glanced down, noting the way the candlelight caught the gold of her hair and transformed it into gleaming filigree, tempting him to touch the gilded strands. The mantua outlined her graceful curves with the familiarity of a glove, the open bodice drawing his eye to the gentle swell of her breasts. As Mrs. Faraday had predicted, the delicate blue shade of the fabric lent a gemlike quality to her extraordinary eyes.

Sebastién blinked and drew an unsteady breath as a treacherous ache spread through him. Her appearance was a calculated assault upon his senses, as was the shy façade she used as a ploy to avoid his questions.

"It seems to me that if I were to look in this direction from the beach, I would see a thick grove of trees and a scattering of wild of primroses, but nothing of the cottage."

"Those at sea may glimpse the cottage on a clear day, but a crew working to avoid the Eddystone rocks has little time to scan the hills. Only the orchard can be seen from the beach."

"Suitable quarters for a pirate king," she said lightly.

As he weighed her comment for a confession, she looked closely at his face and promptly took a step backward.

"I did not mean to offend," she said.

"You did not offend. It merely seemed a curious thing to say."

"I only mentioned it because I am fond of strolling the orchard path, and I feel quite invisible—"

She gasped when he muttered an oath and grasped her upper arms, hauling her up to face him, his greater height forcing her onto her toes.

"Who gave you permission to stroll through the orchard?" *Mrs. Faraday. She allows the girl to wander about while Morgan combs the area searching for her.* "Foolish damn woman!"

"There is no need to be insulting," Rachael admonished. She tugged against his grip.

"You are to stay inside," he instructed. "*Inside,*" he repeated, shaking her for emphasis when she continued to struggle. Her mouth opened then closed. "Test me on this, and you will find your door bolted from the outside."

"Then I will have exchanged one form of imprisonment for another. Perhaps I should depart in the morning and leave you to give my regrets to Tarry."

Rachael tried to shake free of his hold, but his grip on her arms only tightened. He shifted his stance and swept her up against his solid strength, her back braced by his powerful arm. She felt every hard line of him from chest to thigh. Her breasts were crushed against his broad expanse. A pleasant warmth emanated from him, and the suggestion of lithe power, leashed, but deadly.

Staring at the elaborate brocade coat, Rachael was appalled by the unexpected flash of pleasure she felt at being held by him. She breathed in his scent, an aromatic mixture of exotic spices as mysterious as the man himself, and could feel the drumming of her heart when his hand brushed her cheek, smoothing the hair back from her face. Though he had seemed angry, his touch was exquisite in its gentleness.

This was madness. She barely knew him, and yet her heart leapt in reaction to his touch. She felt the tumult of her blood coursing through her veins, and was filled with a sharp, blind ache that begged to be eased. She could not blame her reaction on the wine; she hadn't drunk any.

"How can you leave?" Rachael heard him ask. She looked up at him in bewilderment when he whispered, "How can I let you leave?"

She did not need to see his face to know he was going to kiss her. She felt the rough grasp of his fingers when he cupped her chin, and she lifted her head, driven to meet the hungry passion of his kiss with a sweet fervor of her own.

Who would condemn her for seeking protection or even love? There were enemies on all sides of her. She had felt helpless and without hope, but Wyatt made her feel safeguarded and desirable in ways she had never known.

Sebastién touched the sensitive area in the hollow of Rachael's throat, his fingers gliding over her skin. She shuddered and moaned at the sensation as a fulsome yearning grew within her, a nameless intensity that quickened her pulse and chased away all thought of caution or propriety.

Sighing as his kiss grew demanding and possessive, her lips burned from the heat and depth of the kiss as he tested the resistance of her teeth and urged her lips to part for a fuller invasion. Her arms were locked between their bodies, but she yearned to touch him as he was touching her, with a slow appreciation that was ascending into urgency. Gently born and reared, she was unaccustomed to the riotous tumult of the senses.

Inflamed beyond all manner of thought or calculation, Sebastién moved in to kiss her hungrily, savoring her honeyed taste. It was a treacherous, damned inconvenient desire. The moonlight on her hair, the glowing promise in her dark blue eyes, and her pale, cool beauty had all conspired against him.

He felt her tongue touch his in an unexpected, curiously inexperienced graze that nearly undid him. He nuzzled her neck, lips tracing a trail along her creamy white skin as he moved on a downward path, mouth and hands savoring the bounty of her fragrant, silky flesh. His hand slid the gown up her leg as he caressed her silken thigh. Her skin was like porcelain in the candlelight, fragile and delicate, yet smooth and heated to his touch.

Her fierce, almost desperate response made him pause, and he fought to marshal restraint, unwilling to trust either himself or her. Holding her slightly away from him, Sebastién scrutinized her face. He could have her; that much was obvious. Her ivory skin had flushed a delicate rose, her eyes were dark with passion, and her bruised lips trembled. There was no sly manipulation in her guileless expression, only earnest, painful desire.

"Rachael," he murmured, his accent softening her name to a sensual caress, "Rachael, you must promise me that you will not leave me."

When she murmured his name in response, it was as if he had received a vicious blow to his midsection. Ego and ardor were simultaneously deflated, and the heated blood humming through his veins chilled and turned to sludge.

Yet what other name could she have called him but "John"? Sebastién released her and backed away, hands trembling as he straightened his clothes.

"Did I say—or do—something wrong?" she asked.

"*Non*," he rasped. "I must not divide your loyalties now," he said, forming an excuse that would still allow him to play her hero. "If I make love to you, I will not be able to let you go." That much, he realized with a reaction bordering on dismay, was true. If he gave in to his desire now, she might go unpunished. He could not allow that to happen.

"I . . . I was quite carried away," she said, her face flushing crimson. "You must think me quite wanton. I hope my behavior did not lower your opinion of me."

"My opinion of you has not changed."

"Perhaps we can begin again as friends, when my brother is safe?"

He inclined his head in a noncommittal response, narrowed gaze following her as she fled the room. Her womanly scent lingered like an apparition. As he listened to his own harsh breathing, he reached out and swept the chamberstick to the floor in a sudden explosion of temper.

"*Oui*, we will begin again," he vowed. "*When you know who I am.*"

Chapter Five

Despite the admonition to remain indoors, Rachael decided to take a stroll along the beach. She hoped the brisk sea air would clear her head and calm her restlessness.

The fascination she felt for the mercurial Wyatt had left her shaken and confused. She had never behaved so wantonly and was aghast over her own lack of restraint. Had her base behavior led him to believe that she was unworthy of his esteem? How would she face him again, after the way she had behaved?

Rachael approached the door with candle in hand and was astonished to discover that the handle would not turn. She smiled. Wyatt might have guessed that she would test the limits he had imposed, but he had not reckoned on her resourcefulness. She removed one of the wooden hairpins from the vanity top and inserted it into the lock. Following a faint click, the knob turned freely.

Outside, the air was redolent with the promise of rain, and moonlight spewed in a riot of silver. The south-westerly wind extinguished the candle she carried and tugged at her hair. Rachael lifted her skirts and inched her way down the steep path that cleaved the garden and descended toward the beach, the unseasonably warm weather giving her an urge to run barefoot along the deserted shore.

She was halfway down the path when a sudden, bright burst of light caught her eye. The intermittent flash of yellow originated to her left, almost level with the beach.

Afraid movement would reveal her and divulge the hidden cottage path she traveled, Rachael crouched, waiting for the light to flare again. With senses heightened by fear, she became aware of noises in the distance: the distressed nicker of a horse and the voices of two men.

Peering out from behind the dense growth of thorn, Rachael watched as the men secured a lantern around the horse's neck. Its forelegs had been bound together, forcing it to hobble. The animal tried to shake free of the lamp, but the crude metal box remained fixed securely. Satisfied, the men abandoned the horse and ran down the beach.

Rachael felt revulsion and terror wash over her when she recognized the ploy. The horse would hobble along, causing an up-and-down movement of the light. A ship's captain would assume the light was a beacon and would be duped into sailing too near the rocky coast. A gang of shipwreckers would be lying in wait on the beach.

Plantagenet law provided that the cargo of a ship adjudged a wreck belonged to the inhabitants of the coast where the wreckage washed ashore. The law further decreed that if there were survivors, it would not be adjudged a lawful wreck. In effect, the law promoted murder. Rachael had no fear of fairtraders, but wreckers were a different breed altogether.

Her limbs trembled as she crept farther down the path for a better view of the sea. A square-rigged vessel drifted near the rocky shore and Rachael looked on in horror as the ship's crew recognized the danger too late.

The ship bounced and eddied before it crashed into the rocks with a force that sent the dull crack of rending wood echoing in the night. The beach came alive with shouts of triumph as more than two dozen men suddenly converged on the beach, running into the foaming surf.

The thought that there might be survivors propelled her toward the beach, where Rachael knelt behind a large boulder and looked on with mounting horror at the chaotic scene. The gang was intent upon clean work with no witnesses, and she had to shove her fist into her mouth to hold back her screams as cries of terror and pleas for mercy were brutally silenced by intermittent flashes of steel in the moonlight.

The gang stripped the ship of her cargo and every

item of value with practiced efficiency, including the timber forming the vessel, the ropes from her rigging, and the copper that sheathed her hull. They transferred their plunder into several waiting ships and then headed up the beach in her direction.

One man forged ahead of the others as they marched. Every nerve in Rachael's body thrummed with the awareness of danger as the leader drew close to her and the murky light edged out the shadows hiding his face.

Victor Brightmore stood no more than fifteen feet from her. Rachael ducked, feeling her heartbeat quicken as a flush of coldness flowed over her. Why hadn't she listened to Wyatt and remained at the cottage?

"Well done," he said, praising the group. "A rewarding evening, as befits my return after so long an absence."

Rachael shuddered at the sound of his voice, feeling as if she could not draw air for breath as the assembled men raised their weapons in salute and cheered. Victor sheathed his sword then continued up the beach.

Rachael abandoned her position behind the boulder and scrambled toward the cottage path, keeping to the shadows. Ascending the steep path, her heart pounded in her ears, and her limbs quaked.

The briar and bramble clutched at her and Rachael stifled an anguished sob. What had Victor done with James? Was her uncle merely occupying his time until he could be certain she was out of the way, or had he put his diabolical plan into action?

She heard the sound of a scuffle at the foot of the path and pressed her fist to her mouth again to hold back a scream. Two or more men had stumbled upon the hidden walkway, and an altercation was underway. Rachael sought to distance herself from it, but stopped short when she heard her name.

"Rachael!" The caller hissed, low and urgent, as if he also feared discovery. "Rachael, stop!"

She half turned in the direction of the voice and stumbled and lost her footing, sliding backward in the bramble. Hearing the renewed sounds of a struggle, and the audible grunt of fist meeting flesh as one opponent felled the other, she chewed her lip and clawed her way up the incline, sensing with blunt terror that the winner had turned his attention her way.

Rachael screamed and instinctively fought to defend herself when she was seized from behind and spun around. She met her attacker in a blind frenzy, biting, clawing, and kicking.

The attacker stunned her with a controlled slap to her cheek and enveloped her thrashing limbs in a crushing embrace, increasing the pressure of his hold until Rachael abandoned her futile attack, unable to breathe.

"Did I not tell you to stay *inside*?" a harsh voice grated in her ear.

John Wyatt stared down at her like a dark angel expelled from the depths of hell and looking none too happy about it. It was the first time it occurred to her to be afraid of him.

Rachael cringed when he lifted his hand, and he froze as if surprised by her reaction before gently brushing his fingers against her wet cheek. She had been crying without being aware of it.

"I . . . I'm sorry," she stammered. "You warned me to stay inside. I should have listened."

"Sorry? You might have been dead," he scolded.

"My uncle leads them." Rachael noticed then that he carried an ominous broadsword and his clothing was wet. A small cut over his left eye still trickled blood. A lump formed in her throat and she tried to back away from him, but he still held her, and seemed uninclined to let go. "What have you been doing?"

"You must return to the cottage." He took firm hold of her elbow.

Rachael hung back. "Who were you fighting?" she asked, refusing to be coaxed to move, despite the increasing pressure on her arm.

"You are too inquisitive."

"Why did you call out my name?"

"I did not—" He stopped himself and glowered at her as if she had wrung a confession out of him. "You must return to the cottage. *Now*," he insisted.

"If you didn't call me, who did?" she demanded.

Rachael wrenched her arm free and backed away, eyes fastened upon something he held in his hand: a

71

piece of jewelry. He slipped the trinket inside his vest, meeting her horrified expression with an unrepentant scowl. She continued to back away.

"Who *did* call my name?" Rachael repeated.

Sebastién took a decisive step in Rachael's direction but stopped when a voice interrupted the tense silence.

"I called your name, Rachael."

A bruised and bloodied Tarry Morgan stepped into view. He held a pistol pointed at the Frenchman's broad chest.

"Falconer," Tarry said, as if in greeting.

"Falconer?" Rachael echoed. She uttered a sound of bewilderment, sensing the Frenchman was focused on her reaction to the name.

He bowed. "At last, a formal introduction," he said. "Sebastién Falconer, at your service, *mademoiselle*."

"Your name is not John Wyatt? You're not Tarry's friend?"

Tarry grunted and looked at her as if she had indeed gone mad.

"Let us dispense with games, *Mademoiselle* Penrose. You risk no reprisal from me at the moment; your young friend holds a pistol on me. Pray, be candid."

"I don't know what you mean." She looked from one man to the other in confusion, heart sinking at the enmity on the Frenchman's face. His eyes held hers as if communicating a dare. "I don't understand."

"How dare you use John Wyatt's good name?" Tarry

broke in. "How dare you abuse this girl?"

"No, he has been kind to me, Tarry," Rachael objected. She was baffled when both men gaped at her in surprise. "I thought he was your friend John."

"John Wyatt is dead," Tarry snapped. "He was murdered the night he helped you escape."

Rachael recoiled at the words.

"Falconer abducted you. He believes you are the Customs informer who ruined him and planned to avenge himself against you. He charged me to prove your innocence and said he would not release you without proof."

"Proof you obviously cannot provide," Sebastién commented, arching his brow.

"Is it true?" Rachael asked Sebastién.

He shrugged and folded his arms across his chest. "I've known who you were since the first night. Have I harmed you?"

Have you harmed me? He believed she was a Customs informer. How he had come to such a conclusion, she had no idea. Had he attempted to seduce her as a means of revenge? Had he intended all along to expose and disgrace her? If that was true, then he felt nothing for her other than hatred. He might not have stolen her maidenhead, but he had robbed her of her innocence.

"Believing as you do, the masquerade must have been quite an ordeal for you," she said. "Yet you never lost the advantage, did you?" Even in her inexperience,

Rachael knew he had wanted her. There were moments when he had struggled for control. She noted, with a small measure of satisfaction, that his jaw went rigid at her remark, and his eyes flashed with anger.

"We're leaving," Tarry told her. "I have a horse waiting down the beach."

"I trust you left your horse in the open so the wreckers would have an additional reward?"

Tarry's jaw dropped and the pistol wavered in his hand.

"I thought as much." Sebastién shook his head in disgust as Tarry fixed a look of pure malice on him.

"We'll find another horse," Tarry said.

"And what if the wreckers stumble upon the two of you, *enfant*?" Sebastién asked. "How will you protect her? With your wits?" He shook his head. "You go about unarmed."

"You forget that I hold the pistol," Tarry said through clenched teeth.

"The pistol you stole from *me*. I should warn you, it has no shot left. Unless you choose to employ your sword, you have no weapon." Sebastién smiled unpleasantly. "Other than your wits, of course."

"You bluff. You would not have been held at bay by a pistol with no shot left."

"It suited my purpose. I wanted to hear what the *mademoiselle* might say when her guard was down," Sebastién replied.

Tarry raised the pistol as if to fire it. "I can prove

74

otherwise."

"*Oui*," Sebastién sensibly agreed, "and if I lie, you will alert the wreckers to our presence."

Tarry muttered a curse and unsheathed his sword. Lunging forward, he attempted a savage blow to Sebastién's chest that glanced off the Frenchman's skillful parry and sent Tarry tottering backward.

"Who instructed you in the art of fencing," Sebastién taunted, "your nanny?"

Flushing to the roots of his hair, Tarry launched himself at the Frenchman. So skilled was Falconer with the blade that his actions appeared effortless, while Tarry began to show signs of tiring after only a few minutes.

The Frenchman seemed intent upon wearing his opponent out rather than killing him. Rachael hopped out of the way with a gasp when Tarry's blade almost pierced her shoulder as he stumbled under the Frenchman's relentless assault.

She fell to the ground when Sebastién shoved her out of harm's way and pressed his attack, scoring a flesh wound to Tarry's wrist.

Tarry dropped both sword and pistol.

Sebastién speared the sword hilt and flung Tarry's sword out of reach as Tarry dove to reclaim it.

Sebastién lunged forward, pressing the point of his blade into the soft flesh of Tarry's throat. Keeping his eyes on Tarry as he probed for the sword with his boot, Sebastién gave it a fierce kick, sending the weapon skittering down the steep path.

Tarry's eyes were huge with the realization the fight had ended and he had lost. The echo of his convulsive effort to swallow was visible in Sebastién's sword grip. His eyes followed the cautious movement of his opponent when Sebastién stooped to retrieve the pistol with his free hand.

Sebastién smiled genially. "I found the idea of being killed with my own pistol somewhat repugnant," he confessed.

Rachael dashed to his side and tugged at his arm, intending to plead for Tarry's life.

"Careful! Or you may just kill him yourself," he cautioned as he steadied his hand.

"Please don't hurt him," Rachael begged, voice catching in her throat. "Please let him go."

"I won't leave without Rachael," Tarry warned.

"*Convince him otherwise.*"

The Frenchman's tone prompted Rachael to pull Tarry to his feet and urge him down the path. "Go, Tarry," she said. Tarry shook his head and opened his mouth to protest, but she took one look at the Frenchman's face and hushed him. "*Go.*"

Tarry took a reluctant step in the direction of the beach before he turned and gave Rachael a fierce hug. "I'll be back."

"Go as far away from Cornwall as possible, *Monsieur* Morgan," Sebastién warned. "Spare me a second opportunity to take your life. I will not be so generous the next time."

Tarry began the slow trek down the path. Rachael took a deep breath, steadied herself, and glanced at Sebastién. He was watching her and pointed silently up the path in the direction of the cottage.

When she hesitated, he turned his head and squarely met her eyes, thunder building in his expression until she grasped her skirts and moved with a speed that belied the difficult terrain.

Rachael reached the cottage ahead of Sebastién, throwing wide the door and shouting for Mrs. Faraday. The housekeeper's presence in the hall at such a late hour indicated she was aware something was amiss.

"What's happened?"

"Will you help me escape?"

"You know who he is, then?"

"Yes. My friend Tarry tried to rescue me to-night—"

The woman gasped. "Did Mr. Falconer—?"

"No, he sent Tarry away."

The door slammed, the sound reverberating through-out the cottage. Sebastién entered the hall, cursing when Rachael spared him a brief, terrified glance before fleeing upstairs.

Chapter Six

From behind the barrier of her locked chamber door, Rachael heard the ominous creak of stair boards as someone approached. Feeling the helpless panic of a cornered animal, she spun and surveyed the room with wild-eyed desperation.

As the footfalls drew nearer, Rachael ran to the oak chest of drawers, braced her back against it, and pushed. The chest slid all of two inches toward the door. She groaned and shoved again with all her strength, gaining two more inches.

She was still within several feet of her goal when a knock sounded, spurring her into frenzied action. When Sebastién shouted to her from the other side of the door, she uttered a cry of distress and heaved herself against the side of the chest, frantic to complete the barricade.

The chest lurched forward, scoring furrows in the floor as it went. Rachael cringed at the sound, aware that he had heard it, too. But before she could push the chest the rest of the way, he had tried the knob, discovered it would not turn, and begun a ferocious assault upon the door.

The lock broke, bits of the mechanism showering the floor with a loud clatter. Rachael abandoned the chest and fled to a far corner of the room, where she searched the vanity top for a weapon. She grabbed a thick-bristled hairbrush in one hand and a small hand mirror in the other. When she rapped the mirror against the vanity, the glass exploded into several fragments, and she kept the largest shard as a makeshift weapon.

Sebastién entered the room and began to thread his way around the displaced chest of drawers. He stopped several feet shy of her and folded his arms across his chest.

"So, the arrangement of the furniture does not suit you?"

Sebastién seemed to gloat as he took in her pitiful arsenal of weapons and the evidence of her futile attempt to bar his entrance. He smiled, a chilling baring of white teeth against tanned skin. He did not attempt to come any closer. "We can be honest now, *Mademoiselle* Penrose," he said.

"*I* have always been honest."

Sebastién's eyes narrowed. The casual pose was a pretense. His posture was as rigid as a bowstring, and his jaw flexed with tension. His vivid eyes glittered with distrust.

She didn't know him. She had no idea who he was or what he wanted with her. Duped by his masquerade and the skillful flattery he had lavished upon her, she had been naïve to the point she had almost surrendered to a stranger. She, of all people, should have known that a pleasing exterior could conceal a monster. Hadn't her uncle taught her that lesson?

Rachael tightened her grip on the shard of glass without realizing it and gasped when stinging pain exploded in her grip. A ribbon of blood welled up on her palm.

Sensing movement, Rachael jerked her head up. Sebastién had used the distraction to edge closer to her. Retreat was out of the question; he seemed coiled and ready to pounce. He ducked when she hurled the hairbrush.

"Put that down before you injure yourself," he ordered.

"Surrender my only weapon? I think not." She maintained her hold on the mirror and lifted her chin in a shallow display of bravado.

Sebastién leaned against the chest and crossed his booted feet at the ankles. His smoldering gaze traveled Rachael's length with an intensity that made her breath catch. A molten pool of heat settled in the region of her stomach and fanned lower. She felt exposed and vulnerable. He had already breached her defenses once and was fully aware of how she had responded to him.

"You need not fear me, *ma chère*," he said. "I have no

plans to don a black robe and offer you up as a sacrifice to some pagan god."

"On the contrary, I believe it most prudent of me to fear you," she shot back. His attempt to soothe her only set her nerves more keenly on edge.

"You did not fear me last evening," he reminded her.

His expression had softened eyes vibrant with gold accents. The smile he bent on her was intimate and seductive, and her pulse leapt in response to his slow scrutiny.

It was difficult to breathe with him looking at her like that. This was not Tarry's friend John, but a man who had intended her harm. She must not forget that.

"You were someone else then. Someone I trusted."

Sebastién's jaw tensed, and his expression became unreadable. His persuasive smile devolved into a baleful look. "Ah, but the game has been interesting, *n'est ce pas?*"

"You refer to your game of identities?" Her already dry throat tightened as he suddenly pushed away from the chest and advanced on her, his look verging upon a glare.

"*Non.* I refer to your attempt to deceive me with your preposterous tale of woe."

Rachael started as if she had been slapped. "I told you the truth," she said, her voice rising in indignation. "And who deceived whom? You allowed me to think you believed me."

"It suited me," he said, unrepentant.

"And you always do what pleases you." She made no

effort to hide the mockery in her tone.

His expression grew pensive as he mulled over her words. "*Non*, if that were true, I would have had you in my bed by now."

The bald admission shocked her, and Rachael fidgeted under his amused regard. "What do you intend to do with me?"

"Now? At this very moment?" Sebastién raised one dark brow while he studied her with piercing contemplation.

Rachael frowned, realizing she had waved a red banner before his sarcastic wit. As his eyes bored into hers, she felt a tremor ripple through her in response.

"Move you," he said at length.

"Move me? Why?" A prickling of alarm passed through her.

"Surely you can guess? Morgan's next attempt at rescue may prompt me to return him to his father by cart, draped in lavender." He nodded at her reaction. "I see you comprehend my meaning."

How was she to rescue James if she was to remain this man's prisoner? There was no point in appealing to Falconer's better nature. She was sure he had none. She had told him her story, and he had chosen not to believe it.

"There is no point in imprisoning me or threatening Tarry. You have nothing to gain by it. My story is not going to change."

"That may be," he agreed, "but if you are not responsible for the treachery that took place at Prussia Cove, my search must still begin with you. I have heard your name too often in connection with it. If you are lying to protect yourself, I cannot afford to allow you to roam freely when you act the part of my enemy with such élan."

"I cannot change what you believe to be the truth, but if my brother is harmed while I am your prisoner, you *will* have made an enemy of me."

He looked surprised that she would dare to threaten him.

"I see you comprehend my meaning," she added archly, tossing his words back at him.

Sebastién's eyes darkened in the dim light until they shone like black coals.

The shard of glass slipped from Rachael's grasp, hitting the floor and shattering when he stepped forward and jerked her to him. The elusive, pleasing scent of spices drifted to her nostrils. *Of course he smells like spice. He no doubt traffics in it!*

A soft expulsion of air ruffled her hair when he spoke. "That was foolish. Never threaten me."

He appeared about to say more but pulled back and stared hard at her instead. Rachael trembled and her heart pounded with fear. A sound of misery escaped her, and she closed her eyes against the anger in his voice and the grinding power of his grip.

His hold on her eased and she felt his fingers gentle their grasp on her arm and the warm, feathery brush of his knuckles against her skin. She opened her eyes as he withdrew a handkerchief from his vest pocket and wrapped it around the cut on her hand without releasing her.

The swift change in his manner caused a strange feeling of anticipation tempered with apprehension to rise within her. "Let me go," she said, the huskiness in her voice sounding peculiar to her ears.

"Why?" he asked. His tone was silky. "Other women have found themselves in my embrace; none have expressed grievances. You did not complain earlier."

He had the audacity to remind her! Rachael ignored the irrational pang of jealousy she felt at his reference to other women. "This is not an embrace," she argued.

He chuckled and released her from the vise of his arms, but before she could step away, his hand closed around her wrist and his other hand encircled her waist and drew her forward.

Rachael found herself more fully in his grasp than before. When he leaned his cheek against hers and rubbed the shadowed stubble of his jaw against her skin, inhaling the fragrance of her hair, the simple gesture seemed strangely intimate.

"Now, *this* is an embrace, *oui*?"

She fought the awakening senses that threatened to reduce her insides to a quivering mass as heat from his body seeped through her clothing and settled low. What was wrong with her that he could affect her this way? What was it about this man that made her crave the perilous pleasure of his touch? Why did she still melt in his arms, even when she knew he hated her?

"I find this no more enjoyable than before."

He took her chin in his hand and gently forced her to look at him.

"Little liar," he admonished in a whisper. His fingers brushed the hair away from her face, and he smoothed the back of his hand against her cheek. "Do you expect me to believe that there is any less attraction between us at this moment than there was only hours ago? That has not changed."

Rachael closed her eyes as Sebastién moved his fingers down her neck with a deft touch, causing her to shiver as he neared the bodice of her gown. She tried to push his hand away, but he brought her palm to his lips, pressing kisses upon her fingers. He expended no effort in holding her, while his sensual assault confounded her desire to break free.

"Please . . ."

"I am the same man, beautiful English girl. Only my name is different," he said. He buried his face in her neck, nuzzling her throat, kissing her, his mouth searing her warming flesh. His mastery of her senses was paralyzing, subjugating her will. She didn't want him to release her.

Sebastién spoke in decorative, passionate French as his hands sought to create a romance language of their own. He cupped her breasts, rousing her even through the fabric of her gown while his mouth sought hers, stifling her halfhearted moan of protest with a lengthy, probing kiss. Rachael was swept into a swirling abyss of sensation and her mind whirled with longing.

"Tonight we have no names and no past." He lifted her into his arms and carried her from the room, molding her to him as if they were adjoining puzzle pieces. Raw desire flickered within the depths of his eyes, and she could feel his heart beating in tandem with her own. Sebastién carried her through the dim hallway into a large room with masculine furniture appointed in brass and polished teak.

Rachael felt the feather tick rise to meet her then was caught by his weight and pinned beneath him on the bed.

Sebastién pressed kisses against her flushed skin in an assault on her senses. She battled the traitorous urgings of her body as the muscles of his powerful arms corded and rippled when he turned her slowly, bringing her fully into his grasp.

Rachael's gown slipped from her body as if by sorcery, coaxed by gentle hands.

Sebastién's attention focused on the flesh exposed to his burning gaze, and his breath hitched in his throat, eyes darkening with passion.

Rachael moaned and tried to cover herself, her shyness assuaged by the intense desire on his face. It was obvious that he wanted her as much as she had wanted him only hours before. The fact that he had pretended to be someone else had not dimmed the attraction between them.

"Please . . ." she said again.

"*Oui*," he purred. "I intend to please you."

Sebastién dropped his hand to Rachael's abdomen, stroking her supple flesh with reverence. He slanted his mouth across her trembling lips as his hand dipped lower, drawing a short, involuntary gasp from her.

Shocked by his boldness and unable to govern the fevered response of her body, Rachael tried to turn away, cheeks flaming.

"Do not be shy, beautiful English girl," Sebastién said with an odd laugh.

He kneaded her flesh with skill, tracing a feather-tip pattern over her heated skin, causing an ache to build. Her senses had sharpened to an unbearable pitch, and when his mouth closed over her breast, she arched against him, reveling in the moist heat radiating from his lips and tongue.

Rachael closed her eyes against the delicious shock of sensation. A low moan escaped her throat and her eyes flew open at the plaintive need evident in her voice.

His face was so near that she was stunned. Every bit of stubble, every faint line, every pore beckoned inspection. When he looked down at her, she found meeting his gaze carried as much intimacy as the feel of his warm, possessive hands on her body. His eyes followed the line of her jaw and touched her lips in an almost tangible perusal, then he lowered his head and slanted his mouth over hers in a kiss that seemed designed to extract her very soul from her body.

Sebastién swept her thin chemise aside, and she became aware of the warmth emanating from him, a strange heat that kept her warm as no covering could. Unclothed, he was an ideal of taut flesh and sinew, his bronzed, muscled torso covered by a thatch of short, curly black hair.

Strong arms pressed her down, burrowing her into the wealth of pillows as Sebastién positioned one long leg over her, his knee thrust with casual intimacy between her thighs. An agony of sensation radiated through her stomach, and lower, at the contact, sending burning signals to her nerve ends as his touch continued to coax her senses to life.

Rachael spiraled toward the unknown and could only cling to Sebastién and marvel at the feeling building inside her, a steady, blooming rapture. He pushed her legs farther apart, and she shifted, trying to accommodate the press of his weight upon her. Then he poised above her for an instant, and she arched beneath him, crying out in surprise and pain as his body merged with hers, driving her down with the full thrust of his weight as he broke through the barrier of her innocence and filled her.

An unmistakable look of surprise flickered across his face as she held herself rigid, waiting for the pain to return. When it did not, she exhaled the breath she had drawn at the moment of his entry. The full implication of what had happened became the counterweight to exquisite sensation, and she stiffened.

Sebastién murmured in a voice so low she could not tell whether the words were French or English then lifted his hand and pushed the pale hair back from her face. He did it with such tenderness, she looked away and stared at the wall, unable to meet his eyes.

Rachael clung to Sebastién when he began to move, gaze fastening on his powerful arms as she sought distraction from the overwhelming intimacy of the act and the unexpected tremor of pleasure that was beginning to build.

Suddenly he gave a hoarse cry, then relaxed and rolled onto his back.

Rachael stole a sideways glance, observing the sculpted jaw and shock of straight hair that fell negligently over his brow. With his jet hair, mustache, and cat-green eyes, he had the look of a demon made pleasing to the eye so that he might accomplish evil on the earth more readily.

His eyes were closed and he had raised one arm, the elbow crooked, with the back of his hand resting across his forehead.

A small dark emblem on the underside of his arm caught her eye, and she lifted her head to examine it. It was a body painting of a *fleur-de-lis*.

Rachael stared, fascinated. No one she knew sported such fashion, and it only made him seem all the more exotic and dangerous. She closed her eyes at the thought. Had they just shared an act of passion or of revenge? Would he let her go now?

Sebastién rolled onto his side and looked down at Rachael. She felt the movement and turned her face away, hands worrying the mussed sheets.

"Did I hurt you?" he asked.

"Wasn't that your intention?"

He sighed and turned her toward him with gentle hands. "*Non,*" he said earnestly, with a frown that cleaved a line across his forehead. "You will not have pain the next time."

"There will be no next time!" She clutched the sheet to her chest and leaned over the bed, searching for her gown.

He rested against the bank of pillows and continued to study her. "Do not deceive yourself. There was a strong attraction between us. Sometimes it happens, even among enemies."

She could not decide which was worse, his reference to their attraction as a thing of the past, or being referred to as his enemy. She remembered with acute embarrassment that when he had been "John Wyatt," she had all but begged him to take her. She would not deny that she had wanted him. He already believed she was a liar.

"I do not know what you expect in the way of a reply, Mr. Falconer."

He laughed outright at her stilted manner of address. "Surely the use of my Christian name is appropriate?"

"You once intended to kill me, did you not? I would find it awkward to call you by your given name."

"It will become less awkward with practice."

The self-assured amusement in his voice rankled. She paused in retrieving her gown from the floor long enough to glare at him. "Oh? Which name do you prefer? Sebastién or John?"

His smile soured, and then vanished. "Perhaps I would prefer '*Monsieur* Falconer' from your lips," he gritted. He swung his long legs over the side of the bed and pulled on his breeches, jerky movements betraying his anger.

"You cry foul because you had feelings for 'John' and 'Sebastién' took his place. What you will not admit is that both are the same man. You begged to be seduced, *ma chère*. I simply obliged you."

When he had finished dressing, he reached for the gown she held in her lap. "You are not as likely to attempt escape with only a bedsheet to cover you."

His face remained shuttered as she hurled the gown at him, covering his head in yards of blue silk.

Chapter Seven

Faint, furtive noises awakened Rachael. At first it was the scrape of a chair, then the creak of a floorboard, followed by the sound of footfalls in the hallway. Sebastién would lumber through the place with no thought for those he might awaken, so when the door eased open, she remained quiet.

Mrs. Faraday padded barefoot into the room, wide gray eyes pleading for silence as she crept across the floor, wincing at every sound she made.

"I've been looking all over the cottage for you. I never expected to find you in Mr. Falconer's room." The housekeeper didn't say anything about having found her in his *bed*.

"I never expected to *be* in Mr. Falconer's room." She could not believe she had drifted off to sleep after he had taken her gown and stormed from the room. When he had not returned, she had remained, afraid to venture out and risk another confrontation with him.

"He's broken tradition for you. This chamber is his sanctuary. He never brings his women here."

"I could have done without that honor," Rachael harrumphed. She didn't want to hear about the accommodations he provided for other women he brought to his home, or be reminded that there would be other women after her. She had been infatuated with a man who had used her affection as a way to punish her.

"He was in a fine temper earlier," Mrs. Faraday said. "Did you argue?" When Rachael did not reply, she came closer and pushed a cloak into her hands. "I added a sleeping powder to his wine, but his sleep is fitful, even with the drug. You must leave at once."

"If you help me escape, he will turn his anger on you. He is certain I have acted against him and he is determined to punish me for it."

"He will not harm me. But where you are concerned, he does not know what to believe, or what to do."

She allowed the woman to pull the cloak over her shoulders and fasten the trail of heavy, flat buttons.

"Do not go to your own village. They believe you are a Customs informer; you will find no help there."

"Why do you believe I am innocent when your employer does not?"

Mrs. Faraday shook her head, eyes gone to slate, face

pale and creased. "Perhaps I am a better judge of character. I have a friend who lives in Littlebury who can aid you. Do you know the place?"

"Near Audley End?"

Mrs. Faraday nodded. "Ask anyone there to direct you to Henry Winstanley's home. Mr. Winstanley will see you safely out of Cornwall. He is acquainted with your friend Tarry."

"You should leave as well," Rachael urged. "It is not safe here for you."

Mrs. Faraday shook her head. "You do not know Mr. Falconer, Rachael. He is a good man, but he is the product of a difficult life. If he believes someone betrayed him—"

"I did not betray him!"

"But *he* does not know that. He is usually quite practical, but loses all ability to reason where you are concerned." She moved to the door, motioning for Rachael to follow.

Rachael slipped from the cottage and inched her way parallel to the beach, skirting the steep path. Her footprints would not be as visible there as they would be across the white sand of the shore, nor could a rider as easily follow her on horseback. She would have a few hours to make good her escape before Sebastién awakened from his drugged sleep and discovered what had transpired during his nap.

A low fence with a narrow turnstile in place of a gate framed Henry Winstanley's home. A copper cock perched to one side of the front entrance, while an ornate weatherglass rested on the opposite side. A large lantern upon which stood a weather vane crowned the roof.

Rachael could hear the rush of churning water, the source of which turned out to be a functional windmill in the back garden. A small but elaborate placard at the edge of the property promoted "*Winstanley's House of Wonders*," and declared an admission price of one shilling.

Her hesitant rap on the door drew noise from within, and she heard the deep rumble of a man's voice just before the door was thrown open. A man with a warm smile and astigmatic, almond-shaped eyes greeted her.

"Mr. Winstanley?" she asked.

"And you must be Rachael!" Winstanley clapped his hands in delight and beckoned her inside with a wave of his hand. "I adore reunions!" he exclaimed with an infectious burst of laughter as he propelled her toward a beaming Tarry Morgan.

Tarry held his arms wide and Rachael bounded into them with an exclamation of joy. She clutched him to her breast as if she feared he might disappear.

"Rachael," Tarry protested, laughing, "I cannot

breathe."

He pulled back, gripped her hands, and held her at arm's length. "I had come to seek Mr. Winstanley's aid in rescuing you—how did you manage to escape?"

"The housekeeper," Rachael said. "She drugged his wine."

"Bravo! Clever woman," Winstanley chirruped in approval.

He stepped between them and guided Rachael to a seat. "I fashioned this piece myself," he said with pride, tossing a wink at Tarry as he motioned Rachael into the chair.

She had no sooner leaned back against the polished oak when the armrests snapped downward in a deft, mechanized movement with a hollow groan of metal. She was pinned behind a sturdy bar of solid wood, imprisoned in the chair. Her mouth went dry, and her heart hammered in reaction.

"Tarry!" Rachael cried. She bit back a scream in response to the sensation so reminiscent of the restraints she had endured at Bedlam.

Tarry shouted at Winstanley to release her, and he acted at once, profuse with apology as he hurried to liberate her. She staggered free and whirled to face the chair, afraid it would spring after her like some beast from a nightmare.

"Oh, my dear, forgive me," Winstanley said. "This chair is one of my latest inventions. Tarry was amused by it. I had expected the same reaction from you."

"Amusement? I've been bound in chains and kept behind locked doors. Such hospitality will rob me of what remains of my sanity." She continued to stare at the prank chair, gripped by the terror it had evoked.

Winstanley dragged the offending chair from the room, and returned with an offer to help her select a "less talented" chair. She was aware of Tarry's eyes on her as she eased down upon a simple, armless stool. She met his gaze with a look of misery.

"I am going to challenge Victor Brightmore first, and then I will call Falconer out after him," Tarry announced.

"No, you aren't," Winstanley told Tarry, giving a sharp look. "You and Rachael are to take refuge among your father's friends at court. There is no need to risk further danger now that Rachael's brother is safe."

Rachael's mouth opened in surprise, and Tarry beamed.

"After I was unable to free you from Falconer, I followed the shore and caught up with Victor and his men. I spied on them as Victor ordered where each parcel would be taken. Rachael, they've hidden their plunder all over Cornwall—"

"Tarry, please," Rachael insisted, "what of James?"

"I saw one of the men carrying a bundle, and I could hear the squall of a babe. At first, I thought it came from the ship—"

"There were no survivors," Rachael interjected in a

dull voice.

"I overheard your uncle say to the man, 'Hide him well, that brat is the key to my inheritance'!" Tarry smiled when Rachael perked at his words. "Your uncle suspects you are alive and seeks to keep James out of your reach by juggling him as he would a hard apple. I followed your uncle's henchman and told him that Victor's plan had changed and that the babe was to be handed over to me."

"And he handed James over to you?"

"No. He called me a crude name and rudely suggested that I be on my way. I told him Brightmore had found a safer place to stash the brat, and it would be his neck, not mine, when Brightmore learned that his instructions were not carried out."

"And he handed James over to you then?"

"No. But he agreed to take James to the new hiding place, unaware that he is taking him to my father's London residence," Tarry chuckled. "It may be Victor's plan to pay the Frenchman a visit next." Tarry relayed the last bit of information with particular glee.

"I overheard Victor say that if you were not dead, you were certainly well hidden. He said he knew of one other man who shared his determination to find you. He thought Falconer might know your whereabouts."

"Falconer would not have aided Victor." She said it with certainty.

"Are you mad, Rachael? Both Falconer and Brightmore

want you dead. Why would they not team up and work together?"

"You do not know the Frenchman." Sebastién was not the sort who would trust a stranger. Besides, he seemed to feel that her punishment was his alone to mete out.

"Neither do you!" Tarry said. "You called him 'John Wyatt' and believed he was your rescuer and charming host!"

Rachael blushed. She could almost hear Sebastién say, "*Touché.*"

"I *do* know that he had the opportunity to harm me, but he did not," she said. Why had she sprung to his defense? She could never tell Tarry about what had transpired between them. Tarry would get himself killed avenging her honor, when her own naïveté had been mostly to blame.

"You sound infatuated with him," Tarry accused. "No doubt he thinks you are quite a fool! I'm sorry I interrupted your holiday by attempting to rescue you!"

"This would be a good time to pack for your journey," Winstanley said. He put firm hands on Tarry's shoulders and marched him to the door. "Leave the room and take the tension with you. That's a good boy," he said.

Tarry glowered at Winstanley and shrugged the man's hands from his shoulders before leaving the room in a sulk. Winstanley began to follow Tarry but paused in the doorway and turned back to Rachael with a sympathetic, insightful smile.

"Be patient with Tarry, Rachael," he said. "He dreamed he was a brave knight on a quest to rescue his fair damsel, only to be scorched and humiliated by the dragon."

Rachael felt safe at the center of the whirlwind that was life at court. As she attended her first public gathering, she could not help but gawk at the opulence surrounding her. Women attired in gowns of French silk, satin, damask, and brocade were ornaments on the arms of men dressed in equally stunning finery. Vivid floral patterns splashed across fabrics trimmed with jewels and gold embroidery. Even Tarry was turned out in embroidered gold satin. He tugged at the loosely knotted cravat at his throat as his eyes swept over the pageantry.

"How is James?" Tarry glanced down at the red lining peering out from beneath the scalloped tongues of his shoes rather than look at Rachael.

"James is well, thank you," she replied. Tarry had said very little to her after she had defended Falconer. It was clear he was not in a frame of mind to forgive her for it. What had possessed her to defend a man who had abducted, deceived, threatened, and seduced her? As far as she was concerned, her breach with Tarry was Falconer's fault, too.

The arrival of Phillip Morgan in the hall was a welcome distraction from her thoughts.

"Feet hurt, son?" Phillip asked with sympathy as Tarry winced and shifted his stance.

Tarry nodded, an expression of misery on his face. They had stood for hours, as proper court etiquette dictated. While the Queen had the comfort of an armchair, the only others permitted to sit in her presence were ladies of the rank of duchess, and then only on small stools that looked uncomfortable to Rachael.

"Rachael, you're lovely tonight," Phillip said. "Tarry insisted that the blue of the gown would almost match your eyes, and so it does."

Tarry turned red, but said nothing.

"Have you had word from Eleanor?" Tarry asked.

Phillip had been a widower since soon after Tarry's birth. Phillip's friendship with a woman of long acquaintance had gradually blossomed into love, but just as the two had begun to plan their nuptials, the lady had suddenly vanished.

"Perhaps her son has had word from her," Rachael suggested.

"Rachael, what an excellent idea! Eleanor's son is probably in attendance tonight. I have not seen him in some time."

A plump older woman draped in an exquisitely

beaded gown of lavender silk made her way toward them. The drape was so confining that she called to mind a pigeon as she took tiny steps in stilted shoes. She inspected Rachael, peering through pince-nez.

"Phillip, darling," the woman cooed, eyes never leaving Rachael, "a new companion?" Her eyes appraised the gown Rachael wore. "Where has he been hiding you, my dear?" She turned to Phillip. "And don't you try passing her off as a distant relation," she warned with a peal of laughter. "You've no cousins nearly so lovely."

"No relation, Madeleine. A childhood friend of Tarry's," Phillip explained politely.

The woman's eyes slid to Tarry, who fidgeted under her amused regard. "You've outgrown toy soldiers, I see," she teased with a sly wink.

A renewed burst of color spanned Tarry's cheeks, and the look he bent upon the woman was far from amused.

"Madeleine, Madeleine," Phillip scolded. "You'll have all of London simmering with rumors before the night is out. Might I engage your assistance in locating Eleanor's son?" he asked.

"Where *is* the gracious Eleanor?" Madeleine asked. "I've seen that dashing son of hers, but as for the lady herself . . ."

"You've seen her son this evening?"

"Oh, yes. And so has every other eligible female present," she laughed, fanning herself.

"I was unaware he was at court. His work with

Customs usually keeps him near the waterways."

"So that's what he . . . a Customs officer," Madeleine said, filing away the tidbit. Her eyes strayed to the crowd as she hid her broad smile behind a fan. "I do believe the man you seek has spotted you, or I should say, he's trying to catch a better glimpse of the young lady," she informed Phillip.

Madeleine's fawning enthusiasm was such that Rachael had to resist the urge to turn and gawk as the man approached.

Phillip greeted Eleanor's son warmly. "Tarry, I should like to introduce you to Eleanor's son Jacques, who will be your brother one day."

Rachael caught a brief glimpse of each face surrounding her when she turned to watch as Tarry was introduced to Eleanor's son. Madeleine's face was puffed with pleasure, and Phillip's thin countenance glowed with pride.

It was Tarry's reaction that caused alarm to ripple through her. He went white, and his eyes grew enormous. His breath hitched and he stepped between Rachael and the man when she turned toward Phillip and the subject of his introduction.

She gave a shallow gasp and backed away, shaking her head in disbelief at the familiar black hair, tanned skin, white teeth, and green eyes. Even without the mustache and the stubble of beard, the contours of that face were ingrained in her memory. Phillip's voice floated to her as if from a great distance.

"I would like you to meet Jacques—"

"Falconer!" Tarry exclaimed in a loud voice.

"Falconer," Rachael whispered in dismay.

"Falconer," Phillip finished, his expression puzzled as he looked from Tarry to Rachael.

"I am pleased to make your acquaintance," Jacques Falconer said in a cultured voice. He smiled, his widely set, jade-colored eyes resting on her face. She could detect no recognition in them.

"Pardon me?" Her voice had soared an octave.

"I said I am pleased to meet you, Miss . . .?"

She knew then what had made her want to hear his voice again. His speech was clipped, the English accent pronounced. There was no hint of the Frenchman's fluid, mellifluous vowels and absence of consonance.

He extended a well-groomed hand to her, and Rachael recoiled from it, feeling heat flood her face. She felt trapped and desperate, pinioned by the crowd. *This is what it must feel like to be insane.* She turned and bolted, clawing her way through the horde of onlookers.

Rachael's shocking public reaction to Sebastién Falconer's twin created a scandal, and Jacques refused a third-party apology. He insisted that she agree to a private meeting with him. No doubt he shared his brother's obstinate nature, she reflected as she knocked at the library door of Phillip's London apartment.

"Come in, Miss Penrose."

He was seated in an overstuffed chair near a wall of bookshelves. Although the shadow of dusk had descended over the room, she could see his features plainly enough and was dismayed by the flood of emotion the familiar face awakened within her.

His eyes held a haughty light that marked him different from his brother, but his generous lips turned up at the corners in the same way, and nature had sculpted the fine bones of his face with the same loving hand.

He met her look of appraisal with one of his own, and Rachael diverted her eyes to the books behind him. He startled her with an unexpected laugh, and rose from the chair, extending his hand to her. His eyes sparkled when he smiled, but with a frosty light. Beneath his decorum she sensed a will every bit as strong as his brother's, and the same sort of ruthless purpose.

"You looked for a moment like a small mouse contemplating a gluttonous cat," he commented. "I assure you, I am nothing like my brother. I was sorry to learn that you had suffered at his hands, as I have."

"You, sir?"

He looked at her, the achingly familiar eyes exploring her face as if seeking something kindred there. She was spellbound, fascinated by the uncanny physical resemblance to Sebastién. Jacques indicated two plush chairs near the marble fireplace, guided Rachael to one, and then took the chair opposite.

"My brother would not be satisfied with plunging a rapier through my heart, or felling me with pistol shot. He wants to destroy me fractionally, from the inside out. I must endeavor to destroy him first. With you to aid me—"

"Mr. Falconer," Rachael said, "I am in danger because your brother believes I betrayed him. To participate in a plot against him now would be imprudent of me, to say the least."

He had started to speak over her words, but held back, impatience and irritation flickering over his face.

"He means to kill you, Miss Penrose." There was a roiling tension just beneath his surface. "One would assume you might object. I had hoped you would be willing to aid us again. After the vital information you provided about Prussia Cove—"

"*Prussia Cove!* So that's it. You and your brother share the same misinformation," Rachael said with an exasperated shake of her head. "I had nothing to do with the betrayal of your brother's gang, Mr. Falconer. It was not I who aided you."

Jacques stared at her. "How can that be? The messages received by the Custom House all bore your signature."

"I have enemies as well. Your brother was not among

them until recently."

"You have it in your power to help me rid England of a menace. I cannot comprehend why you would refuse, particularly when he abducted and abused you."

"I know nothing of your brother, except that he believes I betrayed him. I certainly do not wish to continue to court his enmity."

"If you do not act, he will go unpunished."

"The wheels of justice will spin without a turn from my hand," she replied with a weary sigh. "This has been a nightmare, and I want it to be over."

His answering stare was glacial. "If you are unwilling to help stop this fiend, you are no better than he."

She had not come to the interview expecting a verbal attack and started to rise from her chair, but Jacques stood with her, an implicit threat in his stance.

"*Sit down*," he growled.

She sank back into her chair, eyes fixed on his face.

"Let me tell you about my brother," he said. "I want you to know all about the man you are so eager to protect. Were it not for this undeniable physical link, I might be able to deny that I have a brother at all.

"Soon after my appointment as a revenue officer, Sebastién began to transport illicit cargo. He delights in jeopardizing my livelihood by preying wherever I have been assigned, bribing those under my authority, and flaunting his connections whenever I manage to bring him before the Court of the Exchequer." He fastened his gaze upon Rachael. "Pranks, you might say? A harmless rivalry between brothers?"

Jacques laughed, and the sound chilled her. He approached her and leaned forward as she shrank into the chair. A shiny lock of his black hair tumbled forward, and he brushed it back with the palm of his hand. The muscles of his hand were knotted, the knuckles white. He locked eyes with her.

"He is not just a smuggler, Miss Penrose. He is also a wrecker."

Her mind flashed back to the wrecking she had witnessed. Had Sebastién been a part of it? She recalled him walking up the steep path, outfitted with a sword, his clothes damp. She had seen him pocket a piece of jewelry. Had it been payment for his participation in the crime? She made a sound of distress and closed her eyes against the disturbing memory, not wanting to believe it of him. If it was true, he was no better than her uncle.

"That is why you cannot consider yourself safe. I do not act out of blind hatred for my brother. I seek justice for those who have met their deaths at his hands and at the hands of men like him. I seek justice for one young woman in particular, who was to be my wife."

Rachael felt as if she had been gripped about the throat by an invisible hand. The boundless grief in his voice could be measured on his tortured face, that face so like his brother's.

"I had closed down an enterprise of his that ran

tea from the French coast to the basement of a Bodmin pub. My brother vowed that if I ever interfered with him again, I would regret it. I ignored the warning, never realizing those I loved were in jeopardy as well. I might have known the coward would make a young woman suffer in my stead.

"One week later, my fiancée, Adrienne, was aboard a ship bound for England from France when my brother and his crew of cutthroats urged the vessel farther inland than was safe. The ship was smashed to kindling upon the Eddystone rocks. Her crew and passengers were slaughtered."

Rachael's slender fingers gripped the collar of her cloak. "How can you be sure your brother was responsible?"

"He was eager for me to know the deed had been his." Jacques's fingers dipped into his vest pocket, and he withdrew a small locket. "I had given this locket to Adrienne. It was returned to me after the wreck. The envelope containing the locket also bore a brief message: 'Greetings, dear brother.'"

A ragged sound escaped her, and Jacques's attention was torn from the pendant to her face.

"Don't fancy yourself safe here at court. My brother is extraordinarily well connected, or I should say our grandfather has influential friends and Sebastién makes good use of them."

He hesitated, eyes moving over her face as if trying

to read her expression. "If you are still considering refusing to help me, I must inform you that I am aware of your difficulties with your uncle, including your holiday at Bedlam." He shrugged at her look of astonishment. "If you cooperate with me, you will find yourself under my protection."

"And if I do not?"

"I will not lift a finger to help you."

"There are others who would speak on my behalf," Rachael argued, outraged by the threat.

"Who? A lovesick boy and his doting father? There were many who witnessed your reaction when we met," he reminded her. "The impression you gave was not one of stability."

There was no argument for that. She remembered all too well how she had reacted.

"You will be rewarded for your assistance. Your case against your uncle would benefit from the support of a man of my rank. If you refuse to assist me, you leave me no choice but to implicate you in my brother's crimes. Or, you could just as easily be returned to Bedlam."

The threat rang in her ears. All options had been removed from her. If she did not manage to remain free, her brother would die. "What is it you want to know?"

The cold light flickered in his eyes. "How many stay in that cottage Sebastién is fond of hiding himself away in?"

"What do you mean?"

"He must have part of his gang in hiding there, or

nearby. His home is too easily defended, which is why it will be necessary to lure him away. I won't take my men into a hornets' nest."

"I saw only Sebastién, and the housekeeper, Mrs. F—"

"I have no interest in his staff," Jacques said curtly. "What about The Dane?" At her blank expression, he added, "A blond bear of a man. Tattooed."

"I saw no one else," she repeated. "And he would not have shared information with me. He does not trust me." She winced at her words. *He does not trust me.*

Jacques rubbed his chin, and an unbidden memory came to her of Sebastién pulling at the edges of his mustache when deep in thought. "Do you think he would come to you if you were to summon him?"

"Why?" She felt the cold dread of premonition.

"You seem to be his favorite bait."

Rachael stared at him, aghast. "Why would he come to me here in London? Why would he meet me anywhere, for that matter? We did not part on the best of terms."

"You would meet him on the coast, in his own territory, where he has a false sense of security."

Rachael shook her head. "He would recognize it as a trap. You're asking me to risk my life."

"You would be in no danger," Jacques assured her. "You would meet him in a public place. What reason could you give for wanting a meeting with him?"

I'm to be dangled before a hungry shark. "I may be your pawn, Mr. Falconer," Rachael said, "but how you trick your brother into meeting me is your own affair. I hope you lose sleep over it."

She sprang from her chair and hurried to the door. When she reached it, she spun to face him again, and was taken aback by the impression that his eyes had never left her.

"You're wrong on one point," she said. "You are, indeed, very much like your brother."

Jacques's hands clutched the arms of the chair, and Rachael could see that they shook with anger. She slipped through the door and ran down the empty hall. In the distance, she heard a faint, muffled curse and the shattering of glass.

Chapter Eight

Public coaches were not available for night excursions, so Jacques hired a private vehicle for their journey. Once he had formulated his plan, he had been anxious to see it carried out.

His prolonged silence as they made their way south did nothing to calm Rachael's anxiety about the role she was about to play in Sebastién's capture. She had not asked for details. The sooner the deed was done, the more quickly she could begin to forget her own part in it, although she doubted she would ever forget.

The thought of meeting Sebastién in some rough pub near the Devon mainland filled her with anxiety. She had insisted she was innocent of any conspiracy against him, yet here she was, about to betray him. He would never believe her now, and she could not blame him, although he might not live long enough to ponder her treachery. Somehow, that thought lent new depth to her misery.

Tarry was pleased by her participation only because she had said nothing to him about Jacques's threats. If he knew, it would drive a wedge between the two men who would one day be related by marriage.

The carriage rolled to a stop in front of Winstanley's home, where Rachael would lodge until departing for the meeting with Sebastién the following night. Winstanley's place was not monitored by the wary legion of smugglers, so it had been arranged that she would sleep there.

Winstanley ushered Rachael and Tarry into the house while Jacques remained outside to patrol the narrow lane. Henry Winstanley was a talkative host, chatting as he led them to their rooms.

Outside, Jacques huddled against the chill as two riders on horseback approached. He cast a furtive glance at the house before motioning them to meet him a few yards away.

"Is it done, Matt?" Jacques asked of the middle-aged man who had extended his hand for payment.

"Aye," the man replied.

Jacques withdrew a pouch from his vest pocket and

tossed it to him. Matt hefted the bag in his hand, then slipped it inside his threadbare coat. He urged his horse into motion and departed without a word or a backward glance at Jacques.

"Did he earn his pay?" Jacques asked the man who remained.

"We delivered a baby."

Jacques nodded, satisfied with the reply. "I half-expected old Matt to double-cross me. I've sent several of his relatives to the gaol. There's a purse of equal size for you, and your task is simple," Jacques said as he handed the man a wax-sealed envelope.

"A trip to the penny post at this hour?"

Jacques shook his head. "You're to deliver this to the house at the end of the row," he instructed, indicating Winstanley's home. "Ride out and return in four hours. *Ride hard.* I want to see lather on your horse."

Jacques stood alone in the narrow lane long after the rider had departed. He lit a cheroot and gazed up at the starless sky.

A clock somewhere within the house chimed an early hour. Unable to sleep, Rachael gathered her dressing gown around her and made her way down the hall. Light flowed from a small workroom where Mr. Winstanley labored.

As she passed by, he glanced up and beckoned her into the room where he sat pouring over sketches of the lighthouse he had constructed near the Eddystone rocks.

"Are you hilla-ridden, child?" he asked, using the Cornish term for "nightmare."

"My worst nightmares seem to occur during my waking hours," she confided.

Winstanley frowned, turning from his work to face her. "I wish I knew of a way to help you." His eyes strayed to the lighthouse sketches and he eagerly began to riffle through the contents of his desk drawer. His hand closed over a large key, which he dropped into Rachael's lap.

"That is a spare key to my greatest creation, the Eddystone Light. If you are ever in need of a safe place, go there. The lighthouse has enough provisions to last for several weeks. It has withstood many storms; you'd be safe there. My greatest wish is to be on the reef during the greatest storm that ever blew under the face of heaven," he said. "Perhaps you'll agree to a tour after this business in Devon is finished?"

Rachael nodded, unable to keep her mind from dwelling on the impending meeting with Sebastién. She could not shake the feeling that she was being forced to participate in a game missing several key players and one with no clear set of rules.

When the rider appeared, his cries roused everyone from their beds. They stumbled disheveled and bleary-eyed toward the entryway.

"What is it?" Tarry exclaimed.

With a flourish, the rider produced the letter Jacques had given him. Tarry snatched the paper from the man's hand and Rachael peered over Tarry's shoulder as he ripped open the envelope. Her eyes followed the words as Tarry read them aloud.

Miss Penrose:

I will grant the interview you requested. I have borrowed your brother to guarantee my safety. Thus, I am assured that you will not fail to keep our appointment and send a regiment to convey your regrets. Your brother is in the care of a bon ami *who will take action should I fail to return within a reasonable amount of time.*

—Sebastièn Falconer

"Bastard!" Tarry said.

"Give me a pistol," she demanded, furious. "I'll get James back safely even if I have to shoot Falconer myself!"

Jacques stepped forward and offered her a small pistol. "Do you know how to fire it?" he asked.

"I will manage." She stalked down the hallway to her room, no longer feeling any qualms about her participation in the trap being set. She felt no fear, only a stony, unwavering sense of purpose. How *dare* he steal her brother!

Jacques waited until Rachael and Tarry were out of earshot before he turned to Winstanley with a conspiratorial grin.

"My brother doesn't have James," Jacques told him. "I had a man place a foundling on his doorstep with a forged note from Rachael requesting a meeting. Sebastién will believe that Rachael has offered her brother as a guarantee that no trap is being set. It was a way to make him believe he has a hostage."

"You must tell Rachael," Winstanley urged. "She will be out of her mind with worry. She may even try to kill your brother."

"If he suspects a snare, he may try to harm her. She will be more convincing if she believes he has James," Jacques argued. "This way, she is armed and able to protect herself."

He did not confide his concern that Rachael might

be tempted to warn Sebastién of the trap. Her reluctance to take part in the plan had made him doubt her reliability. It had been necessary to make her believe she had something at stake.

Sebastién would have no reason to doubt the infant on his doorstep was Rachael's brother. He would feel safe in attending the meeting with her, and he would never learn that Jacques had tricked her as well. Sebastién would be led to believe the woman he had allowed to escape with her life had plotted against him, which would only add to the torment Jacques had planned for him.

The balmy night turned cooler, and a buffeting wind carried the salt spray inland, filling the air with the pungent scent of the sea. At the small cottage atop the hill, a pair of unsecured shutters slapped against the building.

"Mon Dieu!" Sebastién shouted. "Is there no quiet place?"

Mrs. Faraday peeked into the room just as Sebastién poured himself a liberal portion of rum. It was a familiar scene. He haunted his study and drank too much. His moods were varied shades of black and gray, and what had once been courage was becoming recklessness.

During his initial burst of rage after finding Rachael gone, he had tossed the mantua into the fire with such a display of temper that he seemed to have burned her in effigy. For days, he had said nothing about his departed "guest," but when he had finally spoken of her again, it had been to speculate on whether or not she was the Customs informant. He was behaving like a man racked with guilt.

One by one, his friends had come to warn him that his brother was aware of the location of his hideout and might arrive at any moment with a regiment. The housekeeper had urged Sebastién to leave, but he seemed to care little about what fate awaited him.

"The rum decanter is almost empty," he informed Mrs. Faraday, with a curt nod toward the liquor cabinet.

"I would have to walk the house with a cask strapped to my back to keep it filled," she replied, tired of hearing that particular grievance.

"Another sly nag about my drinking."

The words were flawlessly enunciated. He could hold a fair amount of liquor with no outward sign of it other than a flair for rudeness, which he also possessed when sober.

The shutters continued to bang, and now there was a faint cry mingled with the mournful howl of the wind.

"What was that?" Mrs. Faraday asked.

"The wind," Sebastién said. "The damned shutters." The sound came again, a shrill wail followed by the shriek of the wind. "A cat," he speculated, "come to harmonize with the damned shutters!"

The sound repeated, a short screech dissolving into a petulant squall. The shutters rattled in accompaniment. Sebastién started toward the door, but Mrs. Faraday hurried to intercept him.

"Let me shoo the cat, if there is one."

"*Non*," he said. "I want *le chat* to remember me." He marched through the parted study doors, crossed the hall, and flung wide the front door, Mrs. Faraday behind him.

A shutter cracked against the frame as a renewed cry broke out at his feet and he stared down at a heavily swaddled bundle on his doorstep. Pushing past him with a sound of distress, Mrs. Faraday bent and scooped the small parcel into her arms, hurrying with it into the warmth of the cottage.

Sebastién stepped outside and glanced around the perimeter of the house, his hair buffeted by the strong wind funneling into the cottage through the gaping door.

"Close the door!" Mrs. Faraday shouted.

He immediately obeyed. The arrival of a foundling on his doorstep warranted another drink. Sebastién disappeared into his study and drained the rum decanter in a single swallow, eyeing the empty bottle with regret.

He sought out Mrs. Faraday again to remind her of the empty decanter, and found her in the center of the parlor, heedless of the mewling infant she had placed on the settee. She held a piece of parchment in her hand. Without a word, he stepped forward and snatched it from her. The message was printed in a neat, economical script.

Mr. Falconer:

I request a meeting with you at Tor Pub near Rame Head, at eight o'clock tomorrow eve. I am able to reveal the identity of the true perpetrator of an act you had attributed to me. To assure you that this is not a ruse intended to trap you, my brother, James, will act as your hostage until our business is concluded. Please take good care of him. James is precious to me and he is the only means I have of gaining your trust.

—Rachael Penrose

"Of course, you will not go," Mrs. Faraday said over her shoulder as she unfurled the infant from its cocoon of swaddling.

"Of course I *will* go," Sebastién said. He reread the message, searching for hidden meaning in the words.

"This has the feel of a trap. Rachael would have hidden from you, not sought you out. She's terrified of you."

"Did I ask your opinion?" And who had given her leave to be so blunt in voicing it?

"You must not agree to it," she insisted.

"She would not endanger her brother. She has already suffered much on his account. Or so she says."

The baby lay naked, kicking amongst the layers of cloth and beaming up at Mrs. Faraday, who stared down at her tiny charge, surprise and confusion lighting her face.

"I can offer you absolute proof that a trap has been set," she said.

Her odd tone prompted him to turn and face her, and he raised one brow in inquiry.

"This cannot be Rachael's brother," she said matter-of-factly. "This baby is a girl."

The rotting support beams and patchy, water-stained ceiling of Tor Pub, Rame Head, framed an interior scattered with upturned, mismatched broken furniture and filthy floors of alternating dirt and hardwood. The place looked as if a faint breath expelled against a crucial joist might cause it to collapse.

Sebastién had arrived at the rough pub an hour ahead of the meeting time. The fact that he was here was proof, according to Mrs. Faraday, that he had lost his mind. He wasn't so sure that wasn't the truth of it. The Exchequer had granted his freedom with the stipulation that he return to France. He had initially remained for the purpose of flushing Rachael Penrose out of hiding, but now a different sort of obsession kept him in England.

The meeting was a trap, of course, and Rachael was a key participant. It was worth the risk of hanging to catch her in a plot against him, after all her wide-eyed protestations of innocence. He yearned to expose her for the liar he knew her to be.

It galled him that she thought him dim-witted enough to fall for a crude ruse such as the one she and Jacques had concocted against him. Did she believe she had found a powerful ally in Jacques? He viewed her collaboration with his brother as her final, unpardonable transgression against him.

His keen anticipation of the moment she would enter the pub had not prepared him for the reality of actually seeing her again. She hesitated in the doorway, soft features pinched, blue eyes bright and watchful.

Apprehension clouded her face, and the fragile quality that was unique to her, no matter how plucky she tried to appear, made the rough pub seem all the more sordid and unsuitable a meeting place.

It was obvious she was afraid. She had no reason to believe he would not harm her. Why, then, was she here? She knew he did not hold her brother hostage. For what reason, or reward, had she placed herself in jeopardy?

He had not expected to feel protective toward her, and he cursed himself for being a fool. She had touched upon vulnerability within him he had never known existed, and laid it bare, like a raw nerve. He was at the crossroads where heaven and hell intersected, and the signpost was Rachael Penrose. He needed to expose her for the treacherous witch she was, and soon, before her sins ceased to matter to him.

Rachael was suitably dressed for the location in a long black mantle with deep pockets, the right holding the pistol Jacques had given her. Her shoes were encased in pattens, wooden soles raised on iron rings for easy travel through the heavy mud. She drew the attached hood of the mantle forward in an attempt to conceal her face as she passed through the rough crowd.

Rachael felt his eyes upon her even before she located him in the room. He was not seated near a wall, with his back and sides protected as she had expected. His choice of a center table was bold and reckless. Aware she was the subject of his blistering regard, she took a deep breath and forced herself to approach.

Two steps from his table, she hesitated, and the perceptive smirk that molded his lips goaded her into taking the chair opposite him. The clamor in the noisy pub provided a welcome buffer against the awkward silence. She had no idea what to say to him.

His eyes never left her face as he poured rum into his

glass. The liquor splattered across the top of the knotty table.

"You came here to talk," he said gruffly. "So, talk." He slid the half- empty bottle across the table toward her, along with a grimy glass. "That should loosen your tongue."

"You'll not want my tongue loosened. It may venture my opinion of you."

He shrugged. "Drink to give yourself courage, then."

Was it so obvious she was terrified? Rachael poured a finger of rum into the dirty glass and stared down at the amber liquid. "Why? Because you would prefer to dull my wits?"

The first of Jacques's men entered the pub. A moment later, two others followed, trailed by three more.

"Even an insignificant enemy can be deadly under the right circumstances."

His black-fringed, bright gaze swept their surroundings, and then cut back to her. There was no humor in his smile. "I would not call you an insignificant enemy, Rachael."

The well-aimed barb earned a scowl from her, but she also felt a pang of remorse. He was about to learn she *was* his enemy, despite her having been forced into the role, but she didn't want to be his enemy. She didn't want to be here. She only wanted her brother back.

Sebastién startled her by bellowing a jovial greeting as someone approached the table. She gazed up in awe as a man who looked like a giant from a folk tale joined them. He was a tall, ponderous column of muscle and sinew with a crop of white-blond hair and small, bright blue eyes.

He glanced her way but did not acknowledge her. *He must be The Dane.* He fit the description given by Jacques. She watched as the man revealed that he also sported a *fleur-de-lis* on his upper right arm similar to the mark Sebastién wore.

Sebastién conversed with the man in French, for the purpose of excluding her, no doubt. The blond giant grunted a reply, and Sebastién thumped the huge man on the back, laughing when the other pretended to stagger from the blow.

His manner changed when he was with someone he trusted. His eyes were wide and amused, his face smooth and open. In any mood, he was an incredibly handsome man, but this side of him made her heart ache. By contrast, there was only suspicion in his eyes when he looked at her. If only he were not capable of such despicable acts. If only he had not kidnapped her brother. If only . . .

Still smiling, he watched as the fair giant ambled toward the far end of the pub. When he turned and saw that she studied him, it was as if a shutter had been drawn. His expression became remote. *Guarded.* She was, after all, the enemy.

Jacques's men would seize him at any moment. The knowledge gave her no comfort at all. Instead, it made her want to justify her participation in the plot against him to lessen the guilt she felt. The noise in the pub was becoming a din, and she had to raise her voice to be heard.

"What I told you at the cottage was the truth. I have been my uncle's victim, and I have been your victim. You betrayed me by showing me kindness when what you really are is a scoundrel."

"By all means, be candid, *mademoiselle*."

He was listening with brutal attention to every word she said. The skin had whitened around his mouth, and his vibrant eyes gleamed. A muscle leapt along his cheek, as if he ground his teeth. She spotted several of Jacques's men lining the corners of the pub, their eyes upon their quarry. She was in no danger from him; she could speak her mind freely. He had to shoulder some of the responsibility for the situation in which they found themselves.

"If I am your enemy now, you have only yourself to blame. Anyone willing to endanger a baby is a scoundrel—"

She uttered a sharp cry of surprise when his hands closed over her wrists, jerking her forward and pinning her to the table, palms down. She lay across the knotty wood, the thick plank bruising her ribs, her face only inches from his.

Rachael dared not move, and no one seemed inclined to come to her aid. She cringed as her focus moved outward from the creases near his eyes to the flare of his nostrils above the silky mustache and the cruel set of his mouth. He looked furious. Her throat was dry and she swallowed, wincing. She had bitten her tongue.

"Do I risk having you label me a scoundrel by drawing attention to the fact that I have caught you in a lie? *You* are the one who was willing to offer your brother as a guarantee—or should I say *bait*—so that I might be persuaded to agree to this meeting."

Rachael stared at him, dumbfounded. "I did no such thing! You abducted James and left a note—"

"I should like to see this note," he growled.

"How can you deny it? You must know that I would not willingly venture within a thousand miles of you!"

He released his grip on her as if her words had stung him, and she slumped back into the chair.

"I assure you that if I had desired a reunion, I would not have arranged it in this manner." Outrage and insult darkened his face. She suspected he had spoken in earnest.

"You must know that I would not risk my brother for any reason."

"The fact remains that a squalling, smelly bundle was deposited on my doorstep, complete with a note from you requesting this meeting and offering the child as guarantee of my safety."

"Are you implying that Jacques had my brother kidnapped and delivered to you?"

"Not exactly." He appeared about to say more, but frowned at her instead as a look of suspicion crossed his face.

"I should like to see the note," she said.

"You will have to believe what I say is true, *non?*" His mouth twisted at the irony. "I did not come here to harm you, Rachael. I came because your note claimed you could prove you had nothing to do with Prussia Cove."

"You would have been willing to listen?" The possibility astounded her, but more than that, it gave her hope. She caught a glimpse of something in his flinty eyes that made her pause. Had it been hurt? Regret?

"Despite what you may think, I am not a monster. I would not use an infant as a shield. This concerns only the two of us, and perhaps the real informer." When she perked, he brusquely added, "If you are, as you say, not the guilty party."

"I assure you I am not." The air fairly rang with his unvoiced challenge. "Can I assume that your plan to have me drawn and quartered has been deferred?"

He threw back his head and laughed, eyes glittering; or was it a trick of the light? He seemed in rare good spirits, under the circumstances. But then, he did not know that his brother was preparing to arrest him, with her cooperation.

Had Jacques tricked them both? Had he arranged for James to be taken to Sebastién's cottage? He had known she was reluctant to cooperate. How far would he have gone to guarantee her participation?

"Murder is a more useful threat than a solution, *ma chère.* The world is a harsh, at times ugly place. Why would I want to destroy what little beauty I find in it?"

His eyes rested on her lips, the meaning of his words made clear by the warm light in their depths. Her gaze was drawn to his full, sensuous mouth, and she suddenly recalled the feel of his lips on hers. The memory was unsettling because it made her ache with a yearning she knew could never be fulfilled.

Rachael felt like a rabbit that had wandered into a snare, reeling with instincts that shouted, "Beware!" too late to be of any value. She had come prepared to entrap him, but it was she who had been caught. If Jacques's plan succeeded, Sebastién would believe that she had lied to him all along. Her opportunity to convince him that she had never acted against him would be lost forever.

He did not seem to intend James any harm, but what would happen to her brother if he did not return? Was Jacques willing to sacrifice her brother in order to see his plan succeed? Jacques might be, but she was not. If she warned Sebastién about the trap, he might be grateful enough to return her brother to her.

The tavern swarmed with people, and it seemed to Rachael that every other man was a soldier in disguise. She glanced around the room, noting that men skirted the inside perimeter of the pub. The exits were blocked. Jacques's men were a sober contrast to the rowdy revelers who danced and caroused throughout the small room.

She and Sebastién seemed to be the only two people still seated, while the rest frolicked. Tension mounted within her until she felt she might scream. He was about to be apprehended, or killed. Why did she feel an overwhelming urge to warn him?

She met his eyes and his brow rose in inquiry, as if he sensed her indecision. On impulse, she reached out and grasped his arm. He stared down at the sight of her delicate hand pressed against his muscular forearm and glanced up at her, expression wary.

"Sebastién, this is a trap," she blurted.

Chapter Nine

When his face registered only a subtle change in expression, she concluded that he had not heard her. There must be no misunderstanding between them, even if she had to repeat the bitter mouthful. Not this time.

"This is a trap," she repeated, voice rising. "If you never again believe anything I tell you, please believe me now, for your own sake! There are soldiers—"

"How many?" The urgency in his voice belied his placid expression as he turned to scan the room.

"At least twenty, perhaps more." She stared, perplexed by his calm.

"Weapons?"

"Yes." He fixed her with a look of exasperation, and she cringed and stammered, "P-pistols and swords."

"Led by?"

She hesitated. "Your brother."

Sebastién nodded, his face a mask. He considered her for a long moment, and then reached into the folds of his cloak.

"One more question," he said. "Have you ever seen this before?" He withdrew his hand and opened his palm to reveal an elaborate signet ring.

She sensed that he would not allow her to take it from him in order to examine it more closely. She leaned forward and peered at the ring.

"It looks like one I've seen my uncle wear," she said. She knew better than to inquire how it had ended up in his possession.

"*Bon*" was all he said. He looked inordinately pleased.

"I have a pistol in the pocket of my cloak," she volunteered. She began to reach for it, but he shook his head, freezing her with a look.

"Produce a pistol, and I can guarantee the result," he cautioned. He looked at her with an odd expression on his face, a mixture of warmth, approval, and amusement. "The number of men, the types of weapons, their leader, the owner of the ring—all the truth. I applaud your honesty. Was the last minute warning part of the plan, or just a frill you added on your own?"

"My own idea, entirely." He had mercilessly baited her and enjoyed every moment of it! "May I ask why you came, when you knew it was a trap?"

"I don't know," he admitted. "Perhaps I was intrigued by what you might have to say. Perhaps to discover why you had aligned with my brother." He reached out and cupped her chin, exerting mild pressure until she met his eyes. "Perhaps I simply wanted to see you again."

"Whatever the reason, I hope you found the reunion worth your freedom, perhaps even your life."

His thumb plied her lower lip, sending a shiver coursing through her that she felt all the way to her core.

"It has been a pleasant reunion, *ma chère*, but hardly worth death or imprisonment."

"You're trapped," she pointed out. "Unless you're a magician, your fate is certain."

Undaunted, he indicated the room with a broad sweep of his hand. "Keep your eyes open, beautiful English girl. You may indeed see magic."

She paused to look around her, stunned to realize they were at the center of a throng of smugglers, sailors, and doxies who kept the scattered regiment of soldiers at the perimeter from pushing through their ranks. Jacques's men were unable to reach them at the heart of the hubbub.

"Either you have many friends, or this evening has set you back a good price," she said dryly. "If you fight, some of your friends might be killed."

"No one is going to die on my behalf."

"Then you intend to surrender?"

"*Non.*" He seemed surprised by the suggestion.

"Am I your hostage, then?"

"Would you like to be?"

His smile did not waver when his eyes squarely met hers. He was enjoying himself, and all at her expense. As she glared at him, he lifted the shallow glass of rum she had poured, saluted her with it, downed the contents in a single gulp, and smacked his lips in appreciation.

"I don't know what else you would expect me to think," she huffed. "I am sure the soldiers are content to wait at the exits for you."

"Perhaps," he agreed as he rose from his chair, "but that is not the plan." He stretched to his full height with the languor of a jungle cat, and then strolled around to stand beside her. Smiling, he grasped her elbows and pulled her to her feet.

The action was some sort of signal; cleverly choreographed pandemonium broke out, escalating into a riot. The revelers began to attack one another, shifting the attention of the soldiers away from them.

The crowd cleaved a pathway that closed behind them as quickly as it opened. They made their way toward the barkeep, who stood calmly polishing a tankard, his eyes on them as they approached. When they reached him, the barkeep flung down the tankard and swung aside a tapestry that concealed a narrow opening barely large enough to be called a door.

The portal was swiftly unlatched, and Rachael felt the grip on her tighten. Sebastién's face was resolute as he propelled her toward the opening. She tried to hang back, and then struggled to wrench free, but he locked an arm around her waist and half-lifted her through the opening. He prevented her escape by stooping and pulling his long-limbed form into the tiny, low-ceilinged cubicle after her, using his body to block her exit.

She heard the click of the latch spring and pictured the heavy tapestry being lowered. They were in a narrow, dim room. Sebastién had to hunch over to avoid hitting the ceiling.

Rachael leaned weakly into the corner, the confined space making her feel faint. The stale, dank air was noxious; she inhaled deeply and coughed. He made an abrupt hushing noise as he uprooted a small section of the flooring, revealing a trapdoor. The hinges of the door groaned as it was opened.

The yawning void beyond the door contained a flight of stairs that seemed to descend straight into darkness. Sebastién crouched and peered into the blackness, then straightened, catching her eye as he did, his face carefully blank.

"Where does it go?" Rachael asked in a tremulous whisper.

"It's an underground turnpike. The stairs lead to a tunnel that can be followed all the way to Muldoon's Cove. Fairtraders store goods in the rooms just below. It's one of the few places Customs has not discovered. We needn't be concerned we'll be met by soldiers on the other side."

"*We?!*" Her exclamation was little more than a squawk.

He considered her for a moment. "*Non*, I won't be taking you along," he said finally, with a note of regret. Sighing, he closed the distance between them and gathered her into his arms. "Will you say good-bye to me, then?"

Sebastién drew Rachael close and simply held her. She folded her arms around him, patting his back awkwardly. She did not know what to believe, but he did not seem to be the fiend his brother had painted him. The coarse fabric brushing her cheek and the powerful arms holding her had the power to make her feel safe, comforted. His dusky scent of exotic spice filled her nostrils, and the realization that she did not want to leave the security of his arms confounded her.

He tilted her face upward and brushed her lips with his. Groaning at the gentle contact, his grip on her intensified as his mouth covered hers and his kiss became demanding. The tidy arrangement of curls coaxed into her hair came tumbling down as his fingers tangled in the luxuriant mass. Sebastién raised his hands and cupped her face, resting his palms against her cheeks.

His tongue darted over her lips and pressed against her teeth, urging entry. He tasted of rum. His teeth nipped playfully at the corner of her mouth. A shiver coursed through her as his warm breath caressed her lips, and he kissed the delicate lobe of her ear.

Sebastién molded himself to Rachael until she felt the wall at her back, and when he drew her tightly against him, she felt the hard evidence of his arousal. His mouth was searching, insistent, and she whimpered and tried to pull away, overwhelmed by his passion and her own reaction to being in his arms.

At the small sound of protest, Sebastién tore his mouth from hers and gazed down into the depths of Rachael's eyes. His breath caught in his throat, and he eased his hold on her but did not release her. He scanned her face as intensely as his lips had plundered her mouth.

Rachael closed her eyes as his thumb traced her chin and long fingers swept over her jaw. She opened them again when he kissed her lightly on the forehead.

The seductive spell he had created was shattered when his hand suddenly plunged into the deep pocket of her cloak. Realizing his intent too late, she pulled away with a cry, striking her hip painfully against the wall behind her. She had not moved fast enough.

With a shallow smile of apology, he pocketed the pistol Jacques had given her.

"For the protection of us both."

She tossed back the hair that had escaped the hood of her mantle in anger. "Afraid I'd shoot you in the back?"

"I would be disappointed if you did not try." He inclined his head toward the staircase. "Shall we?"

He was poised as if ready to spring at her if she tried to run. It was obvious he meant to take her along. Had that been his plan all along?

"If I scream, it will alert them."

His smile was indulgent, amused. *Victorious.* "Do you really believe you would be heard? My friends are quite noisy."

He moved closer, and Rachael hugged the damp wall behind her. "You haven't believed one word I've said, have you?"

He continued to smile down at her. "*Au contraire.* You told the truth about the trap. I'm prepared to accept the rest until I can prove otherwise." He indicated the stairs for a second time. "*Apres vous.* I'll follow."

When she refused to move, he reached out and drew her away from the wall, encircling her waist. She felt his superior physical strength radiate through the contact, even though he did not compel her. Sebastién leaned down and his warm breath fanned her ear.

"You can walk, or I can carry you. Your choice."

It was a clear threat, however pleasantly posed. She heard the beat of her heart above the creak of the swollen timber as she began her descent.

"I have given you no reason to take me with you," she protested as they stepped onto the damp, sandy floor of the corridor that led to the beach.

He stopped so abruptly they nearly collided.

"Oh, but you have," he assured her with an enigmatic smile.

Upstairs in Tor Pub, soldiers continued to comb the common room, peering under tables and even going so far as to open several oversized kegs of ale, as if they suspected the people they sought had been temporarily placed on draft to avoid capture.

Victor Brightmore clung to a darkened corner of the pub. He poured himself a brandy and lit his pipe with an unsteady hand. He had been shocked to glance up from his pint of bitters to discover his niece consorting with Sebastién Falconer. He had not expected Rachael to use her feminine wiles to gain the Frenchman as an ally. It was ironic that the one man he had been certain would kill her for him had instead become her protector.

He knew the Falconer twins on sight, although they did not know him. When he began supplementing his smuggling activities with shipwrecking, he had heard a curious tale of twin brothers who hated each other, one a French privateer who was a fairtrader, the other an English revenue officer.

What had started out as a plan to camouflage his criminal activities had mushroomed into a web of murder and deceit. He had organized a gang of wreckers whose penchant for violence had brought their activities to the attention of the authorities. With Jacques Falconer reportedly obsessed with the idea of bringing his twin to justice, Victor had decided that the Frenchman would make a good scapegoat.

When Victor discovered that he and his men had wrecked the ship carrying Jacques Falconer's fiancée, he had arranged to send Jacques a trinket torn from the girl's body, along with a taunting note from his brother claiming responsibility for the crime.

Sebastién Falconer had recently begun making discreet inquiries about him. No doubt the Frenchman had heard about Rachael's little rest cure at Bedlam. The right sources could also confirm that she was not the informer behind the Prussia Cove debacle.

To make matters worse, he had lost his favorite signet ring during a recent wrecking. He was a superstitious man, and the loss did not portend well. Although the ring could not directly connect him to any crime, it was a solid clue to his identity.

The future had seemed a dismal prospect until tonight, when he had discovered that his niece was no longer safely ensconced at court, and therefore no longer beyond his reach. He knew precisely where that underground tunnel would lead them, and it would be a simple matter to pick up their trail from there.

The path to Rame Head wound along a steep cliff surrounded by wooded cliffs of graduating height. The shore that stretched below from Rame Head to Penlee was made treacherous by jagged rock teeth. Due to its geographical limitations, this particular stretch of coast was popular with fairtraders, who were well acquainted with its numerous inlets, bays, and hidden coves.

The tunnel they followed was the most direct route to the beach. It bore a downward gradient that went on for better than two miles before yawning into Muldoon's Cove. Rachael could hear the gurgle of water and the rustle of creatures she was grateful she could not see as they passed through the tunnel.

An eerie yellow pall cast by the random placement of torch-bearing sconces lit their way. Sebastién had forged ahead of her a short distance and had spoken only once, to warn her of glass fragments strewn across their path.

She regarded the tall, powerful man ahead of her. There was an innate elegance in the way he carried himself, his broad shoulders thrown back, spine erect. The cape flowed over his shoulders the way water cascaded over the stolid stone of a magnificent waterfall. What was wrong with her? The man had just abducted her for the second time, and yet she felt safe in his company.

143

It was nearly midnight when they emerged from the mouth of the cave. When she shivered and drew her mantle around her, Sebastién moved to shield her from the frigid blast of the southwesterly wind.

The terrain changed as they traveled. Heather surrendered to white clay hills, and the sea and soil became milky white, reflecting the moon glow as pinpoints of sparkling, opaque light.

When it became apparent the route they followed did not lead to Sebastién's secluded cottage, Rachael halted in mid-stride and stood rooted in the chalky sand while he trudged on ahead of her.

"Where are we going?" she shouted.

Sebastién spun around and drew his hand across his throat in a savage gesture for quiet then walked back to her and arranged the folds of the mantle hood so that her ears and throat were protected from the cold, as if she was a child.

"I thought you were taking me to my brother. I would like to be taken to your cottage at once."

"Why would you assume the infant is at my home unless you had a hand in placing it there?" he asked.

"Your note did not specify a location. It was a guess. The path we are following does not lead to your cottage."

"*Non*, it does not," he agreed. "For a woman who recently fled my home in all haste, you seem anxious to return there."

"I believed I was fleeing the devil," she gibed,

ignoring the edge of distrust she heard in his voice.

His hand brushed her cheek and lingered against her skin. His fingers were pleasantly warm. "And now? Do you still believe I'm the devil?"

Rachael looked up at him and caught her breath as his fingers continued to lightly stroke her skin. She seized his hand to stop the havoc his touch was creating. "I haven't made up my mind."

Her tart response brought a sardonic smile to Sebastién's lips as he peered down at ther. His hand glided down to her throat and lingered, resting against the wildly drumming pulse there. Without another word, he turned and began walking up the beach. Rachael hurried after him.

"Please, you must take me to my brother." She stopped again.

He glanced back over his shoulder. "We need horses."

Sebastién continued on, and Rachael hurried to catch up to him. "Your brother will have every village from here to Land's End watched. It will be safer to make the journey on foot."

He shook his head. "*Non.* Helston is too far to go on foot."

Rachael stopped. "No! I cannot go to Helston. My uncle lives there. It is too dangerous."

This time it was Sebastién who stopped. He looked offended. "You think I am incapable of protecting you?"

"John Wyatt was killed trying to protect me," she reminded him. "My protectors become targets."

"All the more reason to stop your uncle before he gains the ability to buy pardon for his crimes," he replied. "You will lead me to his home, and we will find the evidence we need to expose him. If we do not find evidence, I will coax the truth from him."

Rachael didn't care to speculate on how he might go about "coaxing" anything from anyone. She stared as tears of frustration filled her eyes. Before her stood the dangerous stranger from the night of the wrecking, not the charming rascal from Tor Pub. Her tears welled, and she brushed them away angrily.

"No! I will not take you to Victor's house," Rachael shrilly declared. "What will happen to James if we're killed? Your note said that my brother's safety relies on your safe return."

"I did not write that note." His mouth was set in an obstinate line.

"I want to see James," she insisted.

"Your uncle first," he said, adamant.

"My uncle has apartments in London as well as a home in Helston. He could be in London now."

"*Oui*, but he is not." He renewed his pace, expression grim.

"Is there anything I can tell you that you haven't already discovered for yourself?" Rachael made no effort to hide her annoyance. He was still testing her. *So much for the illusion of trust.*

"*Oui*," he replied easily, "the exact location of your uncle's home."

Rachael's angry response was lost amid the thunder of hammering hooves as a large contingent of riders suddenly converged on the beach.

Chapter Ten

The slight elevation of the low bluff they crossed allowed them to observe as two dozen soldiers combed the beach below. The terrain was a flat, treeless expanse of moor; they could not reach the nearest elevation—another low bluff—without crossing in full view of the men who scouted below.

The regiment had formed a line several hundred feet long in single file formation, allowing them to swiftly cover the path leading to the top of the bluff.

The situation presented the possibility of rescue for Rachael, while at the same time posing peril for Sebastién. She would not be forced to lead him to Victor's home. To escape, she would have to alert the soldiers to their presence, and hope that he would somehow manage to escape.

Sebastién anticipated her move the instant she attempted to bolt. Seizing her arm, he dragged his hand over her mouth to prevent her from crying out.

A tributary of the Tamar River flowed nearby, and he yanked her toward its embankment. The mixture of sea rush and stiff, reedy grass gave beneath her feet and Rachael found herself mired.

Sebastién crouched and uprooted two pieces of the thick-stemmed, hollow grass. He anchored them between his teeth, and then pursed his lips and blew. The soft expulsion of air was audible. He grabbed two more pieces of the reed and held them out to Rachael, who hung back with a mutinous look on her face.

With a low growl, Sebastién captured her chin and jammed the reeds into her mouth while he jerked her toward the bank. The tide was low and there was little crosscurrent. The water was shallow, but the bed formed a natural terrace where depths could vary from five to twenty feet.

Rachael spat the reeds out of her mouth and tried to wrench free of Sebastién's hold. His hand tightened in a bruising grip on her forearm and his other arm circled her waist like a steel band, forcing her up against him. She could hear the flutter of her own heart as it beat counter-rhythm to his.

Sebastién's breathing was measured, as if he fought for composure, but when Rachael struggled again to break free, his arms constricted around her until she feared her ribs would be crushed.

"Remember," he threatened, "your brother's life depends upon my safe return."

Rachael stopped struggling and glared. Relaxing his grip on her long enough to pluck another set of reeds from the bank, Sebastién pried open her fingers and forced the reeds into her palm.

"Use these to draw air through your mouth," he whispered. "We will go only deep enough for the water to hide us."

"The water is freezing," she objected. "I will not put those filthy things in my mouth."

With a growled imprecation, Sebastién seized Rachael by the shoulders and shoved her toward the water. "Then I hope you can hold your breath for a very long time."

Rachael scowled as she jammed the reeds into her mouth, and then nearly swallowed both water and reeds when she gasped at the shock of the frigid water. She strained to keep the stiff reed between her teeth and above the surface of the water, but the soaked mantle and riding suit beneath it weighed her down.

Furious, she began to splash about as noisily as possible while she tried to rise to the surface. How could she make enough noise to attract the soldiers?

Sebastién grappled with Rachael, overstepping the shelf bottom, and they plunged deeper into the water. She was in danger of pitching forward, and he jerked her upright, holding her in a position that would keep her air source peeking above the waterline.

Rachael tried to land a blow to Sebastién's shins, but the flow of water cushioned her motion until she gave up the effort, sapped of energy and seething with frustration.

Sebastién no longer made a pretense of being gentle; Rachael could feel the fury emanating from him through his touch. No doubt if he did not have his arms around her midsection at the moment, they would be on her throat instead. When she tried to shift her position, his fingers dug into her arms and he hauled her closer.

Desperate to escape, Rachael considered her options. What would he do if he thought she was drowning? She drew a deep breath and went limp in his arms, allowing the weak current to float her. As her body went slack, her mind raced, and she inhaled a deep breath and let go of the reed. For full effect, she allowed her head to loll against his shoulder.

Rachael felt Sebastién draw a deep breath and attempt to steady his grip, pulling her close and sliding her up the length of his body. He did not panic and immediately release her as she had expected, and she soon regretted having relinquished the reed. She felt as though she would burst from the simultaneous need to inhale and exhale.

Sebastién cradled the back of Rachael's head, mouth covering hers, and gripped her jaw, applying ruthless pressure until her mouth opened. He forced air into her lungs and she gasped in reflex, biting down hard on his lower lip. He immediately released her.

Rachael propelled to the surface and cleaved the water, choking and spitting. She clung to the grassy shelf, shivering with cold as her desperate gaze searched the immediate area. The soldiers had vanished as if they had been ghosts in search of mortals to haunt. She levered herself toward the edge of the embankment, but her heavy, sodden clothing made it impossible to pull herself onto the marshy ledge.

Sebastién stood on the bank above her, reveling in her predicament as she tried to pull herself out of the water. She had never seen a more obnoxious smile than the one on his flushed, livid face. He spread his feet wide and rocked back and forth, keeping her well within reach as she tried edging along the side of the bank in either direction. She ducked away from his outstretched hand and attempted to dive back down into the water, finding the thought of drowning preferable to whatever punishment he might have in mind for her.

Finally, Sebastién grabbed a handful of Rachael's hair and yanked her close enough to gain hold of her arm. She yelped and struck out at him with her free arm, but he seized it as well, hauling her up and onto the embankment with such force that water exploded all around them.

"I do not know how you have managed to stay alive this long," he exclaimed, giving her a shake.

Rachael tried to twist free and scored a vicious kick to his shin in the process. Sebastién raised one powerful arm as if to retaliate, and Rachael gasped and cried out, cringing.

He checked his reflex, a horrified look edging out the fury on his face. "*Non*," he said. "You will not goad me into behaving like the devil you think I am, even when you make one treacherous move after another against me."

Sebastién shook his head vigorously and his long, wet hair rained water. His hands were still locked on her arms.

"Take your hands off me, Frenchman."

He canted his head with such elaborate grace that there was at once both elegance and menace in the gesture.

"*Pardon*?" His eyes were a frigid, clear green. His skin gleamed with moisture, and the contours of his lean jaw set off the hollow planes of his face. "What did you say to me?"

"Take your hands off me," she said, readily obliging.

"*Non*, all of it."

Rachael faced Sebastién warily, and he acknowledged her silence with a rancorous smile. "You said, 'Take your hands off me, *Frenchman*,'" he supplied. "It had the ring of an insult."

"Interpret it any way you like."

"*Oui*, I will. I wonder if you would have taken such a haughty tone with my brother." He pushed her away with such violence that Rachael stumbled. His lip curled

153

as his eyes raked her. "I have no desire to touch English whores."

She gasped at the insult and slapped him, open palm leaving a white imprint across his tanned cheek. Sebastién's narrowed eyes promised reprisal. Rachael had never seen him so angry, and she uttered a cry, picked up her sodden mantle, and sloshed through the muck, sliding and slipping in an effort to get away.

Sebastién prevented Rachael's flight by connecting his booted foot with her posterior and giving a stout push, propelling her headlong into the mud, where she lay on her stomach, buried up to her chin.

Rachael flopped over onto her back and raised one mud-covered leg in time to send Sebastién sprawling. She heard his muttered oath when he came crashing down beside her, sending a spray of mud flying in all directions.

Rachael was on her feet and dashing toward the narrow footpath of the lower bluff before Sebastién could free himself from the mud. The path widened and became a flat expanse of moor, thick with gorse and the shriveled ghosts of summer flowers.

The moon poked out from the clouds, illuminating her flight. Water-logged garments clung to her, chilling her to the bone. Rachael unclasped the frog closures at the front of the mantle and dropped it as she ran.

If she had not spied Sebastién crouched on the ridge above her, she would have followed the path that descended from a shallow crag overlooking the beach. The cliff also had a steep face with a much sharper descent and no true path other than a sheer drop onto the sand below. It was a shortcut, but a dangerous one.

The sight of him made Rachael reckless, and she abandoned the safer path to dash across the summit toward the more dangerous descent. Sebastién's shout of warning carried to her as she reached the ragged edge of the bluff.

Rachael stood poised at the lip of the crag, indecisive and afraid. There were a few places to gain a foothold, but one clumsy move would send her hurtling down to the rocks and sand below. She was aware that Sebastién's shouts were sounding closer with each passing moment.

Why hadn't he abandoned her and gone on alone? Was it possible that he was taking her to Victor because he had been ordered to? His brother had insisted he was a wrecker, but she had not wanted to believe it. The night she had discovered his identity, she had encountered him on the beach after a wreck. The recollection, and his insistence upon taking her to Helston, fueled her frantic resolve to escape.

The slant of the cliff face was too severe to scale upright. The outer rim was not solid, and Rachael felt the base shift under her feet as she crouched, perching in a partially seated position that would allow her to slide part of the way down. She glanced back and watched in mounting terror as he tore across the space separating them.

Sebastién faltered and then stopped in his tracks. "Rachael," he coaxed, "come away from there." She stared back at him, exhausted and numb. "This is foolishness!" he raged.

"Why would you care what happens to me, Frenchman?"

"I abhor needless death." His rigid jaw shone like granite in the moonlight.

"Oh? That is not what I have heard."

"Bait me all you like," he said, temper flaring.

"Stay where you are," she shouted. "I would rather die than allow you to hand me over to my uncle."

"Is that what you think I plan to do?"

There was something in his tone that made Rachael strain to see his face more clearly. When she moved, loose stones tumbled over the side of the ridge. "I don't know what to believe," she said. "It is unlikely that you would admit to being a member of Victor's gang."

"If I were part of your uncle's gang, why would I need your help locating him?"

"It could be a trick meant to gain my trust. You have proven to be the better strategist by far," she said bitterly.

"I am a smuggler, Rachael. I am not a wrecker. I have no affiliation with your uncle. If you are so eager to die, you will have to jump." His voice was brittle.

"You will not take me to my brother. Why?"

"I'm not convinced you don't know the answer to

that." His voice was sharp. The arm he had extended fell limply to his side. "We are at an impasse, then. You do not trust me. I do not trust you. How can we ever hope to change that?"

"I tried to change it when I warned you that Jacques had set a trap for you."

"How do I know that your warning wasn't part of a larger snare? How can I be certain my brother does not await me at the cottage?"

"You don't; any more than I know your real reason for taking me to Helston."

"I do not have to give you a reason."

When Rachael remained silent, Sebastién sighed. "I can find Brightmore's home without your aid," he admitted. "But if there is any truth to your story, the only safe place for you is with me. I will not leave you with Jacques. He used you to get to me. It is safer for you if my brother believes I abducted you rather than thinking you betrayed him.

"My reason for taking you to Helston is to confront your uncle. I may doubt your guilt, but I must have proof. You must try to trust me, Rachael." Sebastién extended a hand. "We need to find shelter and dry clothing. Will you come away from there?"

A sudden blast of wind cut through Rachael's soggy clothing, and she resisted the driving force of it. A stone rolled under her patten, and she pitched backward, plowing the ground with the effort to remain on her feet.

Sebastién shouted and broke into a run as the shelf under Rachael's feet began to give way.

She felt the foundation crumble and she teetered, searching blindly for a foothold. There was nothing she could grab on to and she felt herself sliding feet first down the slanted, craggy cliff face.

The sharp stones tugged at the buttons of her riding suit and the brush scraped her palms and gouged her exposed limbs. Rachael screamed, unaware it was Sebastién's name she cried as she fell.

Chapter Eleven

Rachael sat up by slow degrees, her head pounding in protest when she moved. A fire blazed nearby, the warmth a welcome sensation. She rested on a bed of fine, clean white sand near a pool of sparkling emerald green. Though she knew the southern coast well, this place was unfamiliar. It was something out of local legend; a secluded natural lagoon bordered by towering cliffs fronted by a storm beach.

"Beautiful," she murmured in appreciation.

Sebastién strolled into sight and dropped down beside her. "You are lucky to be alive," he scolded. "What if you had landed on rocks instead of sand?"

As it was, the skin on her hands and legs had been scraped raw by the rough bramble. When Sebastién's bright gaze swept over her, she was suddenly aware that she wore nothing beneath the garment spread over her like a blanket. With a gasp, Rachael dragged the heavy cloth up to her chin, dismayed by the realization that he had undressed her.

His mouth drew down at the corners as he rose and turned to the fire, idly rubbing his hands as if to warm them. His shoulders shook as if with suppressed laughter. Rachael glared at his back.

"Are you warm enough?" he asked casually. "I can make a bigger fire—"

"I would be warmer with my clothes *on*," she informed him, feeling exposed and vulnerable. *He* was fully clothed, she noted. "I do not appreciate your undressing me without my permission."

"Your clothes are not dry yet. I forgive you for your lack of gratitude," he said. His teeth flashed in a wide smile.

"I thought you had an aversion to touching English whores." "I won't say I'm sorry I slapped you."

Sebastién shrugged. "Perhaps the slap was deserved."

Was that an apology? "Why aren't you strutting around naked? Your clothes were as wet as mine."

Sebastién raised a brow. Within the space of a moment, he had divested himself of his shirt. While she looked on with widening eyes, he began to unfasten the tiny buttons at the side of each knee of his breeches.

"What are you doing?"

His hands froze and he looked at her, all innocence.

"I am going to dry my clothes, as you suggested." The pause was theatrical. "I await your instruction."

"Why don't you dry your cloak first and wrap yourself in that?"

He hesitated before reaching down and locking his fingers on the bulky garment that covered her. As the cloak slid away, Rachael gasped and grabbed the makeshift blanket with both hands. They engaged in a brief tug-of-war, but her hold was so tenacious that he could not wrest the garment from her without tearing the fabric.

"I see you've changed your mind," he said, surrendering the cloak. "I dried it first out of deference to your sense of modesty."

"Give me back my clothes and I will return your cloak," she offered.

"When your clothes are dry." His tone sounded elaborate with patience, as if he spoke to a child.

"You're likely to become ill from wandering around in those wet clothes," she warned.

"I won't expect you to nurse me if I fall ill."

"I should hope not."

Rachael drew the cloak around her and watched as Sebastién draped her riding suit over a low boulder near the fire then he gathered up her chemise and blue-flowered silk petticoat, fingers gliding over the filmy material, a curiously intimate gesture that made heat pool low inside her.

"These are dry," he announced, tossing them to her.

The petticoat caught her shoulder and slid to the sand. Rachael held the edges of the cloak together while she reached for the chemise. She rose to her knees, but when she tried to stand, her legs were shaky, and she noticed her right foot was swollen.

Sebastién dropped to the sand beside her and took her foot in his hand. He made a gentle inspection. "A sprain," he said. "You can soak your foot in the pool to ease the swelling." His hand continued to cradle her foot.

Rachael clutched the frail undergarments to her, even more acutely aware that she wore nothing underneath the cloak. "Please turn your back," she primly requested. Sebastién's hand dropped, and he moved away, presenting his back to her.

The underthings did not add much in the way of warmth or cover. The thin chemise was a transparent wisp of fabric that revealed more than it concealed. Rachael looked down at the display with a pang of dismay, and wrapped the cloak around her again. She selected a large flat stone near the fire and hobbled to it, sitting down with a groan.

Lowering herself to the carpet of white sand, Rachael curled on her side. She was too exhausted to remain on guard, and sensed a truce between them, if only a temporary one. She snuggled against the soft fabric, breathing in Sebastién's oddly comforting, familiar scent.

When Rachael awoke, night had fallen again. The temperature had dropped, and the roaring fire was now a muted glow. There was no sign of Sebastién.

The last observation filled her with panic. She would have been on her feet in an instant if an arm had not suddenly dropped down over her. The arm was corded with powerful muscle, and sprinkled with coarse black hair. There was no doubt to whom it belonged. Her improvised bed now harbored an intruder. She rolled to her knees and gave him a hard shove.

Sebastién awoke with a snort and the well-honed reflexes of a warrior. He grabbed Rachael, rolled, and pinned her beneath him, expression fierce, teeth bared in a snarl.

"Is this a new tactic to get a woman into your bed— sneak under the covers while she sleeps?"

He relaxed his grip and smiled at the indignation in her voice. "Is that how you speak to the man who holds the key to your heart?"

His hand stole under the cloak and Sebastién dangled the key Winstanley had given her to the Eddystone Lighthouse. The length of blue ribbon formed an absurdly delicate collar around his muscular neck. He feigned distress when she glared at him. "Oh, so this is not the key to your heart?"

"It is the key to a safe place," she gritted.

"A place of refuge?" Sebastién looked at the key with new respect. "From what, or should I say, from whom? From me?" When she nodded, he let the key fall from his fingers, and it bounced against Rachael's chest. "I will guard it for you."

She squirmed beneath him, but he did not move a muscle, save those required to form a wolfish grin. "I cannot believe I ever mistook you for a gentleman."

His eyes sparkled. "Chivalry is dead, *n'est ce pas?*"

"If it is, I'm sure you're the one responsible."

Sebastién laughed, and her heart did a curious little leap at the sound. He looked down at her without the guarded expression he usually wore.

"Have you no sense of propriety?" The earnest expression on his face was disarming. Rachael had to resist the urge to smile.

"Of course. I felt it was proper to share the warmth of my body with you."

Although his explanation drew a snicker from Rachael, she could hardly blame him for seeking shelter beneath his own cloak, and his nearness created a restive ache within her. The warmth emanating from him was a languid pleasure, and she suddenly recalled what it was like to be kissed by him, with such acute clarity that her breath caught in her throat and her lips tingled as if in anticipation of his touch.

Rachael shifted, and Sebastién shuddered and gazed

down at her, eyes bright with awakening desire.

"*Mon Dieu*, have you no mercy, woman?"

Rachael lay caught beneath him, staring up into his handsome face. Her right arm was wedged in the folds of the cloak, and when she struggled to loosen the binding, he eased his weight from the fabric and gently extracted her hand.

He squeezed the delicately boned hand resting in his, and then raised it, pressing his lips against her inner wrist. His gaze fastened on the abrasions she had suffered in the fall. These, too, he kissed then brought her hand up and cradled it against his cheek.

Rachael withdrew her hand and raised her fingers to Sebastién's face, sweeping the hair back from his forehead. Then she traced the line of his jaw, touching the sensitive tips of her fingers against the strong planes of his face and feathering a delicate touch over his neck and across his collarbone.

Sebastién inhaled sharply as Rachael made her slow, tactile exploration. His eyes moved over her face although he refrained from touching her. She was so beautiful and so fragile, and after he had seduced her at the cottage, she had felt betrayed by him and had fled. He would never force her or betray her again.

Rachael cupped the back of his neck and drew his head down, planting a clumsy kiss on his lips, as if testing his response.

The tender buss tantalized Sebastién with the hidden promise of passion, and he reached for her and pulled her to him with exquisite anticipation of the ardor he sensed lurked behind the chaste kiss.

Rachael clasped her hands behind his neck as their mouths fused in a searching, impassioned quest. Her lips were warm and petal soft beneath his; they parted at his gentle probing and the kiss deepened. His fingers tangled in her hair as he drank of a heady sweetness more potent than wine and infinitely more intoxicating. He could feel his heart pound as his body tuned to hers.

They broke apart, both breathless, and Rachael ran her fingers over Sebastién's chest, exploring the network of musculature that formed his torso, hands trembling. She seemed shy, and he was charmed by her bashfulness. Sebastién worked her chemise free and swept it aside. The silk petticoat followed. He had cherished her warmth these last few hours and now savored her desire for him as a remarkable, precious gift.

He lowered his head and kissed her again, harnessing the urgent desire that threatened to overtake him, wanting her passion to rise and match his own. Rachael shifted and moaned softly as his lips left a fiery trail of moist kisses over the slender column of her throat. His warm hands smoothed feathery circles over her skin,

willing her inexperienced body into a raging wakefulness. Her eyes opened and she stared into his, as if trying
to glimpse the workings of his mind.

"Do you intend to take advantage of me, Frenchman?"
she asked. Her voice was low and husky with desire.

He smoothed the hair back from her face and gazed
down at her through a haze of burgeoning desire. "If
you insist."

She murmured his name and he molded her to him,
loosening the tight binding of the cloak so that it covered
them but did not hold them separate. Her skin caught
the light reflected by the pool, illuminating her. She
looked like a fanciful creature, a nymph inhabiting an
enchanted cove. The smooth, pale beauty of her flesh en-
tranced him, and he moved his hand slowly over her bare
skin, reveling in the pleasure of the sensation. Her skin
was soft, supple, and warm, like the finest grade of satin.

Sebastién's heated gaze swept over Rachael, his touch
mindful of the scrapes and bruises that marked her fall. She
stirred, trembling, body flushed to a rosy glow from some
inner fire, eyes luminous with need. Her lips parted as her
body arched against him with irrepressible yearning.

Sebastién's need became a sweet agony, the ache in
his loins shouted to be eased; he was stiff and ready. The
night seemed to draw close enough to whisper in his
ear, demanding that he complete this most ancient and
sacred of rites. Instinct demanded that he possess the
woman while intellect and emotion demanded that he

shelter the waif.

"My beautiful English girl," he whispered as his hand swept across her taut stomach and stroked between her thighs. He slipped his fingers inside her to judge her readiness. Her legs parted wider in response to the caress and his palm swept over the smooth silkiness of her inner thigh and cupped her intimately. Only a fool would take this woman in haste.

Rachael arched beneath him and raised her hips as she met the hard evidence of his need. Sebastién fixed his mouth on hers, sealing her gasp of pleasure as he pushed his rigid length inside her, joining them.

He waited, feeling her tight core stretch to accommodate him as her splendid heat surrounded him until his entire being was immersed in the sensation. He slowly began a stroking rhythm that rapidly ascended into a fever of ecstasy. Her fingers clutched at his back as his pace increased, and she gripped his shoulders and moaned as his warm mouth sampled her velvety, fragrant skin.

Sebastién whispered her name as the blistering intensity mounted and washed over him, and he came with a hoarse cry, limbs entwined with hers, their lips molded in a fevered kiss. Rachael softly cried out as she found release, and he clung to her, the emptiness he had felt for so long replaced by a vast sense of peace.

"You must be part French," he mused. "English women are not known for their passion."

"How can you possibly know much about English

women?" she teased. "You don't seem to like us much, as a whole."

"My mother is—was—English." His voice was remote. "I do not know whether she is alive or dead." He made a violent slash across the sand with his index finger.

Rachael nestled in the crook of Sebastién's arm, idly caressing his forearm and running her fingers over his chest. "Is she the model you use to judge all English?"

"She murdered my father and was forced to flee France when I was a child. She took my brother to England with her and left me in France."

"It must have broken her heart to have to abandon her child."

"*Non*," he said bitterly, "she did not want me. My grandfather has been my father and my mother all my life. The only memory I have of my mother is her fragrance." He curled his lip in disgust. "Attar of Roses."

"You should try to find her, Sebastién. Perhaps you don't know the whole story. If one were to believe my uncle, I would be put away as a madwoman."

"I shall forget her, as she has forgotten me."

"Has she never tried to contact you?"

"*Non*. She knew if she returned to France, my grandfather would have her head mounted on his wall. When I was a child, I used to pray that she would come for me, but she never did. She raised my brother to be the perfect Englishman. I do not think she wanted to be reminded of the Frenchman she seduced into marriage and then murdered. Or of the child she left behind in France."

"You must not judge all English by your mother."

"*Oui*," Sebastién replied cynically. "I must consider other examples, my brother, your uncle, your bumbling friend Morgan."

"Tarry is a brave, kind, lovable soul!"

"He's a pompous puppy."

Rachael's eyes flashed, and she made as if to move away from him.

He pulled her back to his side. "I will like Morgan less if he causes me to spend a cold night alone," he warned.

"Tarry has risked his life for me. You cannot hate him unless you hate me as well."

"I never said I hated Morgan. I just find him annoying." He reached out and playfully tousled her hair. "Morgan would not find a declaration of affection from me very plausible."

"I predict that someday you and Tarry will be the best of friends."

Sebastién yawned. "Then I must be well rested if I am to undertake such an ill-favored acquaintance. Go to sleep, my beautiful English girl." He kissed her, arms tightening around her.

Rachael smiled sleepily and relaxed against him, the curve of her body fitting to his, as if she had been made for him. After a few minutes, Sebastién glanced down at her. She had drifted off to sleep.

He gazed at the peaceful, pale oval face only inches from his. He still did not know why he had agreed to meet her at Tor Pub in the first place. With The Dane coordinating his escape, there had been no real risk of capture, but he still risked punishment by failing to return to France. Yet, here he remained.

It had not been his plan to take her with him, but the sight of her in the pub had affected him like a physical blow, and he, a man who rarely acted on impulse, had surrendered to impulse. There was not enough rum in England or France to dull the jumble of feelings she aroused in him. She had become a distraction even when she was not with him because she constantly occupied his thoughts.

He still had his doubts about whether or not she could be trusted, and he was sure she had similar misgivings about him. She might turn out to be the instrument used to destroy him.

Rachael seemed convinced he held her brother hostage, yet Jacques's use of a decoy suggested that James remained hidden and safe. It was possible that Jacques had deceived Rachael just as he had tried to deceive him.

Until he was certain she could be trusted, the only leverage he had over her was the hostage she believed he held. He had no way to keep her safe until he could earn her trust, unless he used the threat of a hostage. Despite his muddled past, he had never viewed his life as complicated. *Until now.*

Chapter Twelve

Sebastién's vast network of allies proved useful as they obtained aid and information from a variety of sources, but only after he revealed the *fleur-de-lis* that marked his upper right arm to each prospective resource.

In one village, a parish priest provided them with horses and fresh clothing. The squire of another hamlet related the news that Jacques's agents had been thwarted in an attempt to capture The Dane. A third contact provided the location of The Dane's hideout. The news that The Dane had gone into hiding in Helston only increased Sebastién's determination to go there, despite Rachael's protests.

His right hand rested on the hilt of his sword as they approached a small, whitewashed cottage and asked to speak with The Dane. His other hand grasped the pistol he had taken from Rachael. The pistol was now only a bluff piece, rendered useless by the water that had flooded its chamber.

After he displayed the *fleur-de-lis* to the man guarding the cottage door, they were hustled into a darkened room occupied by The Dane and two other men. The Dane bellowed a welcome and clasped Sebastién's shoulder with one large hand.

Sebastién motioned Rachael forward, guiding her toward the fair, amiable hulk, who fixed his small, perceptive blue eyes on her. As introductions were made, one of the men sprang to his feet.

"Aye, we all know that name, the traitorous bitch." An ugly white scar cleaved his forehead, evidence of a blow not parried swiftly enough. His burr identified him as a resident of Rachael's part of Cornwall. He reached for his sword but dropped his weapon with a yelp of pain when Sebastién swiftly stepped forward and disarmed him.

"*Mademoiselle* Penrose is under my protection," Sebastién announced, his voice tempered steel. "Attack her, and you attack me."

The Dane was silent, but the other men uttered sounds of outrage.

"Have you forgotten Prussia Cove? She's an informer. Men are dead or imprisoned because of her." Simon, the man Sebastién had disarmed, directed a look of loathing at her.

"She has a powerful enemy who wishes to convince us of her guilt. If I did not believe her to be innocent, she would not be under my protection."

His eyes met hers, and what he saw there prompted him to move closer to her and gather her beneath his shoulder. He placed a possessive, reassuring arm around her waist.

"I've only recently learned what happened at Prussia Cove," Rachael told them. "It is likely that when your gang was routed and led away in chains, I was being taken to London, where I, too, was imprisoned."

"Not at Newgate," Simon said. "My brother's in that filthy hole 'cause of you. If you had been at Newgate, I'd have heard of it. *Liar*," he spat.

"I was confined to the Hospital of Saint Mary of Bethlehem. You might know it as 'Bedlam.' I was not expected to survive my visit. The charge that I betrayed the fairtraders at Prussia Cove was made so that if I escaped, I would find no allies."

"Bedlam," the second man exhaled in a low whistle. Peter Dunhilly had seen the place once. The infirmary was opened on Sunday afternoons for the amusement of the public. One could pay a fee and stroll through the asylum to observe the inmates as an entertainment, the way one might view a minstrel show or carnival. No doubt the racket of the place still exploded in her ears as it did in his; the tortured wailing, the metallic clink of a thousand chains, the sound of bullwhips wielded by sadistic attendants cracking in the air.

Many dismissed the ills of the place as being the result of poor management. The hospital administrators squandered the annual sightseers' income, leaving the inmates without food for days because there was no money to buy provisions. It was widely believed that the insane could not feel hunger or cold. Peter had never accepted that theory after seeing the inmates shivering in their straw beds, begging for food. The place still haunted him, and if the slender girl who stood before them had been confined there, he felt only pity for her.

"I come from a village of fairtraders," Rachael said. "My neighbors number among those presently in the gaol. If I had made myself useful to the Agency of Revenues, would I not have asked for their protection from vengeance seekers? Would I be in the company of this man, a known smuggler?"

"Would she be allowed here?" The Dane put in.

Sebastién glanced at The Dane in surprise. He had not expected his friend to champion her. What did The Dane know about Rachael that he did not?

"So, it is not coincidence that finds us in Helston at the same time," Sebastién observed.

The Dane sank down on a walnut settee, folded his

arms across his massive chest, and crossed his jackbooted feet. His gaze fixed on Rachael, and he grunted as he ran his hand over the top of the small japanned cabinet beside him, drawing her attention to it. She frowned. It was an imported chest, with an intricately worked design and brilliantly lacquered exterior.

He gestured for them to be seated. Sebastién dragged an armchair away from the cluster of men and motioned for Rachael to sit. As she settled into the chair, he sank down onto the floor beside her, like a faithful guard dog.

"My friend Falconer once asked me to learn what I could about Rachael Penrose and Victor Brightmore." The Dane looked directly at Sebastién. "While you and the lady were wandering the moors, we searched Brightmore's home." The Dane patted the cabinet beside him.

"We were told it was a common theft," Simon objected peevishly.

"Common men take part in common thievery," The Dane replied with disdain. "There is no plunder to be divided here."

"If there are no spoils, then what will you pay for our silence?"

"The only way to guarantee that a man keeps a secret is to see that it dies with him," Sebastién told Simon. "Never assume a man will buy your silence." Sebastién caught Peter's eye and slowly inclined his head in the direction of the door.

"Come on, Simon," Peter said, grasping Sebastién's silent directive. "Our work is done here. Let's wet our whistles at Green's."

The Dane went to the window and watched as the two men made their way down the hill. He spent a moment scanning the neighboring cottages before turning back to Sebastién and Rachael.

"What is in the cabinet?" Sebastién asked.

The Dane squatted and unclasped the catch on the black-lacquered chest. There had been a lock fastened over the catch, but it had been broken.

"*Correspondence?*" Sebastién asked, unable to hide his disappointment as he reached in and withdrew a stack of papers.

Rachael knelt on the floor beside him, and he handed her the sheaf of papers then turned to the cabinet again and extracted a heavy leather-bound volume. He laid it out flat on the floor and slowly began turning pages dotted with entries in a neat, spidery hand.

"Rachael," Sebastién said, "your uncle kept records."

Victor Brightmore had chronicled his crimes in detail. Not only was there a list of the names of the men who made up his gang, but each member was profiled. Victor had great insight into how a man's foibles could be used to bend him into service. If a man was a fugitive, his file noted it. If he had unusual appetites, a violent history, or a penchant for illicit compounds, Victor knew about it.

In another section, Victor kept an account of the wreckings. Each page bore the name of a vessel, its destination, how many passengers it carried, what was recovered, how the spoils were disbursed, and how the wreck had been accomplished. With shaking hands, Sebastién snapped the volume shut.

"Bastard," he said under his breath.

Rachael heaved an agonized sob and vaulted to her feet, dropping the letter she had been reading. She leaned against the glass of a nearby window and doubled over, arms wrapped tightly around her midsection, as if she had received a blow.

"Away from the window," The Dane said at once. "It is not safe."

Sebastién steered her away from the window and tried to ease her down into the chair, but she clung to him, sobbing against his shoulder. He stepped backward by inches until he leaned against the wall, resting her body against him. Then he looked at The Dane in bewilderment. The Dane retrieved the letter from the floor and held it out in front of him so he could scan its contents.

Dr. Elliott Macaulay had written a letter for the purpose of ending his association with Victor. The letter stated the murder of John Wyatt as his primary reason, but then proceeded to chronicle his deadly partnership with Victor. Elliott recounted the plot to kill Tarry by razing his home, Rachael's abduction and confinement at Bedlam, and the plan to poison James.

One additional revelation was contained within the document. Elliott expressed his concern over Victor's plan to eliminate three members of the same family using a single method, which the doctor felt was too risky. *The poison was a solution where Anne was concerned,* Elliott had written, *but to avoid suspicion, different methods should be used on her children.*

Sebastién closed his eyes and gathered Rachael into his arms. Unable to remain still, he tapped the wall behind him with the back of his head as he stared up at the ceiling.

"My father was a fairtrader turned merchant," Rachael said, her voice muffled by his cloak. "Two years ago, he left to establish a spice trade. He had been in the Indies two weeks when he contracted a fever and died. Soon after, my mother learned that she expected another child. It was a difficult birth. Uncle Victor brought us to Helston and confined Mother to bed, saying she was to be attended by his personal physician, Dr. Macaulay."

"The good doctor," The Dane rumbled.

Rachael sank into the chair, twisting her hands in front of her as she spoke. "During the first few days, she seemed to improve. Then Dr. Macaulay came to visit and brought a vial of medicine. Every morning, Victor would give her one drop of the medicine mixed in a glass of water."

She glanced up at Sebastién, eyes brimming with tears. "She grew worse, weaker each day, and Victor suggested that the dosage of the medicine be increased."

Rachael buried her face in her hands. When she spoke again, the men had to strain to understand her words. "One day, I walked into the room as he was adding drops of the medicine to a bowl of broth. She had already had her medicine that day. He told me that she had gotten worse."

Her voice was still almost a whisper. "Victor left for several hours, and when he returned, Elliott was with him. But it was too late." She paused. "My father's will states Victor will inherit if there are no surviving heirs."

Sebastién folded an arm around her as The Dane quietly exited the room.

"Do not think me callous, *ma chère*," he said softly, "but this is an old grief. I cannot bear to see you suffer it again." He pressed his lips against the honeyed silk of her hair.

The Dane reentered the room. His mouth turned up at the corners when they self-consciously broke apart, but he said nothing. He bent to stack the ledger with the scattered letters and wrapped the materials in a length of oilskin.

Sebastién thumped the cabinet. "What other evidence was there?"

"I do not know," The Dane said. "Brightmore's home had already been ransacked. Someone had dragged this cabinet across the room and broken the lock. Either the contents held no interest for the thieves, or they were interrupted. Only the man who broke the lock knows what else the cabinet might have contained."

He handed the oilskin bundle to Sebastién, who tucked the package under his arm.

"Hide it well, and quickly," The Dane advised. "Do not entrust it to anyone." His instruction drew a probing glance from Sebastién. "You were being followed by two of Brightmore's wreckers. Brightmore was at the pub. He saw you; I saw him. He sent two men to follow you; I sent two men to follow his men. His men were picked up by soldiers scouting the moors."

Sebastién reflected on his activities during that time and pulled a face, certain that his friend was aware of everything that had transpired from the moment he and Rachael had left Tor Pub.

"An odd time for a swim," The Dane joked, confirming Sebastién's suspicion. His face settled into somber lines. "Brightmore knew you were moving west."

"He will assume we are responsible for ransacking his home." Sebastién groaned.

"I do not know what else was taken, or by whom, but he will think you have all the evidence in your possession. The ledger must be kept safe; you may need it to bargain for your lives."

Sebastién eyed Rachael with an open expression of concern. "I should send you to Morgan for safekeeping."

"I refuse to be separated from you until my brother has been safely returned to me," she said.

He dreaded any discussion regarding her brother. The

Dane knew that he did not hold James hostage; they had shared a pint of ale and a hearty laugh over Jacques's incompetence. His old friend knew the workings of his mind and no doubt had guessed there was strategy involved, or Rachael would already know her brother was safe.

"She might be safest in your company," The Dane suggested. "We do not know who can be trusted. Do you believe Morgan can protect her?"

"But the letter proves I am innocent," Rachael said, "just as the ledger proves that Sebastién is not guilty of the crimes attributed to him."

"*Ja*," The Dane agreed, "but men like Simon will kill you and then look at your evidence."

"*Oui*," Sebastién concurred. "You are not safe, even among fairtraders." He did not voice his doubts about Morgan's ability to protect her. She was loyal to the people she loved. Would she ever see him as worthy of such loyalty?

"I won't be a burden if you take me along," Rachael promised. "In fact, I can be useful to you."

Sebastién regarded her with a dubious, amused smile. "*Oui?* What did you have in mind?"

With The Dane in the room, he refrained from mentioning the uses that immediately came to mind for her, but she seemed to guess the direction of his thoughts. An appealing blush crept over her face, as if he had voiced his lascivious thoughts aloud.

"I know of a secure place to hide that bundle," she

said, indicating the package under his arm. "And you will need my help to do it." She gave him a saucy smile and left the room.

He stared after her as The Dane rumbled with laughter.

"Be glad she is not your enemy," The Dane said. "You may have met your match, my friend."

Sebastién wandered to the window and looked out at the neighboring cottages framed by the barren landscape. The letter they had recovered supported her claims. He would have to come to terms with the shame he felt over his treatment of her, but a more immediate problem loomed. The time was fast approaching when he would have to admit he had lied to her about James, and she would hate him for it.

Chapter Thirteen

Their destination was the harbor south of Rame Head on the Devon mainland. For a fortnight, Britain had been battered by Atlantic gales of such force that nothing in memory compared with them. Ships homeward bound had been swept into port in advance of their arrival dates, while hundreds of outbound ships had been forced to return to the teeming, dangerously congested port. The density of craft was such that the harbor itself had lost definition.

Rachael looked beyond the broad mouth of the channel to the Eddystone Lighthouse reposing on its broad stone base fourteen miles off the Plymouth coast. Its polygonal tower rose eighty feet into the air. The functional light loomed forty feet high, reduced to slightly more than a speck in the distance.

Three reefs of ragged red rock tagged "the stone of the reeling waves" sat astride the entrance to Plymouth harbor. The sea eddied continuously around the central rock, as if stirred by some evil hand. The water churned among the reefs and spewed immense curtains of spray while the rocks took the full blast of the westerly winds.

They approached a grizzled man who whistled as he loaded provisions into a small rowboat.

"This tub isn't for hire," he replied when Sebastién inquired about transport to the lighthouse. "I'm the only man with any reason to be heading out there. I'm Paxton, keeper of the Eddystone Light."

"We are friends of Mr. Winstanley's," Rachael said. "He said we could lodge at his lighthouse."

"Mr. Winstanley wouldn't say such a thing," the old man replied with conviction.

As a member of the French aristocracy, Sebastién was unaccustomed to having to repeat a request, let alone have one denied by the likes of a commoner like Avery Paxton. As he took an angry step forward, Rachael reached out and tugged at his arm. "She has a key," Sebastién said with significance.

"I've never known Winstanley to give a key to anyone. May I see it, miss?"

"Of course," Rachael replied.

Her fingers had gone to her throat before she remembered she no longer had the key and watched as Sebastién made a ceremony out of handing it to Paxton.

The light keeper withdrew his own key from a frayed pocket, along with a smudged pair of spectacles. He donned his glasses and squinted as he compared the two keys, brown eyes owlish through the lenses.

"Extraordinary," Paxton said. "You *do* have a key."

Sebastién grunted and Rachael laughed with such coquettish charm that Paxton's eyes flicked in her direction and he stared, frowning but silent.

"You must forgive my companion's churlish disposition," Rachael said. She rolled a smile to the corner of her mouth as Sebastién communicated his ire through a subtle narrowing of his eyes. "You know how the French can be."

"Do not offer apologies on my behalf, *mademoiselle*."

Paxton looked up from his examination of the pair of keys. "But why must you lodge at the lighthouse? There are any number of fine inns . . ."

"Nowhere else is safe," Rachael replied. Sebastién pursed his lips in clear condemnation of her candor.

"Safe from what?" Paxton asked, a little too eagerly.

Rachael foundered. She simply wasn't a good liar.

Sebastién had no such failing.

"Come now," he said, "there are times when we gentlemen must be discreet for the sake of our ladies, *non*? Must you embarrass the young *mademoiselle*?" His jade eyes gleamed.

Rachael balked at the innuendo. His tight-lipped smile told her that this was reprisal for her remark about the French.

Paxton appeared unconvinced.

"Ah, then, if you must know the truth," Sebastién sighed. Rachael gave him a leery sideways glance as he casually wrapped an arm around her shoulders and hugged her. "The young *mademoiselle* and I seek a trysting place safe from the jealous rage of my bride-to-be. My fiancée is wealthy and often has me followed. The lighthouse promises privacy. I am only trying to be discreet, *mon ami*."

Paxton looked embarrassed but nodded. During the awkward silence that followed, Rachael decided that she would prefer Paxton know the truth, no matter what the consequences.

"The Frenchman certainly does not lack imagination," she said dryly. "In truth, we need to hide—"

"*Oui*," Sebastién quickly broke in, "we must hide from my bride, who suspects that I have a less than faithful nature. I promise you, we shall not bring scandal to your revered tower. I must say a proper farewell to my *chérie*." The easy smile formed by his lips did not reach his eyes when he looked at her.

Paxton cast an appraising eye over Rachael. "Why not keep the lady as your mistress?" he suggested, trying to be helpful.

Rachael looked from Paxton to Sebastién. Canting her head in anticipation of his reply, she tapped her foot, waiting.

Sebastién snapped up the gauntlet with devilish glee. Stepping aside, he motioned Paxton into his confidence, although when he spoke it was with particular care that Rachael hear every word.

"The upkeep of such sport is quite costly, and I have yet to be convinced that the goods are worth the purchase price."

Her jaw dropped, and the look she leveled at him promised a reckoning.

"If Mr. Winstanley does not object, I certainly cannot. To your use of the lighthouse, I mean," Paxton said, flushing. "May I ask a favor in return?"

Sebastién nodded, expression wary.

"I ask that you row out to the tower with these provisions and maintain the light while I spend time with my family. You will have complete privacy and you will be safe. The lighthouse has been equipped to resist invasion. There is a chute that projects downward from the gallery rail that can be used to scatter rocks in defense of the landing place."

"Are such precautions necessary?" Rachael asked.

"Mr. Winstanley once had a bad experience, and he designed the Eddystone to be immune to attack," Paxton explained. He noticed her look of alarm. "I've never had a spot of trouble."

"What happened to Mr. Winstanley?" Rachael asked.

"I don't know the details," Paxton replied. "All I

can tell you is that Mr. Winstanley was manhandled by a group of brigands. French privateers, they were—" He suddenly seemed to recall to whom he was speaking, and stopped in mid-sentence.

Rachael laughed out loud at the affronted look on Sebastién's face while Paxton squirmed, avoiding the Frenchman's cold gaze. Sebastién took her by the arm, scowling down at her as she silently shook with laughter.

"These French lack a sense of humor," she told Paxton, who wisely said nothing.

"That is not true, *ma chérie*," Sebastién disagreed. "I have tolerated *you* with good humor." He extended his hand to Paxton. "We agree to your request," he said.

Paxton took the proffered hand, and a firm shake sealed their agreement. "You'd best be off. The Eddystone rocks are red devils after dark."

Rachael settled into the little rowboat and Paxton helped Sebastién ease the craft toward the first cresting wave. Sebastién pulled himself into the boat and straddled the bulk of supplies.

"I almost forgot," Paxton called after them, "Mr. Winstanley is due out to make repairs on the lighthouse in a day or so. I trust you will explain our arrangement?"

Sebastién's head came up sharply at the news.

"Winstanley shouldn't be surprised to find us there," Rachael said. "After all, he gave me a key."

"*Oui*," Sebastién said grimly, "he may expect *you*, but he does not expect *me*. And as rumor has it, he is less than fond of French privateers."

Rachael placed her slim white hand on his, and Sebastién glanced down at their joined hands . When he looked back up, she was smiling.

"Don't worry," she said. "I will protect you."

Avery Paxton paused in front of the Grog and Gavel. His mouth was dry. He walked into the pub and was roundly greeted by one and all.

He visited the pub with the same dependability that the Cornish people had come to equate with rain on Sunday. After several tankards of stout ale, Avery Paxton could be counted on to become the most amusing source of gossip in all of Cornwall and Devon combined.

Sebastién battled a strong crosswind as he steered the tiny rowboat in choppy seas. They came close enough to the great foundation of rock to which the Eddystone Light was anchored that Rachael was afforded a glimpse of its underpinnings: iron rods of at least twelve feet in length in a stone base some two dozen feet tall.

This was no ordinary lighthouse. She squinted up

at the tower as they stepped onto the landing platform that led to the front entry. The ten-sided upper section bore an artist's impressions of the sun and moon, plus various inscriptions, mostly in Latin: *Post Tenebras Lux* ("After Darkness, Light"), *Salutem Omnium* ("For the Safety of All"), *Pax En Bello* ("Peace in War"), and *Glory Be to God*.

Directly below the great lantern with its massive glass windows was a skillfully engraved shower of stars and the inscription *Anno Dom* in bold work, flanked by a reference to the reign of William the Third.

Sebastién urged her forward, whispering that he expected to find the décor of a Parisian bordello inside. As they passed through the main door, she glimpsed another engraving in Latin, this one a proclamation that the lighthouse had been designed and constructed by Henry Winstanley.

The interior of the tower upheld the lavish style promised by its exterior. Rachael had expected to find steep, rust-corroded spiraling stairs, drafty landings, and hard pallets tossed onto cold floors. Sebastién, evidently expecting the same, gave a low whistle when he opened a door and discovered an attractively appointed bedchamber.

The room was richly gilded, with a large closet and a small chimney. While Sebastién noted the barred outside shutters with a grunt of approval, Rachael marveled at the fine woodwork and the quality of the tapestry rugs.

They climbed carpeted stairs to the next floor, where they discovered the "state room," a chamber similar to the

LISA MARIE WILKINSON

one below but with a larger fireplace and enough closet space for a monarch's wardrobe. The two sash windows had also been equipped with shutters to bar and bolt.

The next level, called "the airry," was an open gallery with a huge leaden cistern used to hold rainwater. The cistern could also be used to allow the sea to pass through in the event of a violent storm.

They wandered into the kitchen, a semi-domed room of moderate size. The kitchen was equipped for basic needs and hinted of past use with its casual state of disarray and, lingering cooking odors.

"Mr. Paxton lives here," Rachael guessed.

The room had a huge fireplace, a recessed oven with a level of ash attesting to frequent use, two dressers, and a long trestle table. A large standing bed dominated the remainder of the room. Casually strewn pillows and crumpled sheets told of a lone occupant who found sleep elusive. A stack of books rose in a haphazard pile atop one dresser.

The uppermost volume contained a small, square, white placard that slipped from between the pages when Rachael lifted the book. She flipped the card over to see it was an undertaker's business card. The artwork depicted a skull and coffin and the customary message about the brevity of human life. She replaced the card between two random pages and snapped the book shut.

Rachael moved away from the dresser to a sizable closet along one wall that bore a crude handmade calendar. She idly noted the date: November 25, 1703, displayed next to the charted phases of the moon. A new moon was due.

The hallway leading from the umbrella-shaped room opened onto a narrow walkway, and Rachael followed the walkway until she reached an open gallery that housed a large standing crane off to one side of the tower. The crane was used to bring up goods when a supply boat could not venture near the rocks due to rough seas.

"It is also used as a signal tower," Sebastién informed Rachael with a circumspect look around as he pulled her back inside.

They continued up another narrow flight of stairs and entered a small hexagonal bedchamber. It was barely large enough for two cabin beds and a tiny walnut dresser. The simple room promised comfort, and Rachael claimed the cozy chamber as her own. Joining Sebastién in the doorway, she stood looking into the area adjoining the modest bedroom.

A dining room and a series of large lockers lined one side. Sebastién entered the room and pulled open one of the lockers. It contained a neatly bound cylinder of candles. He opened several other lockers, and all contained candles to light the great lantern. Several nearly depleted sacks of food staples and other provisions lined the opposite wall.

Rachael had no particular interest in the storeroom. She wandered back into the bedroom and sank down onto the bed, the firm mattress barely yielding under her weight. Her head throbbed, her muscles ached, and her eyes burned from lack of sleep. She pulled off her shoes and fully reclined. Within moments, she was in the grip of a deep sleep.

Rachael awoke with a start to the sound of of water churning and a voice elevated in a tortured cry. Cringing in alarm, she sat up in the bed, arms dimpled with gooseflesh. The sounds came from the kitchen below the bedchamber.

Stumbling into furniture, bumping her shins as she sought the door, Rachael flew down the steps, and as she neared the kitchen, what had sounded like an immense flow of water became a moderate sloshing. She realized the cry of distress that had awakened her was actually loud singing.

Sebastién crooned what was undoubtedly a ribald rhyme mated to a robust melody. He sang in a fractured key, in thick, garbled French and with a gusto that made her certain the translation would rival the raunchiest composition any English minstrel had to offer.

She crept the remainder of the way down the narrow spiral of stairs and entered the kitchen area that doubled as Paxton's living quarters. There, in the center of the room, rested a great wooden tub, filled to the point of overflowing with hot water.

As wispy tendrils of steam drifted upward, Sebastién sat luxuriating in a bath. Eyes closed with pleasure, he reclined against the tub's curved end. The water crested at mid-point against his lightly furred torso, and he had one leg arched over the rim, the white-lathered limb dangling.

He seemed to sense her presence just as she was about to flee back up the stairs and into the relative safety of her bedchamber. His eyes snapped open.

"Are you here to observe or to scrub my back?" His eyes danced with merriment.

"With all the noise you were making, I concluded you were being murdered," she said, flustered. She could feel the heat creeping into her face, and it had nothing to do with the steam rising from the bathwater. She was staring at him and could not seem to stop.

"If I were being murdered, you would be the first to know," he quipped.

"No," Rachael gravely replied, "but I would certainly be the second." Her remark hung in the air, a reminder of the danger stalking them. Sebastién grew morose, and she regretted her hasty words. "Since I am here," she said briskly, "I might as well be of some use."

Rachael raised her skirts and crossed the floor. Snatching the soap from his hand, she began to lather his muscle-corded back. Casting a glance over his shoulder, Sebastién shrugged and leaned forward to make the task easier.

He relaxed and tipped his head back, closing his eyes as her hands abandoned scrubbing and began to massage his shoulders.

The play of his muscles beneath Rachael's hands made her acutely aware of him. The breadth of his shoulders reminded her of his easy strength and how it felt to be held by him. As he exulted in the soothing power of her stroking hands, she felt sensual and powerful in her own right.

When the soap slid from her grasp and plunged into the water, Sebstién lunged to retrieve it with such alacrity that a great wave of the bathwater crested above the confines of the tub, slapping Rachael with a flat, warm wall of water. She stepped back with a cry of dismay, soaked from the waist down.

Sebastién whirled and took in her drenched state with an impish smile. She wanted to rail at him, but he looked like a rascally child.

"You're nearly as wet as I am, *ma chérie*," he said with a straight face. "You may as well join me!"

A noise escaped her as she eluded his hand. "I'll have my bath soon enough," she said.

Her folly was in placing herself so near the tub, within his reach. Laughing, Sebastién lunged forward, gripped Rachael's wrist, and pulled her to the edge of the tub. She shrieked and attempted to wrench free, but he locked both hands over hers and pulled with such vigor that her firmly planted feet slid across the floor.

Rachael tumbled forward and fell thrashing into the huge tub, her enraged outcry mixed with Sebastién's puckish roar of delight. Water flew in all directions as she made several fruitless attempts to climb out of the tub, but his long legs and pesky hands thwarted her efforts. Eventually she sat across from him, unprotesting, clothing completely saturated.

"You may as well join me," he said again, with gleaming eyes and provocatively elevated brows.

"That was a childish thing to do," she huffed.

His eyes glittered and Sebastién smiled warmly. "Now which one of us has no sense of humor?" he taunted. "Would you like your words seasoned before you feast upon them?" A tart retort hovered on the tip of Rachael's tongue, and he made a taunting noise. "Ah, so it is not as funny to be the object of the jest?" He clucked his tongue and shook his head. "These English," he said in a rhetorical tone, recalling her words to Paxton, "these English can make a joke of someone else, but they cannot bear to be the brunt of one."

He laughed, slapping at his thigh and sending up a spray of water, most of which managed to catch her directly in the face. Her hair dripped water in torrents. A blob of lather floated down and perched on the tip of her upturned nose.

"Allow me," he said, reaching out to dab at the droplet of foam. "Your nose is restored," he said, cracking a broad smile. "Now, what can we do about your disposition?"

"My mood will improve the moment I am out of this tub," Rachael replied stiffly.

Sebastién feigned incomprehension. "And allow the bathwater to grow cold, *ma chérie*?"

"I'll heat fresh."

"The rainwater from the cistern is precious. What you suggest is wasteful. We cannot draw fresh for every bath. I meant for us to share this one."

"That much is obvious!"

"I do not intend to lug bucketfuls of water from the oven to the tub simply to indulge your whim when two can bathe just as easily as one. It isn't as if you have a need to be modest with me," he reminded her.

"A fine example of French chivalry. The Frenchman heats water for his *own* bath, the lady be damned."

"A fine example of English *priggishness*," he shot back. His expression said he was willing to elaborate if she had failed to comprehend his meaning. He followed the insult with a devilish smile and arched one brow in a challenge.

Rachael locked eyes with him the moment she accepted the dare. Incensed, she began removing her wet clothing, and they continued to stare at each other as she flung the wet articles over the side of the wooden tub. An audible *thwack!* was heard as each article of clothing hit the floor.

Her bare skin glowed pink with a flush caused by the warmth of the water and the intensity of Sebastién's darkened, heated gaze.

"Will you scrub my back?" she asked, with a regal tilt of her head and an aura of nonchalance she did not feel.

Sebastién silently settled her in front of him in the tub, her bottom meeting the hard column of his thigh. She trembled as his hand moved over her back in a sweeping motion. The silky soapiness of the warm water was a balm, and she sighed at the sheer pleasure of it.

His touch was exquisitely gentle; Rachael felt his breath against her ear as he leaned forward, intent on the task. His right hand moved over her rib cage, swept the indentation of her waist, and crept slowly upward to cup her breast.

"That is not my back."

"*Oui*," he acknowledged, voice low.

As his finger traced her nipple, the heat of her response supplanted the silky heat of the soapy water. Sebastién's left hand found her other breast, and she leaned back against him as he dropped a kiss on her neck. His fingertips massaged both nipples until they became ecstatic peaks and she felt an ache begin to build.

"You're wicked," she said with a sigh.

"*Merci*. I try."

"You said we were going to bathe."

"We *are* bathing, my beautiful English girl."

The warm water and his skillful hands were a sensual combination, and she closed her eyes and nestled against him.

"Do you remember the first time we kissed?" she

asked. "When I thought you were someone else?" She recalled the argument regarding her nightly walks that had escalated into unexpected passion. She had found him intimidating then, but at the same time attractive beyond her wildest imaginings.

Sebastién trailed his fingers along her forearm, idly stroking her skin. "That was not our first kiss."

She swung her head toward him, lips parted in surprise. "You never mentioned . . . I was not sure it was real. When I saw you for the first time after I recovered, I felt I knew you, but thought I had dreamed it."

"And I thought the recognition in your eyes was a sign of your guilt," he admitted. Sebastién leaned his head against hers and locked his arms around her. "The thought of what I might have done—" He did not finish.

While she had been in London, Rachael had heard tales of his obsession with finding and punishing her. It was hard to believe that the man who now held her in his arms could have such a deep capacity for revenge.

"Sebastién?"

"*Oui?*"

She turned and pressed an impulsive kiss against his throat. "Thank you for keeping me safe."

"*C'est mon plaisir.* My very *great* pleasure."

The water had cooled, and Rachael shivered as she stretched against him. He lifted her out of the tepid water and moved toward the stairs, leading to the state room. His black hair glistened with the damp, and a tingling radiated through her as his slick, damp flesh rubbed intimately against her bare skin.

A glowing fire had warmed the chamber until it was dry and comfortable. Sebastién drew back the sheets and slid Rachael onto the bed. She waited while he stoked the fire, breathing shallow with anticipation, senses filled with his presence. She noted the play of muscle across his back, his rounded, firm buttocks, and the muscular strength of his legs. His broad torso tapered into slim hips. Standing still, he reminded her of an ancient statue. He carried himself with feline grace when he moved, and he was a creature of such physical beauty that she could not help but view him with open admiration.

When Sebastién had finished with the fire, he turned and made his way to the bed, a smile playing about his lips when he saw that Rachael studied him.

She had almost overcome her shyness with him, and she felt strangely powerful as his eyes lit with appreciation and carnal hunger when they roamed possessively over her body.

"Priggish young ladies close their eyes and hide beneath the covers," he admonished and chuckled when she drew a hand across her eyes and pulled the sheet up over her head. "Come here, my beautiful English girl," he murmured as he slid into the bed beside her and pulled her into his arms.

Sebastién kissed Rachael deeply, tongue probing her mouth as his hands roamed her body, kneading her breasts and stirring her with a featherlike touch across her belly and thighs. Her timid caresses began to explore the mysteries of his body, attempting to work the same deft magic upon him he used so effortlessly on her as she began to learn what gave him pleasure.

"Touch me," he encouraged in a ragged voice raw with passion. His hand guided hers and tutored her movement until she gasped as she felt him grow and harden. She could not tell whether she brought him pleasure or pain until she heard a groan of satisfaction escape him. He shifted, pinning her to the bed with his weight, and nudged her legs apart with one knee.

Rachael felt she could not bear the intense yearning even a moment longer. She gasped with relief and a pleasure bordering on torment when he slowly entered her, staking his claim to the depths of her soul.

Sebastién withdrew and plunged again, Rachael's cry of pleasure lost as he claimed her mouth in a fevered kiss.

Possessed of him, she felt filled, completed, unaware that beyond the initial sensation of pleasure there awaited a shattering; an explosion of feeling that he had only begun to guide her toward. She arched against him, the sensation so pure it was almost unbearable as he slowly taught her his rhythm. Her breath caught in her throat as the feeling intensified and she felt her body seize his as they both reached the apex. A sensation of warmth flooded her, and she cried out and clung to him, exhausted and sated as the aftershocks of passion rippled through her body.

Chapter Fourteen

Rachael smiled at the sound of the deep, even breathing that every so often erupted into a snore. She savored Sebastién's warmth beside her, along with his strength and power, even in repose. *"Mademoiselle Penrose is under my protection,"* he had told the men at the cottage. Yes, she felt that. She felt safe, protected, cherished. *Loved*.

She could not pinpoint the exact moment she had fallen in love with him, but everything about him seemed significant to her now. Despite his bluster, he was a good man, with an innate sense of decency, even if he did not believe it of himself.

Were his intentions limited to righting a wrong where she was concerned, or did his feelings for her run deeper? There was the undeniable physical attraction between them, but her heart had become entangled as well. Rachael could not separate her emotional response from the physical. More than that, she trusted him, and trust no longer came easily for her. She did not worry whether or not James was safe in his keeping, although she was still unclear about which one of the Falconer brothers had actually taken the child.

Now that they had the means to render Victor harmless and bring him to justice, she would insist that she be taken to her brother. Then perhaps she and Sebastién could begin again, as she had once suggested. Rachael nestled against him with a sigh of contentment and reached down to join her hand with his.

Sebastién stood behind the shuttered windows of the state room, bathed in horizontal bands of fading gold light. He watched as Rachael stirred and stretched, a languid, seductive pose that caused heated blood to rush to his groin and an ache to settle in the region of his heart.

There was still the matter of her brother, James. He had believed that she would be more malleable if she thought he held James hostage. But he no longer needed power over her; she trusted him. It was a fragile thing, this truce of trust between them. He was afraid his confession would shatter their tenuous bond. He was becoming a coward.

"I will hate to leave this place," Rachael said.

Sebastién turned to her and lounged against the wall, studying her face, unsmiling.

"I have not been honest with you." He hesitated when he saw a jumble of emotions flicker across her face, but forced himself to cross to the bed and sink down beside her.

Rachael reached up to smooth the hair from Sebastién's face with a loving hand, and her caress flayed the wild animal his guilt had become. He grabbed her wrist, guided her hand to the bed, and held it there.

Sebastién took a rattled breath, but just as he was about to speak, Rachael reached out with her free hand and touched two fingers to his lips.

"Not here. If you have a confession to make, wait until we leave this place." Her eyes pleaded. "This is our sanctuary, Sebastién. We do not know what awaits us beyond these walls. Here we are friends, allies, and lovers. I want at least this much."

"What remains unsaid will harm us," Sebastién warned. "We must speak of it, Rachael."

"We shall, but not here."

He reluctantly yielded. A few hours would make no difference. Besides, he wasn't eager for her look of adoration to turn to one of hatred. He reclined next to her on the bed, trying to divert his thoughts from her brother's whereabouts.

"So, why did the designer of this great tower entrust you with a key?" Sebastién asked. He felt, rather than saw, the faint lift of her shoulders when she shrugged.

"Winstanley is a friend of Tarry's. We met for the first time after I escaped you."

He winced at her words, remembering the rage that had consumed him when he had discovered her gone. "Why is it you never mentioned this place when we were wandering the moors half frozen?"

"You forget the lighthouse was meant as a place for me to hide from you. It is only recently that I have come to care about your comfort."

His laugh was genuine, prompted by her brutal honesty. "Ah, so you denied yourself comfort so that I would suffer as well?"

"So that you would suffer *in particular*."

"If only your uncle knew what a ruthless adversary he has in you," Sebastién teased.

"My uncle has few fears," Rachael replied. "Poverty. Imprisonment." She thought for a moment. "And the sea. He has a morbid fear of the sea."

He remembered stories he had heard of the "wrecker with dry feet." When he had observed Brightmore on the beach, it had seemed odd that the leader conducted his men from the shore.

"That is why I feel safe here," she said.

"He could always send someone," Sebastién pointed out. Her face fell, and he quickly added, "although he might not trust another man to recover evidence that could hang him."

He had hidden the letters and ledger while she slept and she had not inquired where.

A low, keening howl filled the silence. Rachael's face paled at the peculiar sound, and Sebastién sprang from the bed, blocking the window as he scanned the surrounding seas.

"The wind," he said over his shoulder. It rose again in a low moan as it swept the edifice. "I do not like the look of the sea." He turned to face her. "Yesterday was a lull from weeks of gales. I think the worst is yet to come. If we do not wish to be trapped here by violent seas, we should leave now."

"But the wind—"

"There is still enough time to return safely to shore. A greater danger faces us if your uncle hears a rumor about this tower and sends men to investigate." He was aware that Paxton had a reputation as a gossip, but he did not share the information out of fear that he would alarm her.

"What about the light?"

"The light will burn tonight. Paxton or Winstanley will be here tomorrow."

The glassy, false calm of the sea followed by the slowly mounting wind were portents of things to come. Sebastién doubted that the Eddystone Light would be needed during the coming night because no ships would be venturing out in these waters unless fools captained them.

"I will ready the light while you prepare to leave," he said.

"I must have a proper bath first," Rachael pleaded. "I'll heat my own water."

The corners of Sebastién's mouth drew down, and he shrugged. "Be ready to leave within an hour."

He opened the chamber door and disappeared into the hallway as Rachael hurried to prepare her bath.

While Sebastién went about his labors on the up-permost level of the tower, Rachael heated enough water to half fill the wooden tub and left the steaming cal-dron of water to cool while she gathered their clothing. Sebastién had reclaimed his trousers, but his shirt, vest, and boots remained, as did the voluminous cloak.

Lifting the cloak, she slipped her hand inside the pocket and withdrew the pistol Jacques had given her. If nothing else, it might be useful in a bluff. She returned the pistol to the pocket, folded the cloak, and placed it on a chair.

Rachael heard a loud thud on the floor above her, followed by a muffled curse. Sebastién sounded at odds with some heavy object he was attempting to move across the floor, his haste to leave made evident by the racket he was making.

She found a cake of soap with a vanilla scent and stepped into the crude bathtub, slowly submerging in the hot water with a sigh of pleasure.

Closing her eyes and tilting her head back, Rachael relaxed to the point of drowsiness. She drifted off, but was startled into wakefulness when she heard the creak of a floorboard and opened her eyes just as the edge of a broad steel blade was pressed against her throat. She screamed.

"So, you remember me," Simon breathed through clenched teeth as Rachael's eyes fastened with recognition upon the white scar that marred his forehead.

"What do you want?" she choked in a frightened whisper. His eyes roved over her, and she was grateful for the soap-clouded water.

"I want your French lover to regret attacking me," he said. He leaned closer, and the sharp edge of the blade nicked her throat, drawing a bead of blood. "Your uncle tells me he had you confined to Bedlam to keep you from sending every fairtrader in Cornwall to the gaol. He wants his property returned to him, whore."

Simon caught her chin in his hand, and his stubby, callused fingers cruelly pinched her cheek. Rachael closed her eyes as she felt the knife blade trail along her throat in a cold, obscene caress.

"You will scream when I tell you to scream," he said. "Scream loudly. I like the sound." He fastened his fingers in her hair and jerked cruelly. She obliged with a yelp of pain.

Sebastién heard the cry and raged against the ropes that held him. Two men had ambushed him in the up-permost passageway of the light tower, and the floor be-neath the chair to which he was tied was spattered with his own blood. His face burned and ached from fresh bruises. Blood still flowed from a livid cut above his left eye; the eye itself was swollen shut.

The two men had tried to coerce the location of Victor's property from him. Whether Simon had been in Victor's employ all along, or was a new recruit intent upon distinguishing himself, Sebastién had no idea. Once his attackers had secured his bindings, Simon had briefly conferred with his accomplice before rushing to-ward the stairs leading down to Rachael.

"Perhaps you'll regain your memory when Simon starts to work on your lady," the young man left to guard him jeered. The boy had a tic along one gaunt cheek and strange eyes the color of seawater.

Sebastién winced. The adolescent whine of the boy's voice stretched his nerves to the limit. He was prepared to plead for Rachael's life, but there was something in the boy's flat, deliberate manner that made him cautious.

He sensed that this young man would enjoy slashing a throat and watching the blood flow as life ebbed from his victim.

Another scream reached his ears. He writhed, snarling, desperately fighting against the ropes. The young boy with the fathomless eyes of a killer laughed unpleasantly.

"You may have to stitch your plaything back together—if you can find all the pieces."

Sebastién lunged toward the staircase in a blind rage, taking the chair with him. He toppled over, crashing facedown onto the cold stone floor, and the boy swung a booted foot onto the back of his neck, pinning him.

"That was stupid," the boy said. "Try that again, you French bastard, and I'll cut your heart out and feed it to your woman."

"Tell Simon to stop," Sebastién pleaded, unable to bear the tortured sounds rising from below. The blood flowing from his nose smeared across the floor when he raised his head to speak. "I will tell you where you can find what you seek."

The weight of the booted foot was immediately lifted, and Sebastién drew a shocked intake of breath when the boy grabbed the chair and roughly hauled him upright from his prone position, an eerie feat of strength.

"Tell me where you've hidden Victor's property," the boy bargained, "and I'll tell him to stop."

Sebastién did not trust the boy's motives, his word, or his ability to influence the other man. "If you plan to kill us," he said, "you should know that we took the precaution of hiding some items in the village."

Shrieking commenced below, and Sebastién's heart hammered as fear for Rachael overtook him. He hurriedly gave directions to the boy, who ran off to search the lockers for the bundle of evidence Sebastién had hidden among the candles.

Simon let go of Rachael's hair the instant the boy ran into the room waving the oilskin-wrapped parcel in triumph, and she quickly judged Simon's slight, fresh-faced accomplice to be no match for Sebastién's superior strength and cunning. Why had he failed to come to her aid, and why had he given the evidence over so easily to this—this *child*?

Simon snatched up her damp clothes and flung them at her. "Get dressed."

He motioned for the boy to join him in the hallway while she climbed from the tub and hastily began to dress. Her hands trembled and she dropped her chemise twice before she was able to don it.

Outside in the corridor, Simon and the boy argued.

"I don't like loose ends. We were told to kill the Frenchman and take the girl to Victor. If Falconer escapes—"

"He won't," Simon assured him. "We'll cut loose the rowboat. He will be trapped here until we can return for him. He'll drown if he tries to swim in these seas."

"What if Victor finds out we've double-crossed him?"

"Falconer is worth more to us alive than dead. Let Victor have his property. Our reward will be the ransom."

"What if someone comes to the lighthouse before we return for Falconer? Victor may send us to search for the rest of his property."

"What is contained in the parcel is all there was. I tracked the Frenchman and his whore from Helston to Plymouth. I watched them flummox the old light keeper. I followed the light keeper and relieved him of this."

Simon fished in a deep, ragged pocket and withdrew a key. "When old Paxton wakes up, he'll find he has been press-ganged into the Irish Brigades. He won't be returning to the tower," Simon concluded. "What better place to stash a French noble until a hearty sum in gold can be exchanged for his life?"

"If Victor learns of it . . ." the youth trailed off, still unconvinced.

"Sebastién Falconer is a Marseilles Falconer. This is no fifth-cousin ransom. We'll be dirty rich, so rich that Brightmore won't be able to touch us." Simon frowned, eyes roaming over his strange companion's face. "Of course, Falconer will not remain alive after the ransom is paid." The lure of gold seemed to hold no interest for the boy, but the opportunity for bloodshed brought an eerie glow to the vacant eyes.

"Would you let me have him then?"

Simon nodded. "He's yours. The girl, too, if you like," he added generously.

"I would like that very much."

Simon watched the muscle jump in the adolescent cheek as the boy fingered the blade he held. He made a mental note never to leave his own back exposed.

Rachael was numb as they marched her to the door. Simon linked her arm through his, and when she hung back, he jerked her forward with such brutal force she nearly fell.

They reached the corridor and she suddenly felt faint. She shivered, teeth chattering. The boy stared blandly at her, then muttered to Simon before disappearing into the kitchen. He returned a moment later and carelessly draped Sebastién's cloak across Rachael's shoulders. She smiled in gratitude, but the boy looked at her as if he did not see her.

"What a good heart you have," Simon jeered.

"I expect she'll be cold soon enough," the boy said. He was oblivious to her stunned reaction to his callous, offhand remark. "Victor wants her alive, for now," the boy said, twitching as if he had shaken off a spider. "I'll kill her when the time comes, but I won't mistreat her."

Simon shook his head and prodded Rachael on down the stairs. When she halted beside the turn of stair that led to Sebastién, Simon noticed the direction of her gaze and smiled maliciously. Dragging her along, he sidled up to the stairway.

"Victor asked me to express his gratitude to you for taking care of his niece," he shouted. "We will return later, with your payment."

There was no response. The words were no more than a cruel jibe, but to Rachael, who did not grasp the intended irony behind them, they were a terrible revelation.

The interior of the lighthouse whirled by in a blur as they dragged her down endless flights of stairs. Simon's grip became punishing whenever she faltered. Then they dashed across the rocky perch of the landing area, stones filling her shoes as tears of anguish filled her eyes.

The tiny boat awaiting them rocked as the churning sea tossed it about, and the fierce wind nearly lifted the cloak off her shoulders with a single forceful blast. Simon shoved her into the boat, and she glanced up toward the great golden halo of the lantern silhouetted against the moonless sky.

Did Sebastién stand at some darkened window, looking down upon them? She could never have conceived of such an elaborate plan to place her into her uncle's hands. What would his payment be for betraying her? She felt the sting of the howling wind and turned her face fully into the gust, willing the cold, bitter wind to dry her tears.

Within the uppermost reaches of the Eddystone Lighthouse, the unattended lantern continued to cast its light. On a lower floor, a small storeroom was filled with the sound of shallow breathing As Sebastién lay still on the floor, blood oozing from a gash in his head.

He lay sprawled where he had fallen after the demented youngster with the strange eyes had hit him with an andiron. The boy had freed him from the chair, but only after he had freed him from consciousness.

Chapter Fifteen

Victor Brightmore paced the front hall of Sebastién Falconer's cottage. The Frenchman would be dead by now, and Emerald and Simon would drag Rachael through the front door at any moment. As good fortune would have it, Emerald had been eavesdropping when Simon sat in a pub boasting about having ransacked a residence in Helston, and the tidbit had led them to Rachael.

The peculiar seventeen-year-old was one of Victor's gang of wreckers. He had no knowledge of the boy's background or even his real name; he had dubbed the boy "Emerald," after his pale, changeling eyes.

The boy had exhibited an uncanny flair for the wrecking life. He killed without scruple, and now had proven his loyalty by convincing Simon to share his story with Victor.

Simon had freely shared information Victor would

have been willing to buy. Simon resented Falconer's treatment of him, and he was eager to take part in any scheme against Rachael. Victor's conversion of Simon to a collaborator was necessary because Simon had participated in the theft of enough incriminating evidence against him to send him to the devil as a bondservant for the rest of eternity.

If Jacques Falconer had not spread word up and down the coast that the Frenchman had kidnapped James to force a meeting with Rachael, Victor might never have learned that James was also within his grasp. The infant and Falconer's housekeeper were confined to an upstairs bedroom, and one of his men was posted outside the room to ensure they remained there. Having no desire to see his nephew or hear his mewling cries, he had not ventured upstairs.

The wind keened eerily. The frame of the cottage groaned, and the windows rattled under the onslaught of the battering gusts. The light from a candle on a nearby table flickered. As a sudden violent funnel of air shattered a window, he dodged splintering glass and cursed as all the candles in the room were simultaneously extinguished. Only the lantern resisted the savage blast. Victor grabbed it and sat with it perched upon his knee, waiting.

The winds slammed against the small craft, and the

sea rose up in a churning swell around the boat. Tarry Morgan looked out toward the Eddystone Light, which still seemed far away, despite Winstanley's claim that they would reach the landing area in less than a quarter hour. As they had sailed from the Barbican Steps and headed into Plymouth Sound, the rough strength of the sea had intensified.

It had not been easy to convince Winstanley to allow him to tag along with the repair crew. Tarry had searched for Rachael and the Frenchman by combing coast, moor, countryside, and now ocean in his hunt. This trip to the Eddystone Light was a last, desperate effort to find them. Tarry knew that Winstanley had given Rachael a key, and he could only hope she had lived to use it.

As they approached the tower, Tarry grasped the edges of the plank he sat upon when the sea pitched and rolled beneath the vessel. He shielded his eyes and looked up toward the bright beacon.

"The lady still stands!" Winstanley yelled over the howl of the wind. "No storm can defeat her."

Tarry stared dully toward the brilliant light. He shuddered, blaming the wind for the chill that suddenly passed through him.

Sebastién heard the thunderous racket of boots pounding stairs. The gash in his head throbbed and bled as he crouched in the corner brandishing the only weapon he could find, a chair leg. As the footsteps grew closer, he crossed the room and hid in the blind spot behind the door, clutching the piece of wood.

He followed the sound as it progressed down the gallery toward the tiny space he occupied. So, they had come back to kill him. Well, he was ready for the bastards.

Sebastién was teetering on the brink of madness, at the very edge of rage. He had nothing to lose, and it made him dangerous. Rachael had been taken from him. She would be returned to him, unharmed, or a bloodbath would be visited upon those responsible.

The bolt was eased back and someone advanced into the storeroom with caution.

He did not allow the opportunity for a first strike against him and swung the length of wood with vicious purpose, grunting with the effort. The blow caught the intruder across his midsection with such power that the slightly built figure crumpled to the floor in a heap.

"The tiny insect with the deadly sting," Sebastién snarled as he bent down to the boy who had tormented him. The chair leg had splintered from the force of the blow, and Sebastién held only a fractured stalk of lumber in his hand.

"Christ, Falconer!" Tarry groaned. "Is this how you deal with your rivals?"

He froze, staring into the darkness as he tried to put a name or face to the vaguely familiar voice. A lantern extended by a disembodied hand forced light into the darkened chamber, and Sebastién saw a man holding a pistol pointed at him. Then there were other voices, and a crowd of curious faces pressed into view around the door frame.

He backed away from them and crouched in a fighting stance, teeth bared, arms outstretched, fingers flexing in spasms, as if daring them to approach.

Henry Winstanley and his repair crew gave Sebastién all the distance he required.

"I ain't goin' near 'im," one man whispered to the other.

"Aye, I don't want whatever it is 'e's got," the second man replied. A third nodded vigorously, his eyes huge ovals in his face.

"Morgan, are you hurt?" Winstanley asked. He kept his eyes and his pistol trained on Sebastién.

Tarry rose slowly, dusting off his breeches, and probed his ribs with a grimace. "I'm all right," he said. "He just knocked the wind out of me."

"You, sir, are a trespasser in this tower," Winstanley informed Sebastién. "The Crown will not object if I shoot you."

"Wait! I know this man," Tarry said. "I will vouch for him."

Sebastién directed a surprised, distrustful look at Tarry.

"You know him?"

"Yes," Tarry said. "We know some of the same people," he said, with a double meaning that was not lost on

Sebastién.

He gave a shallow nod of understanding and opened his mouth to speak, but Tarry broke in, leveling a look of caution at him when he spoke.

"His name is Duncan. He is a mute."

Although one word from a thickly accented Frenchman might provoke dire action from the French-hating Winstanley, Sebastién still resented being silenced.

"What is he doing here?" Winstanley asked.

"Oh, Duncan is apt to turn up anywhere," Tarry said. "Usually where one least expects him," he added as he locked eyes with Sebastién.

"He looks deranged," one of the men said.

"He's a bit of a simpleton; makes his home out to Polruan. He's harmless," Tarry added, avoiding Sebastién's incensed regard.

"Unless you happen upon him in the dark," Winstanley commented dryly.

Tarry laughed, a loud, nervous giggle. "I'm certain I gave him quite a fright."

"From the look of him, I'd say we weren't the first to frighten him tonight," Winstanley observed. He took a step toward Sebastién, his speech measured, as if he spoke to a dim-witted beast. "There, son, don't be afraid. We only want to help you. That's a nasty cut you've got—"

Sebastién emitted a threatening, guttural sound, and Winstanley hastily stepped back.

"Maybe you'd best tend to him while I see if I can

find Paxton. If he's gone off on another drunk—"

"Perhaps he got Duncan to watch the light for him. The boat is gone. Paxton must intend to return later." Tarry failed to mention that the room in which he had discovered "Duncan" had been bolted from the outside.

"Take your friend down to the first floor chamber," Winstanley said. "There is a small metal box beneath the bed that contains clean linen and a salve Paxton swears will cure everything from pimples to the plague." Winstanley motioned his men out of the room ahead of him and drew Tarry aside. "See if you can find out what happened to him."

Tarry nodded. "I intend to do just that."

Tarry was miffed to discover that his charge had gone off in the opposite direction and went in pursuit of Sebastién, closing the distance two and three stairs at a time. They collided on the upper landing, Tarry noting at once that the Frenchman had managed to recover his weapon.

"I see you found your sword. Where is Rachael?"

"Taken by two of Brightmore's men. I'm going after them."

Tarry's face contorted as his worst fear was confirmed. "Then you'll need my help," he asserted.

"*Non*," Sebastién said. "I want no distractions." He paused. "I intend to kill the men who took her."

"I am not asking if I may go along. I'm telling you I'm going."

"Ah, *oui*," Sebastién said furiously. "You will impale yourself upon some wrecker's sword so that Rachael may blame me for it!"

"You won't get off this rock without me," Tarry warned. "I may just lock you back up in the storeroom and go after her myself!"

Lantern light flickered with the sound of tread upon the stairs. "If you value your life," Tarry advised, "you'll continue to play the part of a mute."

"What's this?" Winstanley said when he saw them. "I thought you'd have Duncan bandaged up by now." He noted the sword that hung at Sebastién's side. "Is he giving you trouble?" Winstanley indicated the brawny men who flanked him. "Do you need help?"

Sebastién's eyes issued a flinty warning to Tarry.

"I've promised Duncan that I will take him ashore once I've tended his wound, but he's eager to leave now, alone. That would be dangerous," Tarry said. His face was set.

"I'll have two men stand guard outside the door while you sew up that gash."

Sebastién suddenly crossed his arms over his chest as if to still a violent impulse.

"Come, Duncan," Tarry said to him as he began the

downward climb to the lower floor chamber. "Come along nicely now."

One of Winstanley's men drifted to either side of Sebastién, and he fell into step with them, although his eyes told Tarry there would be hell to pay later.

"I don't expect any trouble," Tarry told the men as he swung the door shut.

The door had barely closed when Sebastién spun on Tarry in a rage. "You idiot!" he seethed, voice low. "We waste time here!"

"We'd have left a quarter hour ago, if you'd not been so obstinate." Tarry dropped down on all fours and began to rummage under the bed. He withdrew a small square tin and threw it at Sebastién. "Now I've got to darn that stubborn hide of yours before either of us can leave."

"You are mistaken if you expect to lay hands on me," Sebastién warned.

"I should stitch that gaping hole beneath your nose shut first," Tarry shot back.

"Touch me, *enfant*," Sebastién snarled, "and you will be the one in need of a surgeon."

"Then bleed to death!" Tarry hissed. "If this delay costs Rachael her life, I'll kill you myself."

At the mention of Rachael, Sebastién yanked open the tin and extracted a needle, a coil of thin twine, and several narrow strips of clean white linen, slapping the items into Tarry's open palm. Tarry eyed the needle with apprehension, and Sebastién snorted in disgust and snatched the needle and twine back out of Tarry's hands.

"It's no different from mending a tear in your shirt," Sebastién said. He fed the twine through the eye of the needle and handed it back to Tarry, laughing at Tarry's white face. "*Pardonnez-moi*, I forgot that a man of your station does not repair his own shirts."

"I've no whiskey or the like to give you. This is going to hurt like hell."

"Just as well," Sebastién said wryly. "Get me drunk and I will not remain mute for very long." He reached out and gripped each end of the small dresser, fingers growing white from knuckle to fingertip when Tarry began to wield the needle.

"It might distract you if we talk," Tarry suggested. "Do you know where they've taken her?"

"The boy boasted that Victor has made himself at home in my cottage," Sebastién replied, the edge in his voice as much from anger as from pain.

"The boy?" Tarry inquired.

"*Oui*." Sebastién jerked as the needle penetrated his flesh. "A strange one, about your age. When I attacked you, I thought it was him."

He shuddered when Tarry took the final stitch. Tarry used his knife to cut the excess twine and stepped back to survey his handiwork.

"You know, Frenchman," Tarry said, "if I were wiser, I would have allowed Winstanley to shoot you."

Sebastién turned to face him. "Why is that?"

Tarry shrugged as he fumbled through the contents of the tin. "Because you're my rival."

"Your rival?"

"For Rachael." Tarry withdrew the container of salve, collected a small amount of it on his forefinger, and began to apply it to the newly sealed gash. "I had hoped that she would be here. I wanted her to see me as dashing, worldly, courageous, and handsome. The way I suspect she sees you."

"Yet you stopped Winstanley from shooting me. Why?"

"Because I have misjudged you. I've learned you're innocent of most of the mayhem credited to you."

Sebastién swore colorfully and bolted upright. Tarry looked on helplessly as the bandage he had applied to Sebastién's head began to unravel, like a mummy becoming unbound.

"How do you know I am innocent?" Sebastién demanded.

Tarry hesitated. "Because I took part in pilfering enough evidence to hang Brightmore," he admitted in a rush.

Sebastién's hand went to his wounded head. He looked around for a chair, found one, and sat down. "That was you?" he asked, incredulous.

Tarry nodded. "It was my father, Phillip, and I." He began to reapply the bandage. "You will not believe what we found. Bolts of silk drying in the backyard. Bags of tea seasoning in the sun. Records of high-duty items that never saw a pence paid on the import! Brandy imported in oil casks well-plastered at each end and oiled on the outside. No doubt the duty he paid was for oil and not spirits! His receipts list only Portuguese wine, levied at a fraction of the duty he would have paid for French wine, but his cellar was filled with French wine."

Sebastién shook his head in disbelief.

"We found the source of the tobacco black market," Tarry continued, "boxes upon boxes of ready-filled clay pipes. The Crown never licensed Victor as a tobacconist! We discovered three-hundred packs of wool, no doubt waiting to be exchanged for tea or Lyon's silk," Tarry added, knowing the export of English wool had been outlawed to protect the British wool trade. "There was a written record of wrecking—that is how we learned that Victor had used you as a scapegrace for his crimes."

"The Dane found the ledger. How did it happen that you left it behind?"

"We were in the process of carting away the evidence when we heard men approaching. We gathered the most valuable items and fled. The cabinet was left behind."

"What was more valuable than the ledger?"

"A covered chamber pot."

Sebastién wrinkled his nose and looked at Tarry as if he had lost his mind. "A chamber pot?"

"A solid gold chamber pot," Tarry elaborated. "When I pulled away the cover I discovered counterfeit Customs seals. Brightmore has been marking goods with a set of rather official-looking seals. I dare say the Crown will not find the implied royal sanction amusing. They'll want to hang him once for each seal, I reckon," he speculated with glee.

"No doubt he is frantic over his loss." The intense look of satisfaction, along with almost all the color, had drained from Sebastién's face. "Brightmore will believe Rachael knows where the seals are hidden."

"Why do you say that?"

"The men who took Rachael have the parcel containing the ledger. I tried to buy time by saying that we had hidden the rest in the village."

"My father took everything north for safekeeping," Tarry said. "Nothing was left that we can use to bargain for her life."

Sebastién sprang to his feet, stripping away the bandage Tarry had so painstakingly applied. "We've no more time," he told Tarry. "My head is stitched, *cela suffit*. Enough. Have you gotten any better at wielding a sword?"

"I've been taking lessons," Tarry drolly replied.

Sebastién extended his hand. "Rivals can also make effective allies when they share a common goal," he said.

Chapter Sixteen

Rachael sat with rigid bearing on the cane-back chair, flanked by Simon and Emerald. Her hair streamed across her face, but she made no effort to sweep it back, afraid the movement would draw Victor's attention and give him reason to strike her again.

When his men had first dragged her into the cottage, her uncle had been cocky and glib, but the instant he had opened the parcel his men had retrieved from the lighthouse, his sunny mood had vanished.

"You're lying," Victor shouted, raising his voice to be heard above the bellow of the wind. "Where have you and Falconer hidden the rest of it?"

What more could there be? Rachael had never seen him so near panic. "Your man was there." She nodded at Simon. "He saw that the cabinet contained nothing else."

"The Dane didn't open the cabinet in my presence," Simon protested. "I never saw the contents."

"The Nordic blighter!" Victor snarled. "I shall kill that freak some day."

"Or hire someone else to do it for you," Rachael muttered under her breath.

Victor lunged for her, and Emerald stepped neatly into his path. "The Frenchman said the rest was hidden in the village."

Rachael's head snapped up at the news. "That is not true! All we found was a ledger and some correspondence. Someone else had ransacked your home before The Dane got there."

Without warning, Victor raised his arm and backhanded Rachael. One of his rings cut her lower lip, and she tasted blood and despair. Why would Sebastién have made such a claim? The lie had convinced Victor there was additional information to be pried out of her.

"Perhaps Simon or Emerald can convince you to part with your secret," Victor suggested.

Simon leaned toward Rachael with the look of a destructive child abandoned in a room filled with delicate china. She felt his hand descend upon her shoulder, and flinched as the pressure increased until she thought he would crush bone.

"Don't touch her yet," the boy's high-pitched voice commanded. When Simon lifted his hand to Rachael's throat despite the directive, a muscle skipped across the youngster's smooth, gaunt cheek and his fingers sought the knife slung low on his hip.

Noting the darkening changeling aspect of Emerald's face, Victor stepped between the men and motioned them aside. Simon relinquished his grip on Rachael's neck with reluctance, unaware that Emerald's hand had dropped from his knife in response.

"She doesn't know the hiding place," Emerald said. "Else she'd bargain with the information."

"She knows I intend to kill her anyway," Victor said impatiently. "She'd withhold the information just to spite me."

"Let me see what I can get out of her," Simon begged. He glanced in Rachael's direction, his thin-lipped smile baring yellowed teeth.

"Why don't you ask the Frenchman what you want to know?" Rachael shouted at them with reckless anger. It wasn't difficult to guess the drift of their hushed conversation.

"Not possible," Victor said in a low voice. "Perhaps I was hasty in having him killed."

"We left the Frenchman at the lighthouse, alive," Emerald said.

"*What?*" Victor immediately looked to Simon for an

explanation. "I told you to kill him. Why is he alive?"

Simon cast an unreadable look at Emerald. "I thought you'd want him kept alive until your property was recovered."

Victor whispered instructions to Simon then motioned Emerald to his side after Simon had left the room. "Why is the Frenchman still alive?" he asked.

"Simon planned to ransom him."

Victor choked. "He planned to profit from my peril, did he? I've given Simon a task. Follow him and see that he completes it."

"And if he does not?"

Victor briefly considered the question. "Kill him and then finish the task for him."

"And if he completes it?"

"Simon is not loyal. I leave it up to you. Follow your instincts."

Outside, the wind shrieked. The frame of the cottage shook as the sound surrounded the small building like the screech of a banshee heralding death.

Rachael was gripped by a dark premonition as Simon mounted the stairs to the upper floor. A woman's voice sounding like Mrs. Faraday uttered a volley of pleas as a commotion erupted.

A few moments later, she heard Simon's heavy tread on the stairs as he descended, followed by a tall, muscular blackamoor. She dashed toward him, intending to pluck the swaddled infant from his arms, but Emerald blocked her path, and she had to grit her teeth to hold back the scream. Simon's taunting grin may have been vile, but Emerald's cold, unblinking stare was terrifying.

"The housekeeper won't trouble us for a while," Simon informed Victor. "She isn't dead," he added with a nasty smile at Rachael.

"I will need you and another man in one hour," Victor told the blackamoor. "Go find a sword and bring him back with you." His attention strayed to the bundle Simon carried.

James sounded weaker than Rachael remembered, his once lusty cries muted to whimpers. When she reached for the generous folds of blanket that concealed him, Emerald stepped into her path and stopped her with a slow, wordless shake of his head.

"You have a choice, Rachael," Victor said. "James can turn up as a nameless foundling on some Highland doorstep, although I am willing to negotiate with you; I simply want the rest of my property."

"You know I would do anything to save my brother. I know of nothing more than what has already been returned to you! Please!" Her voice broke and she made another attempt to take the baby from Simon, but Emerald shoved her away with a snarl.

"Perhaps Falconer did not tell you where everything is hidden, but you insult me when you claim that you took only the ledger and my personal mail. The Frenchman himself said there was more!"

"He lied!" This was Sebastién's fault! For all she knew, Sebastién and Victor had collaborated all along and the discovery of the evidence had been staged for her benefit, to make it easier for him to lead her into this trap. "You will have to come to terms with the Frenchman on your own," she said finally. "He is no friend or ally of mine!"

Victor studied her for a long moment. His blue-gray eyes widened, and he flashed a perceptive smile, followed by a throaty laugh. "I won't deny the Frenchman anything that is due him. Shall I relay a message on your behalf the next time I see him?"

"Yes. You can tell him I hate him and he can go to hell."

Without lifting his eyes from her face, Victor folded his arms over his chest and summoned Simon and Emerald to his side. His next words were said with deliberate clarity.

"Take James down to the beach and drown him."

Rachael screamed and lunged for Simon, but he sidestepped her, grunting with the effort, and she fell to the floor, desperately latching onto his boot. He dragged her several paces before Emerald bent down with an oath and wrenched her hand free of its grip on Simon's boot. The boy hauled Rachael to her feet and flung her away from the door with a strength that stunned her.

She stumbled and fell backward, the hard landing leaving her breathless. Victor drew his knife and held it to her throat, forcing her to huddle on the floor at the point end of the blade while Simon and Emerald slipped out into the windstorm with James.

"Never claim I am incapable of mercy," Victor said. "If I had given your brother to Emerald, it would not have been a quick death."

Rachael screamed in outrage and cuffed his hand, dodging the blade. Victor lost his grip on the weapon, and it hit the floor with a metallic clatter. When he sprang to retrieve it, Rachael rolled away and bounced to her feet.

As Rachael fought to free herself from Sebastién's heavy cloak, she remembered the pistol. It was useless as a weapon, but Victor did not know that. She snatched it from the pocket and aimed it at him, hand trembling.

He froze, lips flattening into a white line.

"Drop the blade and kick it to me," she demanded, waving the pistol for emphasis. The knife hit the floor and made a scraping sound as it was booted in her direction.

"I think you should shoot him. I certainly would."

A noise of relief escaped Rachael as Mrs. Faraday entered the room. The housekeeper's left cheek bore a livid bruise, and she directed a vibrant look of malice at Victor.

"I need to tie him up," Rachael whispered. "Is there something I can use to bind him?"

The older woman promptly lifted her skirts, stepped out of her petticoat, and began to tear the garment into lengths.

"Sit," Rachael told Victor, indicating the hard chair she had occupied.

Victor grunted in discomfort as Mrs. Faraday anchored his left wrist to the chair arm with the first of the crude ties. "Pity it isn't around your neck," she said.

Once he had been secured, Rachael deposited the pistol within the pocket of the cloak and ran to the door. She struggled against the wind to open it, the portal groaning in protest, then paused in the open doorway, hair flying, clothes lashed by the force of the gusts.

"The rest of your property is hidden in the lighthouse," she told Victor. "The Frenchman betrayed you."

What better revenge than to set them at each other's throats? She would savor her uncle's reaction later, after she had found James.

Simon and Emerald stumbled down the rough trail to the beach, making their way toward a light in the distance. The baby's tireless screams had made both men edgy and in the right frame of mind to carry out Victor's order.

As they rounded a corner and descended to the beach, they found themselves at the center of more than a dozen men. The leader of the regiment held the light that had beckoned them.

Simon recoiled at the sight of the officer's face. The man looked like the wounded Frenchman they had left at the Eddystone Light. But this man was clean-shaven and uninjured. Emerald dropped to his knees in the sand, staring at the Frenchman's double with a look of awe.

Jacques Falconer calmly sat his horse while he assessed the two men, eyes flickering with shrewdness over the bawling infant Simon held in his arms. He rested his hand on his hip and serenely inquired, "Which one of you is the mother?"

Sebastién maneuvered the boat into port against tremendous odds. The force of the gales drove ships into one another, making the harbor almost as treacherous as the open sea. Ships were being ground to matchwood or swept over flooded river embankments into the fields beyond.

The number of vessels beached atop stone quays, ready to sink once the winds and rough seas subsided, was astounding. The wind had veered southwest and had grown in intensity, rising from an unearthly scream to a pitched, sustained bellow approximating the sound of thunder. There was no rain; only intermittent flashes of lightning lit the gray sky.

They dashed toward the village, dodging debris as entire houses fell apart under the weight of collapsing chimney stacks. A hail of tile and slate fragments pummeled them when fragile buildings were blasted as if made of paste and parchment. More solid structures were dismantled piece by piece until cottage and castle alike were reduced to piles of rubble.

The wind veered from southwest to west with a wail of warning for those unfortunate enough to be caught in its path. The tempest forced them to retreat toward a barren wheat field where a lone windmill whirred with dizzying speed. They dropped to the ground as the sturdy old oak they had sought for cover was uprooted by the wind and heaved through the air, as if flung by some unseen, mighty arm.

Trees were destroyed by the dozens. The cries of birds rent the darkness as the creatures collided in mid-air or were thrown against buildings, where they fell to the ground to die in heaps. Livestock caught in the open were lifted and deposited yards away. A man herding his animals to safety was plucked up by the demon wind and hurled violently to the ground.

Sebastién shouted to Tarry over the howl of the wind as they raced across the field, his eyes locked upon an old church. It was the only structure that had not yet buckled or collapsed completely under the onslaught. The wind had stripped the long forsaken place of worship of several decorative spires and the lead lining of its roof.

They rushed inside and forced the massive wooden doors closed behind them. At the entrance, they found candles and a generous supply of sulfur. After a struggle to light the first candle, they placed others throughout the old building.

The stale air within the church commingled the

faint scent of crushed flowers with the acrid smell of smoke from candles, the mustiness of the moors, and the lingering odor of countless unwashed congregations. The pews were dusty. Spiders had woven intricate web doilies into every crevice. Stained glass fragments were scattered in corners, statues had been defaced, the pulpit overturned. A number of empty wine flasks were strewn about the floor.

"Do you suppose Rachael is safe?" Tarry asked.

Sebastién did not have a chance to reply; he and Tarry spun toward the door when they heard the sound of someone struggling to open it against the strong suction of the wind.

Sebastién blocked Tarry's impulse to rush forward by extending an arm to bar his way then shook his head circumspectly while his eyes remained on the door. His free hand dropped to his sword.

A blast of frigid air swept the building as the door opened fractionally and someone stole inside. The new arrival put a shoulder to the heavy door and gave a determined push, forcing it closed. The light from the candles at the entrance died in the draft. A muted glow from the remaining candles bathed the church in muddy yellow light.

The wretched sound of a woman sobbing echoed in the cavernous interior. The woman leaned against the wall and continued to cry, body shaking with the force of her grief. As Sebastién approached the slender form enveloped by a hooded cloak, the hood fell back, revealing the face. It was Rachael.

Chapter Seventeen

Sebastién rushed toward her with a hoarse, inarticulate cry, arms outstretched. Rachael whirled in surprise and sidestepped the embrace with a sound of dismay.

"Don't come near me." Her eyes were bright with unshed tears.

Sebastién stopped, the expression of accusation and horror on Rachael's face making it nearly impossible for him to breathe. His arms dropped to his sides and he stared at her, his expression desolate. When Tarry stepped forward, she walked into his arms with a choked sob.

Sebastién stood by, helpless, feeling the sting of rejection with greater acuity than he had ever felt it in his life. He watched as Tarry gently ran a finger along Rachael's torn lower lip and quelled the urge to demand to know the name of the man who had struck her. Things had changed between them; he no longer had any right to ask.

"You're safe," he said softly. "Thank God."

She pierced him with a look of loathing. "I am sorry to disappoint you after all your splendid effort to deliver me to my uncle."

What did she mean by that? He had expected anger to follow her discovery that he had lied about holding her brother hostage, but nothing like this. *"Au contraire,"* he said. "The sight of you is balm."

Rachael's face contorted at the earnest declaration. Her eyes traveled over Sebastién's swollen, blackened eye and the liberal swaths of blood that streaked the collar and shoulders of his shirt. She inclined her head toward the contusions on his face and his bloodstained clothing. "I do hope that is your blood."

"Rachael!" Tarry gasped, shocked.

Sebastién held her with his gaze. "Rachael, if you will remember, I tried to tell you about James—"

The mention of her brother's name prompted an explosion of rage, and Rachael launched herself at him like a wild thing, leveling a vicious slap at his bruised cheek and clawing at his hair as if she meant to extract it by the roots. She pounded her fists against his hands when he halfheartedly sought to shield himself from her blows.

Tarry caught her and closed an arm around her waist, half-lifting her into the air as he dragged her away from Sebastién. He struggled to subdue her when she fought to renew her attack.

The sudden explosion of breaking glass startled them when a heavy stone hurled by the violent wind shattered a nearby window. The pane crumbled and fell away in shards as the crazed moan of the wind invaded the church. Tarry lost his grip on Rachael and she retreated a distance from them, looking cornered and wild.

"If you ever speak my brother's name again, I will kill you," she told Sebastién. "I swear it." She had to shout to make her trembling voice heard above the wind.

It was the first inkling he had that something terrible might have happened to the baby she had believed to be her brother. "Why? What happened?" he asked.

Her face was gripped by a spasm of deep grief, and her upper lip quivered as she brushed away tears with the back of her hand. "Victor had James killed." She began to weep again, an inconsolable lament that broke Sebastién's heart.

He took a hesitant step in Rachael's direction, overcome by the need to console and reassure her that James was still alive.

"Keep him away from me, Tarry," she shrieked. "I cannot bear to be in the same room with him."

He held up his hands in a tacit promise that he would not press her, but when she suddenly bolted for the door, he pursued her with a speed and agility born of desperation. Sebastién slipped between Rachael and the door she had managed to partially open then put his back to it and slammed it shut with a backward step, facing her while he made himself the barrier to her only means of exit.

"Get out of my way, Frenchman."

He did not budge, nor did he take his eyes from hers. "*Non*. It is too dangerous outside." Rachael refused the hand he extended. Her eyes glittered in the shadowy light, and he saw fear and distrust in their depths. He had hoped to never see her look at him that way again.

"Let me pass," she demanded.

"Make no mistake, I will force you to remain here, if I must," he said, his gentle tone at odds with his words. The look of hatred she leveled at him wrenched through him to his very core. "Your brother is alive," he said.

For a moment, he thought she might attack him again.

"Liar! Victor told Simon and the boy to drown him. I searched the beach, but I found no one. I was too late!"

She shoved hard at Sebastién's chest and attempted to push past him, but he seized her by the shoulders and held firm. He was desperate and close to violence himself, struggling for control.

"Did you see the child?" When she glared at him but remained mute, his temper flared, and he shook her. "I stand accused, *mademoiselle*," he rasped. "You will not accuse me and then refuse to discuss the matter! Did you see your brother?" he persisted. Driven by frustration, he shook her again. He motioned Tarry away when Morgan stepped forward as if to intervene.

"Of course I saw him!" Rachael said. "It could have been no one else but James."

"Liar," he growled.

"Liar *and* murderer," she coldly one-upped him.

The wind outside changed direction again, and a sudden floor-level blast of cold air funneled into the building through the shattered window.

"It is obvious I am unwelcome here," he said through gritted teeth.

Rachael moved with emphatic steps to the door and pulled it open. Flying debris swirled all around her, but she stood, impervious, holding the door open, making it clear she wanted him to leave.

She had no opportunity to react to the look of alarm on Sebastién's face or Tarry's cry of warning before a muscular arm closed around her. The powerful blackamoor held Rachael immobile as Victor sauntered into the church.

He stopped in front of her, flashing a cruel smile as he reached into the pocket of the cloak she wore and withdrew the pistol. He lifted the weapon, blue-gray eyes searching hers while he aimed it at her face.

"*No!*" Tarry shouted.

So, Victor had not yet discovered the pistol was useless. Sebastién pulled Tarry back as another of the wreckers entered the church carrying a lantern and an unsheathed cutlass.

"I was fascinated by your conversation," Victor said. "Do continue." He looked at Sebastién. "You were telling my niece that her brother is still alive?"

The window had been shattered on purpose so that Victor and his men could eavesdrop. Sebastién quickly evaluated his options. James was safe only if Victor believed he was dead.

"He was alive when I saw him last," he said. "I only kept him hostage. If he's dead, it's your doing." Sebastién avoided Rachael's stricken face and steeled his expression, betraying none of the abject misery he felt.

Conscious of Victor's sharp gaze on him, he moved next to Rachael. When she refused to look at him, he took her chin in his hand and tilted her head until she met his eyes. Afraid his voice would betray him, he remained mute.

She spoke in his stead. "I hate you."

There was pain, anger, and defiance in her expression, but what she saw on Sebastién's face seemed to confound her. Overwrought, she began to cry.

"Now look what you've done," Victor chided. "You've made her weep."

"I seem to have that effect on her," he said. Letting her go with a reluctance that was torment, Sebastién stepped away.

Victor scanned the room. "You're at a disadvantage, Frenchman," he said. "My men are armed. If you attempt to draw your sword, one of them will snap her neck and the other will run you through."

"How do you expect to recover your property if I am dead and cannot tell you where it's hidden?"

Victor raised one elegant, sandy brow. "She already confessed that my property is hidden at the lighthouse. I have only to retrieve it."

Sebastién's eyes cut to Rachael. "That was vindictive of you, *ma chérie*," he scolded, inwardly applauding her resourcefulness. If Victor believed more evidence was stashed away, he might not risk killing them until he had recovered it. Sebastién pretended to examine his fingernails.

"Bolts of fabric and casks of wine and brandy can be found easily enough. But a Customs seal, real or counterfeit, fits in the palm of a man's hand, *non*? The lighthouse has many places where such small items might be concealed. How will you know where to look?" He paused as if a thought had suddenly occurred to him. "How will you manage to get in without a key?"

"Shall I have my large friend break Rachael's fingers one by one until you tell me what I want to know?"

"If you harm either Rachael or her friend Morgan," Sebastién said, "you will never have what you seek."

"Oh, and why is that?"

"You will have nothing with which to bargain. They have no value to me dead."

"Now I see what you've been up to, you French bastard!" Tarry roared. "All this codswallop about helping you rescue Rachael was a trick. How much must my father pay to guarantee my safe return?"

Tarry had picked up the gauntlet and played his part well, but Sebastién's heart sank at the sound of Rachael's horrified gasp. She did not seem to comprehend their ploy.

"Morgan and my niece will be my downfall if I do not dispose of them," Victor said. "As could you."

"You forget that I am hunted. I cannot approach the authorities regarding you. In fact, I have already over-stayed my welcome in England."

"Perhaps this matter can be resolved privately be-tween us," Victor mused. He crooked his head and mo-tioned Sebastién into a far corner, away from Rachael and Tarry.

"What ransom have you asked of Phillip Morgan for the return of his son?" Victor asked.

"My business dealings are private." Sebastién stood in front of the broken window and looked down at the glass fragments strewn across the floor as if distracted. The remaining candles had been extinguished, leaving only the dull glow of the lantern.

"Suppose you set your top price and I triple it?"

"In other words, you will buy Morgan from me?" Sebastién had to force his voice to remain steady. Ab-sently, he reached down and began to loosen the pieces of glass that still clung to the framework of the window. "I have already sent a ransom demand to his father. What will he think when he learns his son is dead?"

"Kidnapping and murder carry the same penalty, if you are caught. Why should it matter?"

"There has never been a riskier time to commit murder," Sebastién said. "There are soldiers on the moors tonight."

Victor conceded the point with a nod. "It is a matter of their survival or mine."

"If you recover your property and destroy it, Morgan can prove nothing. Your niece poses less of a threat now than you think."

"That girl knows I am responsible for the death of her brother!" Victor snapped.

"You forget," Sebastién coldly reminded him, "I have as much to fear should she escape me and live to tell tales."

Victor brightened. "Yes, that is true. You held her prisoner, and she blames us both for James's death."

"I plan to return to France. I believe the superior course of action is for Rachael to leave England with me," Sebastién suggested. "There is little she can do to harm either of us from France."

"But what about Morgan? He will persist in trying to rescue her. His efforts can become quite tiresome."

"Morgan will assume she met the same fate as her brother."

"There is also the matter of a family inheritance that cannot be claimed until both heirs are proven dead. If my niece takes a permanent holiday in France, I'll remain impoverished."

"A simple matter," Sebastién replied. "We will arrange the appearance of her death. Morgan can be the one to identify her body. He has more value to you alive than dead."

"Her death must appear to be the result of an accident. The body must wear her clothing, and the face must look enough like her to fool Morgan. Leave that to me. You may seal our agreement by telling me where I can find my property," Victor concluded.

"I think we should, perhaps, go after it together?"

"Ah, so you do not trust me?" Victor followed his accusation with a humorless chuckle.

"I trust no one, not even my own mother."

Sebastién engaged Tarry in a brief conversation while Victor drew one of his men aside.

"After the Frenchman and I have gone, wait a few minutes, then kill my niece and her hapless friend."

"What about the Frenchman?"

"I will take care of him." He drew his cloak around him and followed Sebastién out the door.

Rachael witnessed the brief exchange between Sebastién and Tarry, but Tarry said nothing of it to her after Sebastién departed the church with Victor. Tarry followed them and moved to close the door, but the guard with the cutlass stepped forward to block his path.

"We'll all be warmer if I close it," Tarry mildly suggested.

The man shrugged and stepped back, and Tarry closed the door, casting a surreptitious glance at Victor's men before he slid the bolt, barring the church from outside entry. He rejoined Rachael and wrapped an arm around her while they waited.

Tarry used the pretext of fetching the lantern as an excuse to let go of Rachael before she could notice he was trembling. Perspiration tickled his upper lip. His heart squeezed in his chest, and even though Tarry had guessed the reason why Sebastién had idly cleared the jagged glass from the window frame, Tarry still cried out in surprise when the Frenchman suddenly dove through the open window, vaulting into the room with an audible crunch of glass beneath his boots.

Tarry kicked over the lantern as Sebastién had instructed him. Glass shattered; the harsh yellow glow of the lantern was replaced by the abrupt mantle of night. The ominous clash of steel resounded as swords were drawn in the darkness. Light flashed as opposing blades struck, raining blue sparks upon the floor.

Tarry grabbed Rachael, using his free hand to feel his way along the wall while they crept in the direction of the door, away from the conflict. He pulled Rachael into a crouch when they neared the shattered window and he suddenly heard the thud of feet hitting the floor when someone jumped through the opening.

The intruder inched along the wall and stopped near the church entrance. Tarry heard chafing sounds, and a spark ignited as the odor of sulfur wafted to him, tickling his nostrils and making his eyes water. The light flared as it fed the candlewick. Victor held the candle.

The unexpected burst of light caused a sudden cessation of movement in the church. Rachael screamed when the blackamoor swung his blade in Tarry's direction. Sebastién whirled and ran Tarry's attacker through with one clean thrust of his sword. The blackamoor collapsed at Tarry's feet, ebony skin still glistening from the exertions of battle.

When Victor saw the floor of the church littered with the bodies of his men, he seized Rachael and thrust her out in front of him as if she were made of armor instead of flesh. He lifted a knife to her throat.

"No more tricks, Frenchman," Victor said. "The pistol may have been useless, but this blade is not. Toss the key to me."

Sebastién's gaze blazed fury as he jerked the ribbon free and flung the lighthouse key at Victor. It glanced off Victor's shoulder and landed at Rachael's feet.

"Pick it up," Victor hissed.

Rachael bent down to retrieve the key, and when she straightened, Victor snatched it from her hand. Rachael winced and touched her throat with shaking fingers, dabbing at a thin stream of blood welling from a cut on her neck.

Tarry glanced at Sebastién, whose eyes were riveted upon the scarlet ribbon of blood on Rachael's pale skin. Cold rage and the promise of retribution etched the Frenchman's expression.

"My niece is going to help me recover what you stole from me. You had better pray she knows where it's hidden." Victor dragged Rachael with him to the door. "If you try to follow us, I will kill her." Victor slid the bar and opened the door, gasping and turning his head away from the sudden blast of cold air.

Rachael did not fight Victor. He was too willing to harm her as it was, and her life would soon be forfeit anyway. After her brother's death and the Frenchman's betrayal, she no longer cared what happened to her.

Victor prodded his niece forward through the darkness along the steep path adjacent to the barren field. Rachael could hear the whirr of the windmill in the distance, and the incessant howl of the wind. When they reached the narrow footpath that led down to the sea, she stumbled and fell, and Victor lost his grip.

Victor tumbled, sprawling as he tried to check his fall and recover his hold on Rachael at the same time, but she pushed away and dashed pell-mell back up the path to the church.

She collided with Sebastién, who seized her by the shoulders to steady her, and stood staring down at her for a moment without saying a word before he thrust her at Tarry and continued down the path after Victor.

Tarry urged her to the safety of the church.

"No," she said. "I don't trust either one of them. I'm not letting them out of my sight." She gave Tarry no choice but to follow as she broke into a run down the path.

Sebastién made no effort to conceal his presence from Victor, and his cool, authoritative voice rang out with taunts as he continued down the path.

Victor scrambled to his feet and cut a wide swath in the opposite direction, abandoning the path for the dormant field.

The howl of the wind became a sustained wail. Patches of vegetation set afire by lightning strikes dotted the landscape with glowing, churning color, all combining to form a meager source of light. In the distance, the glow of the lighthouse beacon framed the horizon.

Tarry and Rachael caught up to Sebastién as he surveyed the panorama of the field and the foaming curl of shoreline, searching for movement.

"There he is!" Tarry shouted, pointing toward the beach.

Mouth set in a grim line, Rachael startled Tarry by snatching his sword.

Sebastién uttered a curse and stepped forward when she attempted to push past him. Taking a firm hold on her arm, he spun her around.

"Where does *mademoiselle* think she is going?"

"To kill him."

Expelling an impatient sigh through clenched teeth, Sebastién tried to pluck the sword from Rachael's grasp, but she danced out of reach, slashing the air with the blade as if to engage him in swordplay.

"Just try it, Frenchman," she said. "I'd love to cleave you in two!"

He drew his own sword with a lack of finesse that revealed his anger, and he and Rachael circled each other.

"Damn it!" Tarry shouted in exasperation as he stepped between them. "Brightmore is getting away while you two stand here bickering!"

"Why do you think the Frenchman wants to keep us here?" Rachael shouted above the wind. "He's helping Victor escape!"

"Give Morgan back his sword. *Now.*" Sebastién's

ferocious expression dared her not to obey him.

Rachael tilted her head back to look at him. "I will not."

He moved to forcibly disarm her, but it was Tarry who unexpectedly leaped forward and snatched the sword away.

"We're going after Victor," Tarry told Rachael. "Go wait for us in the church."

Sebastién followed Tarry, and Rachael stubbornly trailed behind him. He spun around furiously when she continued to follow.

"If I have to carry you back to the church and tie you to a pew, I will." There was barely checked violence in his caustic tone.

"And let *you* go after Victor? No. You are not to be trusted. You're a murderer, a liar, a wrecker, a pirate, a thief, and a kidnapper."

"You forgot seducer of women," he prompted dryly.

"That, too."

Sebastién considered the list of transgressions. "What about smuggler and fairtrader?"

"I don't consider those crimes."

He smiled a nasty smile. "How convenient." Stabbing the blade end of his sword deep into the sand, Sebastién gripped the hilt tightly. "Rachael, your brother is alive. I lied to Victor to keep him safe."

"My brother is dead, and yet you continue to lie. I will never trust you again."

"It is a disgrace that a child may have come to harm, but the infant left at my home was not your brother."

"You cannot possibly know whether it was my brother or not," she argued. "My uncle knew it was James."

"The child left on my doorstep was a girl." He lifted his brows in emphasis when her jaw dropped.

"Impossible." Victor had seemed to believe the child was James. Had Victor even looked at the baby? "I do not believe you," she said, but with less certainty.

"We have finally come full circle then."

"What do you mean?"

"There was a time when you were innocent, but I accused you. Now I am innocent, and you accuse me." He shrugged, and Rachael was surprised to realize that he no longer seemed angry, only weary. "You will believe me when I place your brother in your arms," he said.

Chapter Eighteen

Tarry had stumbled upon a miracle in the barren winter field, a wildflower in full bloom. The unexpected sight of the wild primrose captivated him. The flower stood its ground with audacity, a flash of pristine, almost spectral white to trumpet its tiny, extraordinary existence. Tarry picked the flower with careful fingers, cradling it between his cupped hands.

Awed, he touched the soft petals. Never would he have discovered the flower had it not been illuminated by the wilting heat from a nearby patch of burning bramble. The presence of the flower upon the barren, wind-ravaged moor spoke to him of struggle and survival against insurmountable odds, and the need to protect fragile, beautiful things.

Rachael had been his wildflower, he supposed, but

it was Falconer for whom she had blossomed. He knew his childhood friend too well, and she loved the Frenchman, even if she would not admit it to herself. He was no rival to Falconer; he never had been. The Frenchman had known that, too, but had treated Tarry kindly, with deference to his sense of honor and his vanity.

Tarry spied on Victor from a vantage point above the shoreline. The man had not found a seaworthy vessel. On the beach, the waves were enormous and the sand swirled in blinding clouds. He felt the stinging lash of pebbles as the driving wind shifted again, and heard the groan of a madly spinning windmill nearby.

Tarry gently tucked the flower into his pocket and turned his attention back to the shore below, crouching when Victor glanced up and scanned the area. Victor's presence at the edge of the reflective white, foaming curl of shoreline made him easy to spot. For the same reason, Tarry had avoided passing in front of the windmill. Its broad, sun-whitened common sails would frame him in silhouette and alert Victor to his presence.

As the first faint pastels of dawn crept across the horizon, Tarry slipped down toward the beach while Victor was still unable to detect his approach. He crept along the field where the windmill marked a rugged path down to the sea. The wind veered again, and he resisted the force of it, bracing himself as it capriciously shifted direction again, creating a strong crossdraft.

Suddenly he heard the loud creak of timber and felt

the prickle of rising heat. Sensing danger, he spun around, gripping his sword. The cloth sails of the windmill had caught fire, ignited by the friction caused by unbridled speed. Tiny fingers of flame dropped to the ground and danced along the windshaft, spilling over onto the cap as the fire voraciously consumed the aged wood.

Fire swept over the upper part of the structure and grazed toward the body of the mill itself. The storm battered the weakened framework, and when the wind shifted again, the doomed structure was caught in a mighty crosscurrent. The windmill swayed precariously, threatening to topple. It tottered a few steps as the flaming leader boards spewed fire like some mythical beast on a rampage, giving the windmill the strange aspect of having suddenly come to life.

Tarry shielded his eyes against the shower of sparks and dashed for safety as the windmill teetered and then came crashing down. The structure collapsed with a wrenching of sail bars and splintering timber, accompanied by the squall of the miscreant wind. In the split second he was given to note the irony of it, he saw the blaze had spared the massive plank of lumber as the heavy beam came crashing down upon him.

Sebastién slipped his arm around Rachael and cursed

softly in shock and dismay as they witnessed Tarry being struck down by the collapsing windmill from where they stood on the bluff above the field. Rachael's scream was carried aloft by the howl of the wind. Their argument forgotten, they ran down the path together, cutting across the field diagonally.

A faint shower of black ash was dispersed by the strong wind, obscuring the dusky sky. When they reached the rubble of the windmill, Sebastién removed Rachael to a safe distance from the glowing timber and spray of sparks before he began sifting through the debris.

A moan issued from the mound of wreckage and he fell to his knees yanking at the pile, burning his hands and gathering splinters as he hurled the charred, smoking debris out of the way. Tarry moaned again, and Sebastién continued to work frantically until he had cleared away all but the last piece.

Tarry was pinned to the ground by a length of crossbeam. Sebastién struggled to lift the beam and push it aside, and was rewarded when Tarry slowly stirred as the weight was removed. Tarry brought his arms up and rested the upper half of his body upon crooked elbows. When Sebastién reached out and touched him, he jerked, startled by the contact. His elbows slid out from under him and he collapsed in the mud.

Sebastién crouched down, eye level with him. "Are you hurt?" he asked.

"I don't think so," Tarry replied. "I have a burn on

my arm, but there is no other pain. In fact, I can't feel my legs at all."

As soon as he had spoken the words, he and Sebastién traded openly apprehensive stares. "I cannot feel my legs at all," Tarry said again. He stared down at his appendages, face twisting with panic. "I cannot move them," he said in a rushed, terrified whisper.

Tarry's eyes were glazed and his breathing labored. The early dawn had brought a chill, but he was perspiring profusely and his skin was waxy and translucent. Sebastién cried out to Rachael to bring the cloak, but Tarry reached up and grabbed his hand in a desperate grip.

"Please . . . don't alarm her," Tarry begged.

Rachael dropped down beside Tarry and threw her arms around his neck. She eased the cloak from her shoulders and tucked the garment around him.

"Are you hurt?" she asked.

He raised his eyes and cast an imploring look at Sebastién. "I've injured my ankle," he smoothly replied. "I fear I must submit to the indignity of allowing the Frenchman to carry me."

"Nonsense," Rachael said. "You can lean on me."

He looked at Sebastién again, appearing on the verge of hysterical tears. Sebastién was left with no choice but to lie to Rachael again. "He may have broken his leg. I have no experience at splinting. It's best I carry him."

As they spoke, the velocity of the wind began to climb again. The storm was unlike anything Sebastién had ever experienced, and he was filled with a sense of urgency to get them all to shelter.

Rachael kept the cloak tucked around Tarry as Sebastién lifted him. He scanned the seas as they made their slow trek along the beach toward his cottage. There was no sign of Victor.

"I wonder why he has not put out to sea," Sebastién said.

Tarry's eyes flickered open. "He was looking over the boats."

"He'll want the sturdiest one he can find," Rachael warned. "As soon as he finds a boat, he'll be off to the lighthouse."

Sebastién ogled two rowboats when they passed by them. One had holes bored into its bottom planks, and the other looked ancient. There did not seem to be a seaworthy vessel along the storm-wracked beach. He smiled spitefully at Victor's misfortune.

"We should be going after him," Tarry moaned. He gasped, and Sebastién froze. "Winstanley is out there," Tarry said. "Victor will kill him."

"Your friend has very capable assistants," Sebastién pointed out.

"He has a key now, and Winstanley does not expect him," Rachael argued. The look she leveled at Sebastién was patently one of accusation.

"We will take Tarry to my cottage and you will fetch the doctor while I go after Brightmore." He expected

263

her to object, but her eyes were on Tarry and she made no reply.

Sebastién's cottage remained standing, although every window had been shattered, and a fine layer of dirt had settled over every exposed surface.

Tarry was delirious and mumbling incoherently by the time they put him to bed, and Rachael had hurried to fetch the doctor from the village. Her ears still rang with the doctor's mildly surprised response to her emergency: "Only a broken leg, is it? Then why do you need me? Mr. Falconer can splint a leg as well as I can. I taught him. Broken limbs are common in his trade."

Just one more thing he has lied to me about. The doctor had expressed concern over Tarry's fever but imparted little else that she could understand. He had implied that the extent of Tarry's injuries would cease to matter if the fever did not soon break.

Tarry dozed fitfully while Rachael sat staring out at the sea. Sebastién kept invading her thoughts as she kept vigil over Tarry. He had disappeared when Rachael had gone to fetch the doctor. She would never forgive him if he failed to return, or if he allowed Victor to escape.

Time passed slowly, and the empty howl of the wind lulled her with its incessant moan. Exhausted, she was on the verge of falling asleep in the chair when a random creak of floorboards on the lower level roused her.

She unsheathed Tarry's sword by slow degrees to avoid making noise and glanced at Tarry. He was asleep at the center of the huge bed. She crept from the room, pulled the door closed, and locked it behind her.

Rachael stole into the hall and moved with caution toward the landing at the top of the stairs where she heard someone moving about downstairs. Heart pounding, she backed into the shadows of the landing, but the tip of the sword scraped the floor when she moved, and she froze, aware that the sounds below had ceased.

"Yes, I am certain I heard a noise below!" she exclaimed then paused. "No, it could not possibly be The Dane. It is too early for him to be up and about."

She cocked her head and listened. The intruder was quiet now, waiting. Listening. She was committed to the bluff. Rachael turned and moved along the hallway, speaking in a loud voice as she went.

"Really, do you think a pistol is necessary? Your sword should be sufficient!" She paused again. "Shall I awaken the others?"

She came to the landing and stepped out onto the first stair, but the banister blocked her view of the lower level. When she moved down one step, she inadvertently revealed herself to the man who stood at the foot of the stairs, waiting.

Jacques Falconer noted the abrupt halt of Rachael's

descent and the look of dismay that flickered across her face. He smiled and bowed mockingly, the frosty glint in his eyes telling her that her bluff had been called.

Victor knew the Frenchman was following him. Falconer had made a point of lounging in doorways where he knew he would be seen and blatantly stood by observing as Victor had purchased a boat and a pistol in the village.

Victor bobbed along with the sharp rise and fall of the waves as the boat slid out to sea. Though the modest craft had cost him plenty, it was sturdy enough. The Frenchman stood on the beach watching him as if he were an entertainment. Victor indicated the abandoned, unseaworthy vessels that littered the beach with a sweep of his hand.

"Take your pick!" he taunted above the roar of the wind. He lifted the pistol and fired a shot toward the shore, wasting the ammunition but making the point that he was now equipped with a functional weapon.

The vessel careened against the swell of the agitated sea, and it occurred to Victor that he was at the mercy of a vast, angry ocean. He gripped the gunwale and retched over the side. When he glanced back at the shore, there was no sign of Falconer. The realization rattled him, and he clutched his midsection and stared longingly at dry land.

Sebastién had also secured a vessel and had kept it hidden in an inlet along the beach. The craft was of moderate size, constructed specifically for smuggling. It was rigged fore and aft rather than square-rigged, so that its speed was not dependent upon the wind. His lighter, more streamlined craft shot toward the open sea, aided by both wind and current.

Victor had strayed from his course. Rachael's uncle battled a circular sweep of wind and sea that threatened to capsize him. Within a matter of minutes, the wind veered from southwest, to west, to northwest, and then shifted by degrees until it regained a westerly draft. The fickle blast freed Victor from the whirlpoollike pull of the sea, and he made steadily for the lighthouse, swept along by the gusting wind.

Sebastién's craft shifted crazily, opening a yawning gulf between the two vessels. He stumbled along the leeward side as his boat slammed into a barrier reef where the ship faltered, listing dangerously, her hull pierced by the sharp rocks. She had lost her main mast and mizzen-mast due to the hard gales, and seawater slowly flooded the bottom of the boat. He swore in frustration as the sea continued to flow into the vessel. His ship was bilged, and Brightmore would reach the Eddystone Lighthouse within minutes.

Sebastién's light craft plowed against the ledge of rock as the wind toyed ruthlessly with it, and he was forced to dive overboard to avoid being carried down with it. The churning sea swept him up and he struggled toward the shore, swimming against the fierce pull of the current. He was a strong swimmer, but in these seas there were no advantages.

Stumbling onto shore, Sebastién shivered from cold and gasped for air. Kelp and sea grit clung to him and saltwater stung the gash in his head.

The awesome strength of the wind had increased. Sand swirled all around him, stinging every exposed inch of flesh. Sebastién looked toward the lighthouse, distressed by his failure. Winstanley and his men were on their own. Brightmore would eventually return to landside, and he would be waiting for him.

Sebastién trekked to the top of the bluff, where he had a better view of the comings and goings at the lighthouse. He half-crawled up the steep cliff path, fighting against the wind for balance. The village below had been reduced to scattered piles of rubble, and few buildings remained standing. Anxious faces peered out of shattered windows as villagers waited for the storm to end.

Easing down to the ground, Sebastién looked out to sea. Victor was having difficulty nearing the landing platform; the sea playfully swept him back each time he came close to it. The rippling depths threatened to channel the small craft into the foaming waters around the dangerous reef, and the current was at its strongest near the rocks.

Sebastién had a sailor's quirky reverence for the sea, and he could not recall a time when the aspect of it had been as extraordinary as it was at the moment. The sea wore a white crest of spume that extended to the waves rolling in along the current. The sight was like the foaming muzzle of a rabid animal. The roiling black waters formed enormous swells that pounded the rocks as breakers lashed the exterior of the lighthouse.

The sand burned his eyes and the tang of saltwater filled his nose and mouth. The banshee howl of the wind rose again in a horrific shriek and Sebastién felt his heart accelerate as instinct urged him to his feet.

The Eddystone Lighthouse was under attack, but not by any human foe. An immense curl of water had gathered into a monstrous swell and was flowing toward the mighty tower like some ancient sea serpent in a mammoth curtain of rushing sea. It was buoyed along by wind and water, gathering momentum as it approached the tower.

Sebastién knew the exact moment Victor became aware of the danger because Victor glanced over his shoulder, save the advancing menace of a wave, and foolishly stood up in the boat. He turned toward the approaching onslaught, briefly immobilized by the sight before he exploded into a frenzy of action as he tried to escape the inescapable.

A gigantic groundswell of water rolled over the little boat. It tumbled, spinning end over end at the core of the rushing water as the huge wave coursed toward the lighthouse. The wall of water pounded the edifice, flinging the boat against the stone.

The magnificent tower seemed to quake as it resisted the shock. Sebastién was so stunned by the suggestion of movement that he shouted in disbelief and waited for some sign that the sea would calm now that it had tasted sacrifice. But the swirling black void seemed to gather strength for a fresh assault. Sebastién stood on the bluff, numbed by a peculiar flash of precognition as a phenomenal wave glided toward the tower.

When the wave hit, there was no gradual stone by stone surrender. One moment the lighthouse stood, proud and defiant, and in the next the sea loomed empty and triumphant, washing over the lengths of iron rod that still protruded from the great stone base. The iron rods were all that remained of the magnificent structure. Henry Winstanley's wish to occupy his tower during the worst storm imaginable had been granted. The sea lay tranquil.

Chapter Nineteen

Sebastién's pace quickened as he approached the cottage. Although his limbs were heavy with exhaustion and the wound on his head throbbed, the worst of the storm was over, in every sense of the word. Rachael and her brother were safe from their uncle, and her reunion with James would be the first step toward healing his tenuous relationship with her.

He looked forward to being vindicated. The English authorities would soon have proof that he had not been involved in the wreckings that had plagued the southern English coast. His status as a French privateer made the punishment for his transgressions against England somewhat negotiable, but the crime of shipwrecking was one that would have earned him a swift execution.

Jacques might be able to confine him to the gaol

until their grandfather could arrange a pardon for his "patriot exploits," but Jacques could no longer accuse him of being a wrecker.

Sebastién trudged wearily up the path. The sight of the horizon without the magnificent Eddystone Lighthouse to mark it was a somber one. How would Rachael react to the news of Victor's ironic fate? Would she look upon the time they had spent at the lighthouse fondly, or with regret?

His cottage had sustained a minor amount of damage, but he had never seen a more welcome sight. It had sheltered the woman he loved during one of the worst storms the English coast had ever seen. Every lichened stone and fractured pane of glass bore his gratitude.

He entered through the front door with a lighthearted shout of greeting, but the door slammed behind him before he could think to react. He tried to draw his sword, but his strength and speed could not compete with that of the two uniformed men who confronted him.

He heard the metallic clink of chain as one man bent a relentless grip around his neck and shoulders while the other slipped a rusted pair of irons around his wrists. Enraged, he bucked headlong into the man who had chained him. The soldier staggered backward, crashed into the wall, and collapsed on the floor. The other man outweighed Sebastién by at least two stone, and was well rested, uninjured, and unfettered.

He landed a fist in Sebastién's midsection, and Sebastién doubled over, winded and in agony. The other man recovered and the two set upon their shackled prisoner, beating and kicking him viciously until he slumped between them, bleeding and barely conscious.

Once his men had quashed his brother's rebellion, Jacques made his way down the stairs. Sebastién hung limply between the two guards.

Jacques came face to face with his twin and stood looking at Sebastién as if puzzling over an enigma. Sebastién became aware of his brother's scrutiny and stiffened, standing rigidly under his own power.

"Englishman," he said, "you are a trespasser here."

"This property now belongs to The Crown," Jacques informed him.

"Oh? When did you offer me a price I could not refuse for it?"

"Such high spirits for a man under arrest," Jacques said. "I wonder what your mood will be the day we hang you."

A board on the upper floor creaked. Rachael came as far as the edge of the landing and stopped, staring aghast at Sebastién. The sweep of her eyes took in the shackles and the new injuries suffered at the hands of Jacques's men. She looked at Jacques, expression filled with censure.

"Tarry is delirious," she said. "I fear his injuries are far more serious than a broken leg." She directed a look of indictment at Sebastién.

His troubled gaze lifted to her, and he was dismayed that she remained rooted to the top stair. He had no intention of trying to pacify her while in the presence of his smirking twin. "Where is Victor?" she inquired in a low voice.

"Dead."

Her face twisted with impatience and frustration. "Do you really believe I can accept your word for it?"

"He drowned. His body was washed away. The lighthouse is gone." He could forgive her cynicism, but he stiffened in outrage when she and Jacques exchanged knowing glances.

"Oh, Sebastién," Rachael sighed, voice hitching as she shook her head.

"Go and see for yourself," he snapped. "The tower was swept away."

"At least his lies are colorful," Jacques muttered.

"*My* lies?" Sebastién sputtered. "You were the one who convinced her that I had taken her brother hostage. Apparently someone hated you even more than I. A baby girl was left on my doorstep so that I would know a trap was being set. James is safe. You know that."

"I know nothing of the kind."

The possibility of what Jacques might be planning suddenly occurred to him. "For what crime am I being detained?"

"Murder." There was malevolence in Jacques's tight-lipped smile. "And you are not being 'detained,' as you put it. You are to be tried and summarily executed."

"You have no proof I am a wrecker." Jacques

conceded the point with a nod. "It is impossible to prove you guilty of wrecking. You are to be tried for the murder of James Eaton Penrose."

"Impossible," Sebastién countered furiously. "You will never find his body."

Rachael made a strangled sound, and when he looked up, she had disappeared. Had she interpreted his words as a confession? Determined to go after her, he struggled against the men who held him.

Jacques signaled for his men to shackle his brother, and both men fell to the ground on top of Sebastién as he fought against this new indignity. They dragged him up again, slamming him into a wall and winding him in the process.

Jacques barked a curt order, and Sebastién's tormentors stepped away. He was left leaning against the wall for support.

"I meant to say that his body will not be found because he is alive. Let me explain to her." When Jacques did not respond, his temper exploded. "You know her brother is alive. If you refuse to acknowledge it in her presence, at least admit it to me!"

"She would never believe it now," Jacques said. "She is convinced she saw James taken from the cottage by Victor's men. Who am I to try to convince her otherwise? Moreover, why would I want to?"

"Then how do you plan to execute me? You cannot prove me a wrecker. You may as well claim that I killed

my housekeeper as claim that I murdered James Penrose."
It was the most outrageous thing he could think of in
the heat of the moment. His tongue flicked over his
bloodied lip. "If your goal is to kill me, Englishman,
you had better succeed."

"I don't plan to fail," Jacques said, locking eyes with
his brother. "I will not make mistakes such as the one
you just made." At his brother's stony look of inquiry,
he obligingly added, "Your housekeeper will be compensated for her assistance."

"You will learn that there are those who cannot be
bribed." Let Jacques look for Mrs. Faraday; she could support his claim that the baby left on his doorstep was female.

"Everyone has a price," Jacques glibly replied.

"The lady is a sharp judge of character, and you are
not so difficult to read."

"The lady has never met me. I may make a positive
impression upon her."

"You will not fool Mrs. Faraday—"

Sebastién's eyes widened in surprise as Jacques suddenly bellowed in outrage and lunged at him. He was
unprepared for the attack and took the full impact of
the blow on the concave underside of his jaw, grunting
in surprise and pain as the force of it drove him to his
knees. His shackled ankles threatened to topple him
when he shifted his balance in an effort to rise.

Jacques drew back his arm and dealt Sebastién
another savage blow. He fell to the floor amid a clanging

of chains, the fetters rendering him prone and vulnerable. The shattered glass from the broken windows pierced his clothing like thrusts from a thousand knives.

"Where is she?" Jacques screamed at him.

Jacques grabbed him by his bloodied shirt and hauled him upright, nearly choking him with the violence of the action. "By God, I will kill you!"

Sebastién clumsily raised his chained hands to block the assault, but the blows were too numerous to defend against. Jacques flung him away in a rage, and he tripped over the length of chain.

Sebastién fell against the wall with a grunt of pain as the stitches in his head broke loose. He dragged air into his lungs, and a sharp stab of pain jarred his rib cage. The pain repeated with each subsequent breath he took.

"I will give you one chance to tell me," Jacques warned. "Where is your 'housekeeper'?" He looked crazed. A lock of black hair fell over one eye, and his teeth were bared in an ugly snarl.

"Why should it matter to you? A poor widow from the coast would mean nothing to you."

For the first time since the curtain of rage had descended over him at the mention of the housekeeper's name, Jacques paused to look carefully at Sebastién's face.

"How can you not know?" Jacques asked, incredulous. A hardness settled around his mouth and he made a derisive sound. "Is the name Eleanor Faraday Falconer more familiar to you?" he prodded with cruel simplicity.

"Faraday was our mother's maiden name."

Upstairs, Rachael gasped at the soul-wrenching out-cry as Sebastién's howl of rage seemed to spring from the very foundation of the cottage. The porcelain bowl she held slipped from her hands and crashed to the floor, and she stepped over the shattered mess, shoes grinding rem-nants of the bowl into grit as she ran from the room.

Rachael heard the cry again when she reached the landing, and the sound was so terrible that it destroyed her resolve to remain upstairs. Running down, she found herself on the perimeter of activity centered around Sebastién and froze at the sight of him, her exclamation of dismay lost in the din.

Two of Jacques's burly men grappled to subdue him, and although chained at the wrists and ankles and bru-tally beaten, he was possessed of uncanny strength. She had witnessed such strength and singleness of purpose before, in the more violent inmates at Bedlam. She could not imagine what had precipitated such behavior in Sebastién, but rushed forward blindly, determined to pull him back from the brink.

Sebastién fought to wrench free of the men who held him while keeping his eyes fastened upon his objective: his brother. Jacques stood a safe distance away, staunching the flow of blood from his nose with a handkerchief, wary gaze upon his raging brother. Jacques was marked by a strange pattern of red-white welts across his face and along one arm; welts that bore a telling resemblance to the chains worn by Sebastién. Jacques shouted for a pistol in a raw, authoritative voice.

"What do you intend to do?" Rachael shouted in alarm.

"Defend myself." Jacques pushed her aside, grabbed the pistol from his aide, raised the weapon, and took deliberate aim at his brother.

Rachael had no doubt that Jacques would murder his brother in hot blood. Sebastién inexplicably continued to bait his twin, and after a quick glance at their faces, she uttered a sharp cry and thrust herself between them.

"*Non*, Rachael!" Sebastién shouted.

"You will not do this!" she spat furiously at Jacques.

"He attacked me!"

"If you do so much as touch him again, you will answer for it!"

"He means to kill me if he gets loose."

"A threat from a prisoner does not justify killing him."

Jacques's eyes blazed with resentment. "He'll die soon enough," he muttered.

Rachael shuddered at the palpable hostility that flowed between the two men.

"You had better pray I find your witness, alive and

in good health, or you will see me again before you meet the hangman."

Sebastién lifted his chin and looked at his brother with open scorn. "If I am the mad dog you think I am, perhaps she is already dead."

Jacques needed no further provocation. He slapped the pistol into his aide's palm and barked: "Confine this animal! Get him out of my sight!"

As Sebastién was ushered to the door, Rachael noticed his stiff, cautious movements and the wince of pain that fleetingly crossed his face before he adopted the guarded expression that had become all too familiar to her. The urge to speak to him tugged at her, but she did not know what to say. She felt corrupted and confused by the strength of her emotions.

If he was guilty, his crimes were unpardonable. The Dane had found proof that he had been unjustly accused of leading the wreckers. Had Sebastién kidnapped her brother and indirectly caused his death, or was Jacques responsible? Had he allowed Victor to go free? His claim that the lighthouse had been swept away was easy enough to prove or disprove. When he had been uncertain of *her* guilt, he had been willing to assume she was innocent until proof to the contrary had been found. He deserved no less.

As the men led Sebastién from the cottage, Rachael ran to his side and took his hand, possessed by an indefensible need to comfort him.

He studied her face, and then raised his free hand,

moving his fingers slowly over the slope of her cheek. She
felt the cold tingle of metal links against her flushed skin,
and her uncertainty exploded into raging doubt. Her eyes
filled with tears when she opened her mouth to assure
him that she had not judged and abandoned him.

Sebastién's fingers formed a barrier to prevent the
words from spilling from her parted lips. He did not
smile, but nodded somberly in understanding.

"*Out!*" Jacques shouted, and his men shoved Sebastién
through the door before any words could pass between
them.

"How easily you forget your brother," Jacques
sneered at her as he slammed the door.

Rachael leveled a look of antipathy at him. "How
easily you forget your own."

"How else can I put an end to the wrecking? If the
gang loses their leader, it will be like severing the head of
a bloodthirsty beast."

"Sebastién has never been a wrecker." Rachael
studied Jacques a moment. "Did Sebastién kidnap my
brother?"

She found her answer in the hesitation before he replied.

"Sebastién is guilty of many things," Jacques said
evasively. "I have arrested him for the crime that will be
the easiest to prove."

"Don't you mean to say, the crime for which proof
has already been assembled?"

His jaw tightened at the accusation. "Your brother

is dead," he cruelly reminded her. "Do you want the man responsible to go free?"

Rachael canted her head and considered Jacques, eyes narrowed in speculation. "I want the man who actually took James—or had him taken—punished. That man is either Sebastién or you. God help you if you've killed my brother as a means to destroy your own."

Jacques's eyes searched Rachael's face, and he suddenly grew angry and defensive. "He will not escape justice this time! You're a fool to believe whatever he wants you to believe. You have no proof he is innocent!"

"Proof!" Rachael cried. "I will show you proof!"

She stormed out of the room, and when she returned a moment later, tossed the shipwrecking ledger at him. When he made no attempt to catch it, it struck the table-top and fell open to a random page.

"This is proof that you have been wrong about your brother. You cannot prove Sebastién is a wrecker, and you will have a difficult time proving him responsible for what happened to James. I will leave you to your reading. I fancy a walk along the beach. I'd like to see if a landmark is missing."

You will have a difficult time proving him responsible for what happened to James. Jacques's head came up sharply as he remembered Rachael's words. He recalled a similar comment made by Sebastién. He had implied that Jacques would have an easier time proving that he killed his housekeeper.

Had the words been a confession? Jacques remembered, too, that one of the last things Sebastién had said had been "perhaps she is already dead." He roared in outrage and swept the ledger to the floor with a shaking hand.

His cry brought a wild-eyed aide into the room with his sword drawn. Jacques was perched at the edge of the small secretary, face ashen.

"I wish to undertake a search for a former servant of this household, a housekeeper known as Mrs. Faraday."

"A woman's things still occupy a servant's chamber just off the kitchen," the aide dutifully informed him. "It could be that the lady plans to return." He paused. "Or, it could be that she no longer has need of her belongings."

The aide flinched when Jacques cursed and kicked at the desk. His foot caught the ledger and he nearly tripped; only the quick reflexes of his aide kept him from falling. He snatched up the ledger and handed it to the man.

"Sir, what shall I do with it?" he inquired, turning the volume over in his hands.

Jacques eyed the ledger with distaste. "Burn it."

Chapter Twenty

No one knew with greater certainty than Jacques that James Penrose was alive, but he did not plan to initiate a search for him until Sebastién had been executed. James Penrose was in Phillip Morgan's care, probably somewhere in or around London, and there he would remain for the time being.

There was no risk that the female infant would resurface. The foundling had been placed on the steps of an orphanage after he had extracted a confession from Simon and sent Simon and his strange sidekick as far away as his authority would allow.

He was certain Sebastién was a wrecker; he had Adrienne's pendant to prove it. The necklace had been evidence enough for him, but not enough for the Court of the Exchequer. His attempts to have Sebastién tried as a wrecker had repeatedly failed, and now it no longer mattered to him that his brother would die for a crime he had not committed. Sebastién was guilty of a heinous, personal crime against the woman Jacques had loved.

The only detail that pricked his conscience was how to break the news of Sebastién's death to their mother. Eleanor had spent her life pining for the son she had been forced to abandon.

Jacques remembered many attempts to retrieve Sebastién during his childhood, all thwarted by Hugh, who finally resorted to threats against Eleanor and her "Englishman son" if she did not end her attempts to contact Sebastién.

Eleanor had disappeared following Phillip Morgan's proposal of marriage. After years of unsuccessful appeals to Hugh to be reunited with her son, Jacques thought it likely that his mother had returned to France with the intention of demanding her right to know her son.

Jacques had sent Tarry Morgan north to Phillip Morgan's London residence, with Rachael as his companion. Rachael had agreed to the journey out of concern for Tarry's health, but when she recognized it was a forced departure under heavy escort, she had seemed to guess his plan to have her out of the way and had coldly informed him she intended to return in time for Sebastién's trial.

From the moment she had discovered that the Eddystone Lighthouse had, in fact, been washed away, Jacques had suspected she might side against him on behalf of his brother. The decision to send her north had been followed by his decision to move Sebastién to a location from where news would not flow as speedily.

At his brother's order, Sebastién had been bound, blind-folded, and taken to another village in the southwest of England near Lizard Point, where he was not as well known. As a secondary strategy to weaken the bond between them, Jacques had arranged for Rachael to leave for London without being told that Sebastién had made several requests to see her. If she did by chance reappear before the conclusion of the assize, she would be told that he refused to see her.

A trial was imminent. Assizes were staged twice a year; only the very influential had the power to request that one be held off schedule. He had called in several favors in order to bring about a special commission. By moving Sebastién during Rachael's absence, it was un-likely that she would be able to discover the new location of the trial before he was tried and executed.

His plan fell just short of outright murder, and he was anxious to have it done.

Sebastién squinted against the light when he was brought out of the tiny cell into the barred waiting area. The dirt-floored cage that contained him had been damp and dark, with barely enough room to contain a human being. Jacques noticed that his gait was stiff when he moved, as if walking upright had become difficult.

"For all the attention you've been given," Jacques said, "you look no better for it."

Several days' growth of beard shadowed his brother's face. The unkempt black hair that fell across his brow was matted with dirt and dried blood from a deep gash the physician had resutured. His eyes were lackluster, flat and distrustful. His clothing hung torn and filthy on his lean frame, and his cheekbones were ruddy from a fever. Jacques had sent for a physician to ensure that his prisoner remained alive long enough to try and execute him, and the irony did not escape either of them.

"I am touched by your concern," Sebastién replied in a hoarse growl. His lips had cracked and bled, and his face was marked by new bruises.

"It will not suit my purpose to have you die before you have been judged. I have no desire to make a folk hero of a criminal." There was no mistaking the blazing defiance in the eyes staring back at him. Jacques fidgeted in his chair.

Sebastién narrowed his eyes against the light, a twisted smirk on his lips.

"If you think my death will end smuggling and stop the fairtraders, you are stupid. A man in your position must know by now that if a gallows was constructed every quarter of a mile along the coast, the trade would still go on briskly."

"This coast will finally be free of the man who led

the bloodiest band of wreckers Cornwall has ever seen. Cornwall will be a much safer place after you have been committed to the ground."

"The man who led the wreckers drowned the day you arrested me. I witnessed his death. That is why the wreckings stopped."

"How will you prove it?" Jacques sneered. "With a promise of gold to anyone who will lie for you? Or will you use force and send that blond, tattooed monstrosity—?"

Sebastién sprang forward with an agility that belied his condition. "The Dane," he said with brutal clarity, "is a friend of mine. Be careful what you say; I have nothing to lose. I don't need to bribe or threaten. All I need is to have my evidence weighed against yours before an honest judge."

"You won't bribe or bully your way to freedom. I will send you to the gallows this time."

"I will live to see you fairtrading for your daily bread after Customs casts you out as inept!" Sebastién predicted in a low growl.

Jacques flushed with anger. He crossed his arms against the urge to strike out at the helpless, shackled man before him. There was a more effective means of retaliation. His jaw flexed, and his smile was a feral baring of white teeth.

"You should reconsider your case," Jacques said. "Where is your proof? Who are your witnesses?"

Sebastién swayed, and the chains clinked in faint echo

of the movement. His eyes, sharp with wit, were focused upon his brother's face. The guard cleared his throat, and the cry of vendors on the street outside drifted to them in the silence as he waited for Jacques's next words.

"Rachael has been aligned with Customs all along," Jacques said. "She's made quite a fool of you." He saw pain and uncertainty flicker across his brother's face before he could mask it.

"Liar," Sebastién growled.

"Oh, but I assure you, it's true. She fled to London immediately after your arrest. I hope you haven't been waiting for a visit. She has no plans to return south, and no interest in your fate."

Sebastién once again denounced him as a liar.

"If I were lying to you, would I know about the ledger?"

Sebastién's head jerked up at the question. "If you've read the ledger, then you know I am innocent."

"Innocent, no. I only know that you are resourceful," Jacques said evenly. "You will not have enough time before the trial to commission another forgery."

"It was not a forgery! Did you read it?" The guards reacted to the rising tone of his voice as he took a faltering step toward Jacques, his movement restricted by the chains. "Where is it?" Sebastién demanded.

"It is a mound of ash in your parlor fireplace," Jacques informed him, with a note of triumph.

Sebastién uttered a low, guttural cry and lunged at him, but the guards were upon him in an instant. They had been tensed like tight coils, ready to spring at the first hint of trouble from their mercurial charge.

"Take me back to the cage," Sebastién said in a hoarse voice, "before I tear him limb from limb!"

They escorted him to the outer common cell door with Jacques following closely.

"Once you return to your dark hole, you should reflect upon why Rachael gave your evidence to me. Real or not, it might have saved you, yet she gave it to *me*. She and I spent many pleasurable hours at court together, if you will recall. She's played you for a fool, *brother*." The last was said as if he had uttered a curse.

Sebastién could still hear the taunt hours later.

The coach carrying Rachael and Tarry rolled up the narrow drive, coasted through the sharp turn of the servants' entrance, and stopped. Phillip Morgan's modern London residence was a simple rectangular design, tall and narrow with a hipped roof that sloped upward on all four sides from eaves to ridge.

Rachael had never visited the London Morgan residence before. Tarry had always preferred the family estate in the south, but since Victor had reduced the Morgan ancestral home to ruins, Tarry was forced to recuperate in less familiar surroundings.

An efficient, hand-picked staff managed the London residence. Phillip Morgan's ability to assemble order out of chaos was a skill emulated by his staff, and within minutes, the entire household was assembled. Rachael fretted over Tarry when he was removed from the coach by the butler and two footmen. A doctor was summoned posthaste, and Tarry was put to bed.

The staff bustled about, every action focused upon the health and comfort of their employer's offspring. Rachael followed the flow of human traffic and ended up in the kitchen, where the cook pressed a steaming cup of tea into her hands with the claim that the herbal concoction was capable of banishing all manner of woe.

Her hands shook as she accepted the dainty cup and saucer, spilling the scalding liquid on her hand. Her lower lip trembled, and her eyes filled with tears.

"Oh, my dear," Mrs. Lively said, "are you burned, miss?"

"No," Rachael said. She lowered her head, embarrassed that a stranger should see her thus. "Heartbroken," she confessed.

"Now don't you worry about young Tarry. As soon as Master Phillip returns, he'll see that all's put to right. Your young man will be fine."

"He isn't my . . . I mean, Tarry and I have been friends since we were children. Where is Tarry's father?" The news that Phillip was not in residence distressed her. She had counted on asking for Phillip's intervention on Sebastién's behalf.

"He's as much a mystery as the Lady Eleanor herself," Mrs. Lively confided. "Lady Eleanor turned up again just days ago, all weary and agitated after weeks of not a word, and then Master Phillip went missing. The whole household is abuzz over it."

Rachael tried to listen, but was distracted by her own troubles. She did not have much interest in news of Eleanor. She had never met the woman. Her thoughts were centered on Tarry's recovery, and Sebastién's survival.

" . . . tiptoeing up and down the hallway so as not to disturb her," Mrs. Lively was saying, "so afraid she'll disappear again before the master returns. She's been in such a state that we've been tempted to lock her in the guest bedchamber to keep her here."

A young chambermaid rushed into the kitchen, face flushed with excitement. She thrust a folded, sealed piece of parchment at Rachael.

"From the Lady Eleanor," she announced with importance.

Rachael frowned as she broke the wax seal and unfolded the paper. The young maid avidly watched her face for some clue of the contents of the note as she read Eleanor's request that they meet.

"The lady awaits you in the second floor parlor."

Rachael turned the letter over as the young servant beckoned for her to follow.

The hall smelled of roses. Not of one bud, but a distillation of many potent flowers captured in full bloom.

As Rachael crossed from the outer hall into the parlor, her eyes swept the room, expecting to find vases filled with flowers, but there were no containers filled with flowers of any kind. Nor was there anyone in the parlor.

The scent was almost a tangible presence, as was the handsome portrait that hung centered upon a far wall, softly lit by glowing lamps on either side. Rachael hesitated at the door, confronted by the irrational urge to flee. What did Eleanor so urgently require of her?

Rachael's eyes scanned the well-appointed room. Old tapestries depicting forest scenes decorated the walls, and an extensive teapot collection of glazed stoneware and Chinese porcelain rested in a gilded cabinet. Vibrant damask and velvet fabrics covered comfortable furnishings.

She looked again at the portrait, drawn by a vague sense of recognition. It was a masterfully executed oil, complemented by a scroll-cut, dark wood frame. The subject was a middle-aged woman, soft-eyed and reflective, thin lips turned down at the corners as if from some abiding sadness.

The melancholy matron in the portrait was not someone she knew, yet Rachael was drawn to the painting, steps tentative and fueled by a sense of discovery. She came close enough to view the network of brushstrokes that formed the whole. At this proximity, the likeness was very realistic; even pores and eyelashes were visible.

Rachael stared, bewildered, jaw becoming slack as she envisioned the comely, affluently attired lady in a different guise; slightly blowsy and clad in the humble attire of a servant. There was no mistaking the wan, preoccupied expression, or the handsome features.

"Quite an amazing likeness, don't you agree?"

Startled by the familiar voice, Rachael spun to face the woman who had entered the room. The elegantly clad, self-possessed lady bore little more than a faint resemblance to the frumpish, nondescript caretaker from Sebastién's modest cottage.

So, this is Eleanor. This is Phillip's intended bride and Tarry's stepmother-to-be. Rachael's mind raced as it cleared of shock. *Jacques's mother. Sebastién's mother.*

Eleanor moved toward Rachael as if intending to embrace her, but Rachael backed away,.

"You are owed an explanation," Eleanor said with a sigh, gray eyes intent upon Rachael's face.

"Not I," Rachael said. "You owe *your son* an explanation, madame!"

"I never intended to deceive anyone," Eleanor said. She uttered a small sound of distress and sank down onto a settee.

"How could you? You've only justified his mistrust of you," Rachael said.

Eleanor winced and bowed her head.

"Surely you knew his feelings; you share his past."

"His 'past,'" Eleanor repeated bitterly. "His past is no more than a fabrication by a vengeful old man! I know Sebastién believes that I killed his father and then abandoned him, but that is not the truth!"

"Then why did you approach him as a stranger instead of revealing your identity?"

Eleanor dragged her hand across her eyes. "Had you been in my place, would you have told him who you were?"

"Were you afraid of him because of his reputation as a wrecker?"

"No, not that," Eleanor sniffed, indignant at the question. "His reputation has several authors, your uncle and Jacques among them. I never believed he was a wrecker. I was afraid that he would reject me. I wanted him to know me and then find the right moment to challenge what his grandfather had told him. I planned to tell him who I was, but—"

"Jacques holds him responsible for crimes I know were committed by my uncle. And now his fate rests in his brother's hands."

"Jacques does not have the means to harm his brother. He has no proof—"

"Sebastién has been arrested! Your son awaits trial and execution."

Rachael detailed the charges against Sebastién in a hushed voice, and was dismayed when Eleanor responded with an unladylike snort of amusement.

"Jacques will have an easier time proving that he is a wrecker," Eleanor said lightly.

"At the very least, he will be tried as a kidnapper. James fell into Victor's hands after being abducted by

Sebastién."

Eleanor stared, her expression one of incomprehension. "Your brother has not come to any harm, Rachael," she said. "To my knowledge, James never left London. The infant left at the cottage was a female. Phillip will know where your brother is."

It was the truth. In her heart, she knew it, and she had withdrawn her trust at the time Sebastién had needed it most. *"What remains unsaid will harm us,"* he had told her at the lighthouse. She had stopped him from speaking when he would have confessed the truth.

"You must come with me to Cornwall to save your son."

"Do you honestly believe he would accept my help now?"

"Your son is a proud man, but he is not a fool. He wants to live. This is your opportunity to redeem yourself."

"And how will Jacques react to my intervention?" Eleanor twisted her hands.

"I see that Jacques has your full support," Rachael charged. She moved to the door. "Good day, Mrs. Falconer," she said.

"Rachael, I have not decided anything yet," Eleanor called after her.

Rachael spoke without turning to face Eleanor again. "Madame, I expect that your son is quite used to being abandoned by you."

Rachael hired the services of a hackney coach to take her home to Cornwall. As he had prospered, her father had invested in property, and her family had spent eight months of the year in Cornwall and the rest of the year in London.

Winter had arrested the wild growth of shrubbery that bordered the modest estate. Either vandals or the storm had broken all the ground floor windows.

Rachael found a key to a servants' entrance hidden under a large white urn at the back of the garden and used it to gain entry to the kitchen area. The faint odor of spices lingered like long forgotten memories. Staples still lined dusty pantry shelves.

She found a lantern and coaxed a dull glow from it. As she toured the house, she felt a renewal of grief. James had been born here. She had no idea where he was now, or if he would ever return. If only they had remained here after her father's death rather than allowing Victor to move them south under his care.

Shadows bent across the walls, and Rachael half-expected to encounter a ghost at every turn, but the house was empty. *She* was empty, and alone. She had never experienced anything like the bond she had shared with Sebastién. If he died, her soul would wither and die, and what remained would be a brittle shell.

Rachael was so wrapped up in her musings that she did not hear the rapping at the door for several minutes. She answered the summons with caution, expecting a curious neighbor, a banker inquiring after the property, or even a beggar pleading for alms.

The individual at the door was a resplendently robed man of the cloth. He was olive-skinned, no more than forty, with a beaming smile that revealed very white teeth, a wide gap between the front two. His slender nose tilted upward at the tip, and he had a small birthmark in the hollow of one cheek. A silver crucifix dangled nearly to his abdomen. He wore spectacles, and good humor and intelligence animated the warm brown eyes behind the lenses. Rachael curtsied and stammered a shy greeting, ushering him inside.

"Please accept my apology, Father," she said. "I have nothing to offer as refreshment. I've been in London and have only just returned."

He casually wiped away an accumulation of dirt on a chair before he sat down.

Rachael took the chair opposite him, and folded her hands in her lap.

Seeing her unease, the cleric leaned forward, placing a cool hand upon hers.

"I had a hunch you might return home. Perhaps something stronger than intuition," he amended with a smile, fingers touching the crucifix. "I am in need of your aid, Miss Penrose."

She watched his short, fleshy fingers pat the cross. Then his hand dropped away, and he arranged the skirts of his heavy robes, as if reluctant to broach the subject he had come to discuss.

"I would be pleased to help you, if I can," she prodded.

"I must confess I am not certain you will want to aid me if you consider Sebastién Falconer your enemy."

"Sebastién? No, he is not my enemy. Of course I will help you . . ."

He cleared his throat. "I do not wish to mislead you. I am speaking of aid in the spiritual sense. I understand the man is destined to die." At her crestfallen expression, he scooted closer to her and placed his hands over hers. "I am Father Porter, and I am here on behalf of a young parish priest in Black Head. Do you know the place?"

Rachael's eyes swept over the cassock, then returned to the hands that held hers, and she managed a small sound of affirmation. Porter had dashed her fragile hope that forces were being assembled to save Sebastién. Her enthusiasm for the priest's mission had fled, and she struggled against the impolitic urge to ask him to leave.

"Yes, I know it," she said dully.

"My duty does not lie with Falconer, but with the priest assigned to minister to him."

A glimmer of light struck her eyes when he released her hand and produced a folded piece of parchment with a broken seal.

"This note comes from a newly ordained priest in

Black Head. The young cleric is distressed by his inability to bring any measure of comfort to 'the incarcerated Frenchman,' as it says here. He appeals to me for aid. I fear that if I cannot discover how to advise him, Mr. Falconer will die with his soul in turmoil, and my young priest may be disillusioned enough to abandon his calling."

Porter handed the letter to Rachael. It confirmed that the young priest felt his failure keenly. There was a specific request that Father Porter help him locate someone who knew the man well enough to establish a way to communicate with the withdrawn Frenchman.

"So, the trial is to be held in Black Head," she mused and glanced up at the priest. "An innocent man is being tried," she told him. "How do you go about reconciling a man to an unjust execution?"

"If you know he is innocent, why were you in London when he is on trial in Black Head?"

"His brother sent me there. His plan is to try and execute Sebastién in secret before anyone can vouch for his innocence. If you had not come today, I would not have known the location of the trial. She reached out and touched his hand on impulse. Her fingers touched a cool, hard surface. "Even so, it may be too late. There is a ledger that proves Sebastién is not a wrecker, but how can he prove he did not kill James?"

Rachael raised her head and realized, from the expression on Porter's face, her ramblings made no sense at all to him.

"It is such a long story, Father." She sighed.
He smiled. "I am told I am a good listener."

Full darkness descended while Rachael guided Father Porter through the labyrinth of her memories. Now she was alone in the dark, drafty house. She curled up on the parlor sofa with the lantern on the floor beside, but, although she was weary, sleep would not come. Rachael heard every creak of the settling house and the bay of every lonely animal, with her thoughts drifting back to the afternoon spent in the company of the priest. As she lay with knees bent upon the sofa, she suddenly felt uneasy.

Her unconscious mind had seized upon the contradiction almost at once, directing her eyes again and again to the short, fleshy fingers of the priest.

In her mind's eye, she again saw the ornate, expensive rings on the third and fourth fingers of Father Porter's right hand; overlooked clues to an identity the man had otherwise taken pains to conceal.

What ordained priest would willfully disobey the vow of poverty? Even an insubordinate priest would not wisely flaunt such a breach. Who was he, then? What had been the purpose of such an elaborate deception? She slowly sat up on the sofa, wondering what her pliant tongue had cost, and whom it had cost.

Chapter Twenty-One

Sebastién had found a weather crack in one of the rough boards that formed the east wall of the cage. There was a two-hour respite in the afternoon when faint light pierced the dark hole that had swallowed him.

Today the beam was solid and steady. It thrust through the minute fissure in the wood and crisscrossed the cramped space at an angle, slanting diagonally to the floor. Although it provided no heat, it was a reminder that a world existed beyond the earth and timber coffin.

Sebastièen sat on the dirt floor with his long legs drawn up, eyes fixed upon the beam of light. He had looked upon that thread of sunlight daily, and never once had he felt hope or even experienced a desire for freedom.

Why escape? To be hunted again? To be looked upon with hatred by those he loved? To confront those who had deceived and then abandoned him? Rachael had forgotten him easily enough. It had been a recurring theme in his life; the women he loved had always betrayed and deserted him.

Many of his most trusted friends had already met a fate similar to the one he faced. He would die soon enough; his own brother would see to it. Why struggle merely to exist, when he would never again feel alive?

Sebastién lifted his head when a key turned in the latch, followed by the groan of hinges as the cell door swung open. Light flooded the squalid chamber, and he squinted. The tension in his face slowly relaxed, and he opened his eyes, narrowing them against the painful influx of light as he greedily inhaled the fresh air.

Pity and revulsion filled the eyes of the man who paused in the entryway looking down at Sebastién. He did not attempt to stand, being fairly certain his legs would fail him. Instead, he peered up at the man in the doorway, resentful that his visitor's presence obstructed the flow of light and air.

He had first met the man only a few days ago, but there was something about him that encouraged trust. The man was well into middle age, brown-eyed, bespectacled, with an olive complexion and a bright, gap-toothed smile. His upturned nose was too dainty for his broad face, and his left cheek bore a birthmark. The black silk riding ensemble he wore spoke of wealth and station, and his heavy gold rings tossed a wink of burnished light as he absently stroked his chin.

"*Monsieur* Porter," Sebastién rasped in acknowledgment.

Porter stood staring down, frowning pensively. "I have a bargain to propose to you, Mr. Falconer," he said.

Porter stole a surreptitious glance at the attending guards, and then took a deep breath before he crept into the dark, fetid cage and pulled the door firmly closed behind him.

"Father Porter" had provided the only clue to Sebastién's whereabouts, and although the village of Black Head was modest in size, its taciturn, close-knit population was reluctant to share its secrets with an outsider. Not even a murmur of scandal rippled through the village with regard to a priority assize involving an infamous French privateer. Black Head was possessed by the sort of eerie calm that preceded a gathering storm.

Rachael set out to locate Sebastién by frequenting taverns and other meeting places where snippets of information might be gleaned as strong ale loosened tongues. One such establishment was Kilkenney Tavern, a place popular with soldiers, messengers, tide waiters, Customs officials, and other assorted types.

The tavern was not crowded when she entered the

common room. Her slim hope of finding information that might lead her to Sebastién was capriciously answered when she spied Jacques seated at a corner table.

He did not notice her until the straggle of humanity surrounding him parted like some biblical sea and she swept toward him with a look of determination on her face, all rustling skirts and pricked nerves. In a bold move, she took the seat opposite him without waiting to be asked.

"At last!" she said loudly. "I've finally lifted up the right rock and found you."

His answer was a rude, resounding belch. Long fingers caressed the tankard he held, and when he raised the cup to his lips, his hand shook.

"I was certain you were not privy to my whereabouts, Miss Penrose," he said, speech slurred. "How resourceful of you. You must have missed me terribly." His eyes were watery and bloodshot, but his gaze was alive with insolence.

His coarse appearance invited Rachael's biased, critical inspection. His longish hair hung dirty and matted, and his lean, muscled frame had lost mass. There were bruised hollows under his eyes, and his skin glowed with an unhealthy sheen. He looked haunted, ill, and desperate. The dapper, expensive cloak he wore did nothing to dispel her impression of a haggard wretch pretending refinement.

"Seeing you thus, I cannot bear to contemplate your brother's condition," she muttered.

"I am certain he would be touched by your concern," he sneered, eyes piercing her with animosity. "What brought you here? Curiosity? Will you be in attendance at the trial tomorrow, or is the hanging the focal point of your visit?"

She reacted to his biting sarcasm with icy poise. "I am here because I want to see him and you know where he is."

"Oh? You want to see him? For what purpose?"

The mild elevation of black brows and the spark of challenge in his eyes tugged painfully at her heart. His expression was one she had often seen Sebastién use.

"*For what purpose?*" she repeated, mocking him. "So that he does not believe I abandoned him! Will you deny me that much? I have no ragged army at my heels, no plan of escape, no miracle to save him. You punish me simply because I love the man you despise."

He was silent while he considered her words. "It was never my intention to punish you, Rachael," he said softly.

His speech was a garbled mishmash of flowing vowels and swallowed consonants. Drunk. He was drunk and had no idea what he was saying. He studied her face, his own clouded and inscrutable. Then, just as quickly, the brief flash of compassion was gone. The misery and fleeting uncertainty she had glimpsed in his expression were quashed as his jaw tightened.

"If you wish to see my brother, the visit will come at a price."

"Name it," Rachael responded without hesitation.

He reached out and stroked her hair, the backs of his

fingers gliding along the length of her jaw in an overt caress.

Rachael drew back, appalled. "You've mistaken inebriation for ardor."

He said nothing, but sat staring at her with the trace of a smile.

Rachael felt color flood her cheeks. "You seek a new way to hurt your brother," she accused.

"You underestimate your appeal," he scoffed as he withdrew his hand. He grinned wolfishly and slumped in the chair. "You judge me too harshly," he protested. "I simply wanted to express my gratitude for all your splendid aid." There was a peculiar archness to his voice.

Rachael had unconsciously leaned forward in her effort to understand the garbled, drunken words and sat back abruptly, as if she had been slapped, her bearing rigid.

"You know I've never willingly aided you. How can you think—?"

"The ledger." It was a gruff, terse bark. "I destroyed it, just as you had guessed I would."

His words were slurred, yet unmistakable. He watched as shock and then fury animated her face as she digested the information.

Rachael's face betrayed her intention to strike him, and his hand seized hers in a resolute grip when she acted on the impulse.

"Cause a scene and you will regret it," he warned with a bland, false smile as he scanned the room. "Do not make the mistake of misjudging me."

His hold eased and Rachael snatched her hand away. She was beyond propriety, pride, or panic. He had seen to it that she had nothing left to lose.

"Mr. Falconer," she said coldly, "I advise you to listen carefully to me. If I doubt you comprehend my meaning, I am prepared to raise my voice until anyone in the lane outside can make clear to you what you did not hear or understand."

His jaw worked, his teeth snapped together with an audible sound, and his eyes narrowed in warning.

"You have deliberately kept me from Sebastién," Rachael said, voice rising. "I thought the ledger would convince you of his innocence. Had I known you would destroy it, I would have taken pains to conceal its existence from you."

"Sit still and be silent," he ordered in a low voice, gaze sweeping the room.

"Am I embarrassing you? Good."

"Sit down," he said again.

Instead, Rachael stood, and he sprang to his feet as if he had anticipated her move. She noted that he was not armed.

"Your brother did not kidnap mine, and you know it! Your brother is not a wrecker, but you refuse to believe it! You planned to have the hanging done before anyone who knows the truth could interfere. You are the lowest form of coward!"

"Continue, and there will be consequences," he cautioned.

Weaponless and intoxicated to the point that he swayed on his feet, he did not inspire fear.

"I want to see him!" she demanded.

He seized her arm and shook her, but she continued to berate him, trying to wrench free as he dragged her along with him.

Rachael hung back as they neared the door, guessing that his intention was to remove her from the safety of the crowd, and their difference of purpose evolved into an outright skirmish.

Rachael launched an attack on his shins, making full use of the pointy-toed shoes she wore, although he managed to retain his hold on her while she repeatedly kicked.

"You demand to see my prisoner, Miss Penrose?" he growled. "I can do better than that. You will share his cage."

"Fine! I would rather share his cage than your bed!" she shouted in reply, with a contemptuous toss of her head as he thrust her through the doorway and into the street.

After they left the tavern, he was silent and his hold on her lapsed into a mild prodding, as he propelled her across the lane toward a series of storefronts. When he produced a key and steered her to a wealthy merchant's abundantly stocked shop, she was too surprised to resist.

They entered the shop, and he marched her across the floor then stood at the top of a dark landing from which sprang a narrow set of stairs. It was obvious that he expected her to follow and descended part of the way. When he did not hear her tread on the boards behind him, he spun, reaching for her with an impatient hiss of exhaled air.

Rising panic overcame her daring, and Rachael jerked away as his hand groped for her, compromising his balance and sending him sprawling down the stairs. She heard his descent, wincing in spite of herself as his fall was punctuated by assorted thuds, crashes, bumps, and curses.

"Merde! Fils d'une chienne! Son of a bitch!"

Poised to flee, Rachael was riveted to the floorboards by the disembodied voice as it continued to issue a string of florid curses, all uttered in cogent, flowing French.

Too shocked to speak, she turned back to the stairs. Why would Jacques have imprisoned his brother in some shopkeeper's basement? She took the steps one at a time, fearful of what she might find at the bottom.

The fourth step brought a wash of illumination over the tops of her shoes. The basement was filled with bolts of silk, undoubtedly some smuggler's booty safeguarded by a merchant in exchange for a portion of what it would fetch on the black market.

A lone figure rested at the foot of the stairs, leaning against a displaced bolt of red silk. He had rolled up the right leg of his breeches, and his right shoe and stocking lay discarded on the floor beside him. He probed his right ankle with careful fingers, grimacing as he made his inspection.

"Sebastién?" Rachael stood looking down at him, openmouthed.

He froze at the sound of her voice, his concentration arrested by her presence. He gave a shallow nod. "Do I dare admit it now?" he asked. Now that he no longer impersonated his brother, he sounded unmistakably sober.

Rachael rushed the rest of the way down the stairs and dropped to the floor beside him. Framing his face with her hands, she drank in his beloved features. All the nuances that made him who he was were evident in his face. They had always been there. If only she had read his eyes and ignored his words!

His face was thinner. The full mustache and dashing beard were gone. He looked younger, more vulnerable, although he still had a formidable quality about him. What she had mistaken for the ravages of conscience on Jacques's face was the toll Jacques's abuse had taken on his brother.

"What has he done to you?" she asked, her eyes welling with tears.

Sebastién shook his head in rejection of her pity while he drew her to him with a strength that surprised her. Their conversation in the tavern played through her mind, including the amorous overture he had made to her. Had he been testing her? She knocked at his arm and pulled away then rose to her feet and stood looking down at him.

"I must be an endless source of amusement to you," she scolded. "How could you play such a mean-spirited trick?" Rachael felt the urge to box his ears, and said so. "I am not certain an apology will suffice," she added in a chastising tone.

"Did I offer one?" Sebastién leaned back as he regarded her, eyes glowing with amusement.

"Nor did you offer any aid while I made a complete fool of myself in the tavern!"

"You did not seem to require my assistance," he taunted, smiling.

"Scoundrel!"

"You called my brother far worse," he reminded her. At the memory, he tipped his head back and his chest rumbled with laughter.

The underside of his chin had been scraped raw by a dull blade, and the loss of the beard looked recent. "What sort of mischief are you up to? Why do you go about masquerading as your brother?"

The amusement left his expression. "I fancied a change," he replied. "The latest news from Paris is that facial hair is no longer considered *de rigueur*."

Her narrowed eyes conveyed her displeasure over his evasiveness.

"You see before you a changed man," he said. "The razor made all the difference, *non*?"

Rachael frowned. "I doubt that the removal of your beard has improved your character," she dryly observed.

"After all, a rodent without its whiskers is still a rat."

"*Touché*," he conceded lightly.

Had he escaped? Didn't he trust her enough to confide in her? With a ragged intake of air that was almost a sob, Rachael lifted her hand and tilted his head back with gentle fingers while she inspected the rough wake of the blade.

Her gaze moved over his face and then strayed to survey the storeroom. There was nothing to indicate that the dim, airless basement littered with bolts of silk and unmarked crates had served as a hideout. She voiced her thoughts aloud, attention riveted upon Sebastién while she waited for an explanation.

He said nothing, only turned away and began examining a swollen, discolored area below his right ankle. Why was he being so distant and secretive? Rachael wondered.

"Were you injured by the fall?"

"*Non*," he replied in a detached voice as he probed his inflamed ankle. "Rat bite."

Rachael edged closer and gingerly touched the seeping wound, discovering puncture marks at the center of the livid flesh.

"How long has it been?"

"I don't know," he replied, with a bemused shake of his head. "I was bitten the night I was arrested. I do not know how long ago that was."

Rachael nodded. She knew all too well the agony of days that passed seamlessly into nights. "The rats at Bedlam . . ." She shuddered at the memory, unable to speak of the experience.

"My attacker fares well." Sebastién swept an arm around Rachael's shoulder and gathered her close. "He grows fat on the scraps he steals from me, and has retained his foul temperament. And his whiskers," he wryly concluded as he stroked his naked chin.

A low chuckle escaped her. "How do you know which one attacked you?" she asked with a dubious sideways glance. "Have you given them all names?"

"This one is bolder than the rest. I know the look of him. Man or beast, if you wound me, I will remember you."

His fierce expression made it obvious his words held a deeper meaning.

"We can take comfort from the fact that your pet rodent has not taken fits and died," she said. "It might have passed a sickness to you."

He pursed his lips in a grim smile. "I planned to summon Jacques and leave my mark upon him at the first sign of fever," he confessed.

"Yes, and he would have tried you for that, too, with the imprint of your teeth as evidence," she joked.

"In that event, I should seek to mark him where it will cause him the most embarrassment should he be asked to display his evidence." A malicious grin molded his generous mouth, and wicked lights danced within the depths of his eyes. He rubbed the underside of his chin. "Well worth the consequences," he mused. "They can only hang a man once."

Sebastién sobered and lowered his head as the gravity of his words destroyed his mood. His hands trembled and he glanced up at Rachael before crossing his arms in an elaborately casual manner.

"They cannot hang a man they cannot find."

His head came up at her words, and his jaw tightened. He reached for her, and then drew back, denying himself the contact. In a display of frustration, he pounded the floor with a fist.

"Nothing is ever as simple as it seems, Rachael," he said finally, scowling.

Despite several opportunities to reveal his identity to her at the tavern, he had chosen not to do so. "You never intended to let me know it was you and not Jacques, did you?"

His answering gaze was as cruelly direct as his reply. "*Non.*"

Rachael flinched at the brutal admission. "Why?" she asked, resenting the wary intensity in his catlike eyes as he regarded her. Her despair quickly escalated into anger.

"I *will* have an answer, damn you! Why would you allow me to believe you were Jacques? I've gone for days without sleep. I abandoned Tarry to search for you. I've made inquiries of dodgy strangers. I've paid bribes. I was prepared to beg your brother to allow me to see you. I've thought of nothing but you!"

"Then you're a fool," he interjected, without heat.

"Is it your plan to make me hate you so that I will not grieve for you?"

Sebastién's eyes narrowed. She had struck a nerve.

"Selfish bastard!" Rachael exclaimed. "You are the fool if you believe I will abandon you now. It was your will to win me, Frenchman, and you'll not escape the consequences of it!"

"You no longer hold any interest for me," he churlishly replied. "It's true, you were a challenge, but the challenge was met."

He was trying to protect her, but if he stayed true to this course, he would destroy them both. Rachael eyed him with mounting skepticism.

"I demand to see the mark."

His reaction was swift and under different circumstances, she might have found his profoundly insulted air amusing.

"What?"

"You heard me. I demand to see the mark," she repeated.

"*Pour quoi?*"

"Why? Because I don't recognize you. My Sebastién would fight for his life. My Sebastién would consider me reason enough to want to live."

He seemed to have no answer for that, and his silence enraged her even further. "It must be difficult for you to know where one deception ends and another begins. I think you've become so adept a liar that you fool even yourself!"

"What do you mean by that?" he demanded. A

telltale flush of crimson had fanned across his cheeks.

Impulsively, Rachael seized his face between her hands and kissed him with all the angry passion inside of her. She felt his ragged indrawn breath of surprise and the sudden leap of his pulse beneath her fingertips. The stubble of his new beard chafed her skin as she ground her lips against his.

Although she feared he might reject her, her lips formed an exultant smile when he groaned and wrapped his arms tightly around her, as if afraid that she would withdraw from him.

Sebastién crushed Rachael against him, clinging to her as he parted her lips with the thrust of his tongue and tasted her as if he drank from the sweetest fountain, their breaths mingling as their mouths fused hungrily.

"Don't claim you don't love me, Frenchman," she whispered breathlessly. "Your own lips betray you."

Sebastién stared into Rachael's eyes, composure completely eroded. He darned his fingers in her heavy hair and pulled her head back. His brows were hawklike above his flashing eyes, and there was a cruel set to his mouth.

Gripping the back of her head, Sebastién held Rachael immobile as his mouth hovered over hers, and she could feel the play of his breath over the sensitized skin of her lips. His unsmiling, aggressive intensity alarmed her, and she flinched, suppressing the urge to wrench free of his hold and retreat.

Sebastién swept her hair back and rested his hand

on her shoulder, fingers splayed and angled toward the delicate buttons of her frock. Elegant fingers toyed with the first of the shiny glass buttons near her throat.

"How shall I express my affection?" he cooed in a low, menacing tone. "Shall I tumble you here among the silks?"

Ignoring her gasp of indignation, Sebastién snatched at a button with a ferocious tug. It popped free and hit the slab floor with a dull chink. Rachael dodged when his fingers moved to the next fastening.

Her throat burned as tears welled and clumped in her lashes, obscuring her vision. She blinked and felt moisture spill over onto her flushed cheeks. After all the perils she had faced, why, at this moment, did she not care whether she lived or died?

Sebastién abandoned the buttons and swept Rachael into an unyielding embrace, arching her back as he bent and captured her mouth in a ravening kiss that felt like a brand. He buried his face against the soft flesh of her neck, breath warm against her throat. His arms folded around her, drawing her impossibly close. Through it all, she remained pliant but unresponsive.

Aware of her lack of response, Sebastién paused and looked at her closely then uttered a bleak sound of frustration and pushed her away. Cupping his face in his hands, he sank to the floor.

After an endless moment, his open palms slid wearily down the length of his aristocratic, fine-featured face, as if in covert removal of a mask.

"I cannot hurt you, even to keep you safe. God help me," he said, muffled voice sounding shaken. "How will I convince anyone of the truth when I cannot even convince you of a lie?"

"It is enough to know that you do love me," Rachael whispered. She lowered herself to the floor beside him. "You've escaped. We'll leave England—"

"There was no daring escape, and no pardon," he said, manner brusque. His expression softened when her face fell. "My first thought was to find you and take you to France," he confessed. "I would have kidnapped you again."

"Kidnapped? I would have gone willingly. I would go with you now," she urged. "You can as easily flee your jailers as return to them."

"I must return to the cage tonight," he said, with a flinty look that warned her he would not negotiate the point.

"You seem willing to compromise me in every way but with the truth. How can you love a woman you do not trust?"

"I trust you with my life," Sebastién said earnestly. "This has nothing to do with trust." His face twisted with despair. "You would not be driven away, would you? I wanted to spare you further danger . . ."

"I have learned tenacity, if nothing else," she said wryly and rested her head against his shoulder.

"You would be safer if you had fled this place believing you had escaped Jacques," he said.

"There are things I treasure more than my safety."

"There is nothing I treasure more than—"

Sebastién stopped himself, eyes sweeping over Rachael as his expression hardened with resolve. "My freedom is by arrangement. I am only free while Jacques is gone to fetch the magistrate south. It was my plan to circulate among his men as Jacques, to learn what I could. Perhaps one of his men saw the ledger before it was destroyed. But my impersonation of my brother did not reap the results I had hoped."

"I denounced you in front of everyone in the tavern," she recalled with a groan. "I ruined your plan."

"You did not denounce *me*," he reminded her. A shallow smile softened the lines around his mouth.

"You cannot intend to simply surrender and allow your brother to murder you!"

Something in the directness of his gaze heralded an unpleasant revelation.

"Rachael, I am not free," he said. "My activities are being observed. If I attempt to leave England, I will be shot. Anyone caught with me or assisting me will be imprisoned. If my identity is revealed while I am outside the cage, I will be shot. The official explanation will be that I tried to escape."

She shuddered. He might have been killed had she recognized him and acknowledged him in public.

"Jacques plans to accuse you of killing James, but James is safe in London," she said. "You cannot be condemned for a crime we can prove never took place."

Sebastién looked Rachael fully in the face, expression wary. "Who told you your brother is alive?" The line of his jaw tightened when she hesitated. "*Eleanor Faraday Falconer*," he bit out.

He spoke the name as Jacques had said it to him, with discrete emphasis. The shadow he cast on the opposite wall wavered in the feeble light, like a ghost trapped in the room with them.

"How long have you known?"

"She disappeared before I could confront her," he said bitterly. "Jacques accused me of killing her." He swore under his breath.

Rachael recalled the fight between the brothers the night Sebastién had been arrested, and now she knew what had precipitated his violent assault upon Jacques.

"You must not judge your mother too harshly. She was desperate to know the son she had lost."

"The son she *abandoned*." The correction was cutting.

"Perhaps she has suffered her share of misrepresentation," Rachael argued. "She vouched for your good character to me, even when she was your 'housekeeper.'" As she rested against him, she felt tension surge through his body. His features were rigid.

"I prefer her in the role of domestic to that of concerned parent," he said coldly. "I suspect Jacques plans to accuse me of leading the wreckers as well as the kidnap of your brother. She will not challenge her favorite son for my sake."

Rachael was silent as she recalled the outcome of her meeting with Eleanor. She had come to the same conclusion, but could not bear to share her insight.

"I will speak on your behalf," she said.

An amused, indulgent glimmer lit Sebastién's eyes and he reached out to affectionately tousle her hair, fingers gliding through the strands. He watched the play of her hair over his skin as if mesmerized.

"*Non*," he demurred. "The judge would find his evidence in the way we look at each other. Even the truth will seem like a lie."

"We could petition the Crown . . ." her voice trailed off when he emphatically shook his head.

A tremor of alarm rippled through her. "I am the only one who knows you are in Black Head! Those who might come to your aid will not know where to find you!"

"You found me." His smile was sanguine.

"But I would not have known where to find you if not for Father Porter. He was the one—"

His shocked exclamation stopped her. "This 'Father Porter,'" he said, "how do you know him?"

"I don't," she replied uneasily. "He sought me out in London on your behalf."

"Shall I describe him to you?" Sebastién inquired.

Chapter Twenty-Two

"Squire Porter and Father Porter are the same man," Rachael concluded after hearing Sebastién's description of his visitor.

"Squire Porter" had been his only visitor, and their two meetings had been conducted without Jacques's knowledge.

Sebastién's initial suspicion that Porter acted as Hugh Falconer's agent was proven wrong when Porter's offer of a brief respite from incarceration had come with conditions that bound him as securely as chains.

"When I told Porter that Jacques had destroyed Victor's ledger, he suggested that others might have seen it."

"I saw it," she put in eagerly. "The Dane saw it—"

He held up his hand to forestall Rachael's enthusiasm. "Porter said my witness should be unimpeachable; one of my brother's own men, or the like. Morgan told me he and his father saw the ledger. Some of the evidence against Brightmore was taken north by Phillip Morgan."

"Then others must have seen it, as well," Rachael said.

Sebastién considered her words, and some of the strain left his face as he accepted the hope she offered. He drew her to him and kissed her, cupping the back of her head while he gently, leisurely explored her mouth.

He started to remove his shirt.

"What are you doing?"

"You demanded to see the mark," he said, wagging his brows and winking, his playful manner more reminiscent of the man she knew and loved. "So, my beautiful English girl, I am going to show it to you. And a few other things, as well."

Rachael laughed, her peal of amusement ringing out in the cavernous basement. He paused at the sound, a look of expectation on his face.

"I no longer need to see the mark," she said. "You've just proven your identity to me."

Sebastién paused and sent Rachael an inquisitive look. "Ah, the kiss," he said. A self-satisfied grin warmed his face, but the look of self-assurance faded to puzzlement when she smiled and shook her head.

No one but Sebastién called her his "beautiful English girl." She loved him so much that her heart swelled and ached with it, until it was almost painful. Her secretive smile turned saucy and she reached out to help him remove his shirt.

"I don't *need* to see the mark," she said, "but show it to me anyway."

The ornate carriage stood out among the many brightly hued, yellow-wheeled flying coaches that littered the lane.

Jacques's attention shifted from the busy roadway to the public hall where the proceedings against his brother would soon be underway. The hall was filled to capacity. A crush of spectators pressed into the entrance, making it almost impossible to enter or exit.

Expecting a sparse turnout, he had first been mystified, and then furious to discover that some unknown hand had posted bills throughout the southern coast announcing the trial. Anyone who knew the accused was encouraged to journey to Black Head. The bill, with its ambiguous promise of rewards for information, had guaranteed an overwhelming public response.

Sebastién was already inside the hall, guarded by a double contingent of sentries. His brother's behavior in public had been decorous. *The stuff of which folk heroes are made.*

The appearance of the handbills and Sebastién's infuriating composure were not his only worries. The official who would preside over the trial was not the sympathetic, politically ambitious judge with whom he had previously aligned. He had been informed that an alternate magistrate was en route, no doubt one immune to bribery.

The late arrival of the magistrate's replacement irked Jacques. The anxiety he felt was nothing like the sense of closure he had expected to feel on the day his brother was finally brought to justice for the murder of his fiancée, Adrienne, among others.

He kicked at the shiny black door panel of the expensive carriage. A long fissure appeared in the veneer, like a scar on a dark face. He stared at it before turning his back and leaning against the exterior of the carriage, the muddy heel of his right boot lodged along the step.

He was surprised to see Rachael threading her way through the crowd in his direction, hitching up her skirts to protect them from the mud as she crossed the road.

"If you've come to plead for him, you needn't bother," he shouted.

Rachael reached Jacques, breathless and rosy-cheeked from the chill air. Her thoughtful scrutiny of his face made him feel ill at ease.

"I don't believe you are an evil man," she said. "Only a misguided, bitter one. In fact, I pity you."

About to utter a glib retort, Jacques stumbled forward with a startled exclamation as the door panel he had been leaning against was thrust outward, nearly throwing him to the ground.

He recovered his footing and spun around, ready to voice his indignation as the passenger alighted from the carriage and waited with elaborate patience for him to step out of his way. The epithet he had been about to hurl was replaced by a double take, followed by a stiff, pompous greeting.

"Judge Porter, sir—your lordship. We are ready to begin the trial."

"Oh!" Rachael gasped. She blinked in surprise at the late arrival. "Oh!" she repeated, flustered.

The man's brown eyes twinkled behind the stern spectacles when he briefly met Rachael's gaze.

Jacques stood between them, looking from one to the other. "Do you know each other?" he asked sharply.

"He . . . reminds me of someone," she said.

Porter lifted the hem of his magnificent scarlet and ermine robe, adjusted the tilt of the elaborate, powdered haystack of a wig he wore, and then moved with regal bearing toward the public hall. His only comment to Jacques was a pointed glance at the damaged door panel of his private carriage.

Rachael gawked as Porter ascended the stairs and disappeared into the building. She turned back to Jacques and smiled prettily before she broke into a run, hurrying across the lane and up the stairs into the hall. Frowning suspiciously, he followed.

Rachael entered the building and crept along a bench near the back of the hall, searching for Sebastién, who was seated at the front of the assembly. The fleeting look of astonishment that crossed his face when he recognized Porter was replaced by a rigid stare so potent that Porter soon stopped looking in his direction.

Porter instructed Jacques to declare the charges and summon his first witness. Simon and Emerald were led in together, Simon's left leg bound to Emerald's right by a length of chain. The pair shuffled noisily down the narrow aisle and sat down upon the bench facing the crowded hall. Simon looked around with a sullen expression while Emerald sat serenely, fathomless eyes roaming over the assembly with interest.

Rachael drew an unsteady breath when Emerald's eyes locked with hers and recognition filtered his expression. His mouth formed the rictus of a smile, and a chill passed through her.

Jacques's opening speech alleged that Sebastién had led the gang of wreckers responsible for the atrocities that spanned the southern coast of England, particularly Cornwall and Devon. Victor Brightmore was barely mentioned as a minor player as Jacques described the bloody swath the wreckers had cut across the land and the devastation they had wrought.

Sebastién stared straight ahead during Jacques's meticulous assassination of his character. The crowd stole covert glances at the accused while they listened with rapt attention to the charges.

Rachael wanted to rail against the injustice being done. As if sensing her distress, Sebastién suddenly shifted his attention to her. He arched a brow and smiled sardonically before his brooding gaze returned to his brother.

Rachael glanced around the room at the multitude

of curiosity seekers and almost failed to notice The Dane, who sat swathed in a flowing brown robe that gave him a monklike appearance. The hood was drawn up to conceal his shock of white-blond hair, and generous folds of fabric concealed his tattooed arms.

He acknowledged Rachael with a slight inclination of his head, and deliberately allowed her to glimpse a flash of steel beneath the folds of his robe. She recalled the escape from Tor Pub, and began to scan the crowd with a new awareness. Many of the same folk who had aided Sebastién in his escape from the pub were in attendance, strategically placed throughout the crowd. She wondered if Sebastién was aware of their presence in the crowded hall.

Emerald was called to the witness bench, and Jacques's eyes rested pensively on the strange boy while the shackles joining Emerald and Simon were unlocked and the two men were separated. Jacques frowned slightly and withdrew a handkerchief from his coat pocket. The hall was drafty and cold, but beads of moisture dotted his forehead when Emerald pierced him with his oddly discerning gaze.

A brief, cunning smile animated Emerald's face as the boy observed the Frenchman without expression, face blank as he looked from one brother to the other. The chilling effect of Emerald's scrutiny prompted Sebastién to break eye contact with him and Jacques to turn his back on the boy.

Porter curtly ordered Jacques to begin questioning his witness. Jacques alternately mopped his brow and tugged at his cravat as he paced before the spellbound crowd. Emerald's head followed the movement of the man before him with the precision of a pendulum swing.

"Is it true that you and Simon were members of the gang of wreckers led by my . . . by Sebastién Falconer?"

"Simon and I belong to the same gang," Emerald said.

His pacing stopped at Emerald's obtuse response. Jacques spun around.

Rachael's faint smile at Jacques's obvious misgiving drew Emerald's yellow-green gaze. The boy then turned his attention back to Jacques, who had begun to pace again. Emerald visibly tensed each time Jacques edged closer to the bench upon which he sat.

The boy's soft speech and placid manner were at odds with the gruesome description of his activities. The crowd listened to the flat drone of Emerald's voice as he recalled his participation in his first wrecking, when he was fourteen.

"The gang didn't want me—said I was too scrawny," he recalled. "I knew I had only that one night to prove myself. It was my idea to tie the girl to the forward mast. She made a handsome human figurehead, she did, all twistin', pleadin', and screamin' as the sea swallowed the ship and her with it."

Rachael turned away in revulsion, but she could not block out his monotonous voice as it continued to drone above the shocked hum of the assembly.

"I chose her," he said with pride. "The gang never doubted but what I belonged after that. We found out who she was from the ship's log after the wreck, and he couldn't believe his good luck. The trinket was part of my share, but he said he'd pay me triple what the locket was worth. It had more value to him 'cause it had her initials. 'A.L.A.,'" he blandly recalled. Emerald peered into his palm as if he still held the locket in his hand.

Rachael did not grasp the significance of what Emerald had revealed until she glanced at Jacques. He stood white and trembling, face contorted with grief. The woman Emerald had selected to become the human figurehead of the wrecked ship had been Jacques's tragic Adrienne. It was obvious from his reaction that he had not known the circumstances under which his fiancée had perished.

Jacques erupted into sudden motion, lunging at Emerald with a snarl of rage. The chains did not hinder the boy's reflexes; Emerald sprang from the bench in a single lithe move and thrust out his leg. Jacques fell heavily across the bench, and Emerald leaned down and shoved him to the floor when he struggled to rise to his feet.

Bringing his manacled hands forward, he slanted the chain across Jacques's exposed throat and pulled viciously on the length of iron as he braced his booted foot against the back of Jacques's neck.

Everyone in the hall was so stunned by the unexpected attack that for a moment no one moved. It was Sebastién who recovered first, springing forward and seizing Emerald, forcing him to allow the chain to slacken. He lifted the boy off Jacques and hauled him a distance away, hurling him to the floor with a violent shove.

Emerald rolled toward Sebastién, gnashing his teeth and emitting growling sounds. Sebastién's guards, their courage bolstered by the daring their prisoner had displayed, seized the boy before he could press an attack upon Sebastién.

Jacques crawled away and leaned against the wall, gasping and heaving for air. He dismissed Sebastién's hesitant offer of assistance and struggled to his feet.

An eerily composed Emerald sat down again on the bench as Sebastién was led back to his seat. Jacques's livid face promised retribution while he gingerly touched the angry red latticework of scored flesh left by the chain.

Jacques was silent, as if he could not decide whether to throttle Emerald or ask him another question. After a moment, he turned to Porter.

"I cannot question this monster," he choked out in a hoarse voice. He waved a hand in Emerald's direction rather than look at him. "He and my brother tortured and murdered the woman I loved."

The accusation brought Sebastién to his feet in protest.

"Sir, you will sit down," Porter instructed.

"*Non*. If my brother cannot question this witness, I must."

"Under the law, he has no right to question any witness," Jacques objected.

"You do not need to cite the prohibition against counsel or defense for those accused of felonies to me, sir," Porter said sharply.

Rachael leaned forward and grasped the rough wooden edges of the bench in front of her, her heart torn by the pain so evident on the faces of both Falconer brothers. A strong arm slipped around her, and she glanced up with gratitude at The Dane, whose face was creased with worry.

She followed his gaze and realized he was engaged in silent communication with Sebastién. Sebastién very deliberately shook his head. The Dane looked incredulous, even angry, and Sebastién reinforced his message with a quick, definite shake of his head. Some faces in the crowd that had been animated with purpose took on expressions of dismay.

"He refuses to save himself," The Dane muttered under his breath. "He believes escape is an admission of guilt."

"He will not allow Jacques the satisfaction of being able to say he sought escape because he was guilty," Rachael said. "He will have this out, no matter what it costs him."

The Dane glanced at her in surprise, and then nodded in agreement. "Few understand him so well," he remarked. "But if one brother dies, so will the other."

Rachael shuddered. Abandoning her seat beside The Dane, she quietly moved to the front of the hall where she would be closer to Sebastién.

Porter warned Emerald that any further outburst would result in punishment, and added in a low voice that Sebastién would be allowed to question the youth.

Jacques's reluctance to yield the floor to his brother

was palpable as he sank into a chair and folded his arms across his chest when Sebastién stood.

Leg chains scraped the floor when Sebastién cautiously approached Emerald. The boy's eyes narrowed as Sebastién limped clumsily in his direction.

"Do you recall the first time we met?" Sebastién inquired.

Emerald frowned as he picked at the rough cuticle of his thumb until blood pooled around the nail.

Sebastién crouched until he was at eye level with the boy. "One would think your first encounter with such a bloody villain as I would have left a lasting impression upon you," he said.

Rachael heard the sarcasm and barely controlled fury in his voice, but she still jumped in reaction when he suddenly slammed his fist down upon the bench next to Emerald's chained thigh. The boy quaked and his upper lip drew back.

"You would do well to search your memory, *enfant terrible*," Sebastién warned in a gravelly voice. "Mine may be the last face you see in this life. It is likely that we will hang together."

"There is one difference between us," Emerald said. "You are afraid to die. I am not."

Sebastién was left momentarily speechless. He considered the boy, a mixture of pity and disgust on his face.

"Perhaps," he softly conceded. "But I have the courage

to tell the truth." He leaned toward Emerald. "Do you?" He straightened and moved a distance away, the pale eyes following him. "My guess is that you and Simon have been promised your lives," Sebastién said, tone casual. "But was anything said about freedom? After all your splendid cooperation, will you still be led away in chains and kept in a cage for the rest of your life?"

Emerald cast a wary look at Jacques, who languished in his chair, face turned away from the youngster's perceptive gaze.

"No matter what you say here, your fate will be the same," Sebastién said. "You have nothing to gain by lying. I think you know that."

Emerald's eyes traveled over the crowd and fixed upon Rachael, who had taken a seat in the front row. She looked back at him without flinching, her face taut with tension.

"Then I will tell the truth," he said simply, with an apathetic shrug. He sighed and looked directly at Sebastién, eyes half-closed as if against painful light.

Sebastién glanced over his shoulder at Jacques, who leaned forward in his seat with a look of alarm on his face.

Chapter Twenty-Three

W ho led the wreckers?" Sebastién asked.

"Victor." Emerald said the first name as if the last was unnecessary. "Brightmore," he added in a bored tone, when the crowd continued to look at him eagerly. Emerald smirked at Sebastién's dumbfounded expression. "I thought you wanted the truth."

Emerald spilled secrets with the same élan he had spilled blood. He had seen the ledger, and confirmed that Sebastién had never been part of the gang of wreckers. Victor's interest in Falconer had been as a scapegoat, and as the man who would eliminate his niece for him.

Sebastién's jaw tightened in anger when Emerald related how Victor had channeled the Frenchman's wrath toward Rachael. The tip that resulted in the arrests at Prussia Cove had been Victor's doing. He had been delighted to learn that Jacques Falconer's intended bride had been aboard a ship they had wrecked. It had added fuel to fire the hatred between the brothers, and directed suspicion away from him.

Jacques's chair scraped the floor when he came to his feet with a shouted objection.

"The ravings of a madman!" Jacques exclaimed. "We may as well move these proceedings to Bedlam!"

"He was your witness only moments ago," Sebastién reminded his brother. "He was credible then, *non?*"

"He's the lowest form of criminal," Jacques balked. "No doubt he's been paid for his aid."

"Do you really wish to discuss bribes?" Emerald asked him in a low, nasty voice. Jacques grilled him with a look of loathing, and Emerald smiled. "Didn't think so."

"What of the other charges?" Jacques asked Porter. "Do we assume he is innocent of all charges simply because the boy lied about the wreckings to spite me?"

"Of course not," Porter replied. He looked at Sebastién. "Will you admit to smuggling, sir?" he inquired.

"Admit to running tea and spirits? *Oui,*" Sebastién readily agreed. "I do not deny smuggling. I have already been punished for it. The record will show that my ship, cargo, and crew were seized as payment."

"It does not serve justice to punish a man twice for the same crime," Porter said thoughtfully. "Unless, of course, you've committed new offenses."

Sebastién had not had the opportunity to smuggle one pound of tea, one bolt of lace, or one barrel of brandy since meeting Rachael.

"*Non*," he earnestly admitted. "I've been too busy."

Laughter rippled through the crowd. Porter suppressed a smile, jowls broadening with the effort.

"There is still the matter of the kidnap and murder of a child," Jacques interjected with desperation.

"Not true! The child he speaks of is my brother," Rachael declared.

Sebastién whirled around, startled by the nearness of her voice. The chains tinkled in a gentle reverberation of movement.

"My brother is alive. He was not abducted or harmed by this man." She looked at Jacques. "If only you had read the ledger," she told him. "One day, you will realize what you have tried to do, and it will destroy you. What you are attempting here is murder."

"I challenge the integrity of this witness," Jacques said loudly. "She has spent most of her time in my brother's company. And, no doubt, in his bed."

The crowd tittered, and Rachael flushed in embarrassment.

Sebastién leaned toward Jacques with a look of entreaty on his face. "I saved your life earlier," he said. "I do not ask you to spare mine, only that you do not cheapen Miss Penrose in front of this crowd. Leave her out of this, and I will not oppose you."

"No!" Rachael protested. "My silence will not be the instrument your brother uses to destroy you."

Jacques frowned, and his eyes searched his brother's face. He nodded in agreement.

"May I be permitted to speak, your lordship?"

Rachael cringed at the familiar voice and turned to face the back of the hall. The tall, sandy-haired man brought a flood of unpleasant memories of dank, musty cells, draughts laced with bitter substances, and threats of death.

Elliot Macaulay kept his eyes averted. His hands twisted the cocked hat he held as Phillip Morgan roughly hauled him forward by the front of his cape.

Morgan addressed Porter directly. "Your lordship, please pardon my untimely entrance. I would have arrived sooner, but I've been tracking this ignoble coward."

"I will excuse the interruption if you've come to shed light on this case," Porter replied.

Elliott stood before Porter with his head bowed.

"My son, Tarry, and I recently came into possession of property belonging to Victor Brightmore," Phillip said.

Phillip produced a paper and waved it before the crowd. "My solicitor has prepared an itemized list." He turned to Porter. "Brightmore owned a set of Customs seals that lack sanction and authenticity. His home concealed illegal goods. He kept a ledger that supports the conclusion that it was he and not Sebastién Falconer who led the wreckers."

Sebastién stared at Phillip's narrow back as Morgan

told of having read the letter Elliott wrote to Victor detailing Victor's plan to murder Rachael and James, and Elliott's participation in having Rachael committed to Bedlam.

Jacques leaned back in his chair and closed his eyes. When Phillip paused, he opened his eyes and looked at Porter as if trying to gauge his mood.

"Can you produce the letter?" Porter asked.

"I can do better," Phillip blithely replied. "I can produce its author."

It took no more than being pointed out before the crowd to provoke a confession from Elliott.

"Yes, it's true that Victor planned to do away with his niece and nephew. Rachael was confined to Bedlam while Victor tried to work out a way to be rid of them both without attracting suspicion. He could not use poison after she revealed Victor's plot to young Morgan."

"This has nothing to do with the Frenchman's crimes," Jacques objected.

"Victor kept meticulous records." Elliot sniffed. "You have only to read the ledger for yourself."

Jacques tugged at his cravat, as if he suddenly found the room oppressive. Rachael shook her head at the irony. He would not dare admit to having destroyed the ledger.

Porter leaned forward, his brown eyes bright. "We can no longer dispute the existence of the ledger when so many claim to have seen it," he said. "I am tempted to suspend these proceedings until the ledger can be found."

Rachael heard Sebastién's shocked intake of breath as Phillip Morgan reentered the hall, trailed by Eleanor, who held an infant in her arms.

Sebastién took a faltering step toward his mother and stopped. He was angry, so angry that his eyes glittered and his lean jaw tightened with wrath. Rachael grasped his arm and he started at the contact, eyes drawn from his mother. He blinked and placed an arm around her, as if to absorb her calm.

"Give James to his sister," he said coldly. "I'll not see him abandoned in some back alley." Eleanor obeyed, her grim face as white as parchment.

"Sebastién," Rachael soothed, "please try to understand how difficult this is for her."

"One kind act does not mitigate the past and she knows it."

"If that is what you believe, then thank God I was not raised by Hugh Falconer," Jacques said.

"Had you been mine to rear, you would have been drowned in infancy," a stern, authoritative voice bellowed from the back of the hall.

"*Grand-père*." Sebastién greeted Hugh Falconer with a respectful inclination of his head.

Hugh Falconer was a striking man. His coloring

was as stark and vivid as his personality. Cotton white hair framed his sun-darkened face, and his eyes were more green than blue. A square jaw alluded to an obstinate nature and white, even teeth made him look more feral than friendly. His small, upturned nose was lost amid the wrinkled terrain of his face.

He was tall and slender, with a wiry build. The handsome black riding suit he wore was outlined by a generous amount of gold braid, lending his appearance a stringent, military air.

Rachael might have escaped his notice entirely had it not been for Sebastién's arm placed possessively around her waist. Hugh's eyes clouded with contempt as they raked over her.

"You're not the first Frenchman to be tempted by ripe English fruit," Hugh told him. "Was she worth it?"

"Rachael had no part in this," Sebastién replied.

"Rachael . . . Penrose?" Hugh guessed.

Hugh's eyes moved over her again and she was glad Sebastién had not withdrawn the support of his arm. His rasping cackle was barely a laugh. "Were you aware that your English whore works for Customs?" She felt the arm around her flex and tense. "Oh, do you prefer that I speak in French?" Hugh asked.

"If you are going to insult her, I would prefer that you not speak at all."

"She has helped to ruin you."

"I am not ruined," Sebastién replied. "Close to

hanging, perhaps, but the Falconer legend will only be enhanced by an execution. That should please you."

"There will be no justice for you in this court," Hugh charged in a gravelly voice. "Your accuser was raised on the right knee of England!"

"You do not aid my cause," Sebastién warned, indicating the miffed-looking Porter with a shallow nod of his head.

Hugh seemed to notice the judge for the first time. He dipped into his vest pocket and withdrew a creased piece of parchment as he approached the bench. He handed the worn paper to Porter.

Porter frowned as he adjusted his spectacles, unfolded the paper, and read the message scrawled upon it. He looked up in surprise, glanced over at Simon, and then returned his attention to the paper.

Hugh crossed the room and rejoined his grandson.

"Some blackguard named Simon demanded a ransom for you. If I had not seen a posted notice of your trial, you would have been executed before I could learn of your predicament."

Sebastién's brows drew downward as a frown creased his forehead and he looked at Simon, who slowly reddened under his steady, incensed regard.

"You intended to collect a ransom for me?"

"Victor told us to kill you," Simon explained. "I promised a share of the ransom to any man who would cross Victor and deliver a ransom note. We did not expect you to escape."

Emerald tugged at the bloodied cuticle of his thumb. "We did not expect you to *live*," he archly disclosed. He laughed in response to Simon's glare of warning.

Simon appealed to Hugh. "I sought only to spare your grandson's life," he said.

"*Menteur*," Sebastién spat. "Liar!"

"Have you any other witnesses?" Porter inquired of Jacques.

Jacques's gaze swept over Simon and Emerald. He sighed. "My witnesses are from the rogues' gallery," he said. "If they disagree, which one of them will you believe?" He shrugged. "I'm not sure what *I* believe at this point," he said.

"Your brother expects to be exonerated," Porter said.

"*Oui*," Sebastién staunchly concurred.

"What remains, then, is a question of the degree of guilt supported by the evidence," Porter said. He glanced over at Sebastién. "Will anyone speak for you, sir?"

Rachael looked up at Sebastién, but he resolutely shook his head. His eyes settled on The Dane, who still waited for the signal Sebastién would not give. He turned back to Porter.

"*Non*," he said.

Rachael groaned, and The Dane mouthed an obscenity as a flush of annoyance crept over his fair skin. Desperate, she looked to Eleanor, whose eyes rested on her son with a look of entreaty.

"Could she really be so different from the woman

you knew as Mrs. Faraday?" Rachael whispered.

Sebastién's arm tightened around her, and she felt tension vibrate through his frame as he held her. He drew a deep breath and released it slowly. "Perhaps my housekeeper will speak," he said.

Eleanor stepped forward, only to be restrained by Phillip's hand.

"Porter knows you," Phillip cautioned. "You cannot present yourself as his housekeeper. If Porter believes you are attempting to deceive him, your son will suffer the consequences."

"The housekeeper will come forward." Porter scanned the crowd with an impatient scowl.

Eleanor looked at Phillip in alarm.

"You cannot present yourself as his housekeeper!" Phillip urged again in a low voice.

"Perhaps not," Eleanor replied, "but I *can* truthfully claim to be his mother!" She slipped past Phillip with a determined set to her jaw.

Hugh stared as Eleanor came forward and gasped in outrage when she stated her name, complexion suddenly as white as his hair.

"I don't fear you any longer, Hugh," Eleanor told him. "You've already done your worst to me by stealing my son." She turned her attention to Porter, effectively dismissing Hugh. "Sebastién Falconer is my son," Eleanor told Porter. "His father was Henri Falconer of Marseilles."

"I cannot consider you an unbiased witness," Porter

said gently. "You *are*, after all, his mother."

"She is no mother to him," Hugh spat. "She is here to dishonor the Falconer name!"

Phillip took an angry step toward Hugh, but Sebastién thrust out an arm to forestall him, the length of chain dangling noisily from his wrists. He was intent upon the exchange between his mother and grandfather.

Hugh spun toward the judge with an indignant scowl.

"This is a private matter," he said. "I will not shake my family tree while English peasants sit beneath it."

"One might suspect you have something to hide, *Grand-père*," Sebastién said in a deceptively light tone.

"Your son wishes to hear how you murdered his father," Hugh said coldly.

Eleanor drew a sharp breath and gaped at Hugh.

"What lies have you told him?" She saw that Sebastién waited. "I was barely seventeen when I met your father. I was enchanted with Henri," she recalled with a wistful smile. "He was quite charming."

"It was a mistake to allow him to visit England," Hugh muttered. "Henri would be alive today if not for the Englishwoman he married against my advice."

"You told me she murdered my father," Sebastién reminded Hugh. "You have never told me how he died."

Eleanor's luminous gray eyes grew dull and her face twisted with emotion.

"I understand your hatred of me now," she told

Sebastién. Her chin lifted. "I would never have harmed your father, Sebastién. I loved him."

"She may not have plunged a dagger into his heart," Hugh put in, "but she barred the physician from the room when Henri needed treatment. My son might have lived."

"Who made such a claim? Fantlereau himself?" Eleanor challenged. "If so, the miracle was promised *after* the patient died!"

Eleanor held up her hands in frustration at the condemnation in Sebastién's expression. "Your grandfather would have you believe I coldly resisted treatment for Henri, but that is not so." She ignored Hugh's disparaging snort. "Henri had been thrown from his horse and then trampled by the beast. His injuries were so terrible that Fantlereau, Hugh's physician, was called."

"Fantlereau was a student of Fagan," Hugh added.

"But he did not have the skill of the King's personal physician," Eleanor argued. "Fantlereau sought favor by courting members of the French aristocracy. I learned his true nature when I found myself fending off his advances after Henri's accident, and he dared to suggest that I would soon be a widow. He was cruel, ambitious, and dangerously inept." She turned her attention to Sebastién. "He bled Henri. Henri was badly injured from the fall, and the bloodletting only weakened him more. Fantlereau would have continued to bleed him, but I locked Fantlereau out of the chamber because he was only adding to Henri's suffering. Your grandfather has always blamed me for his death."

"I had envisioned sinister figures grasping daggers or poisoned goblets of wine," Sebastién said in a flat voice.

"Ignorance and greed killed your father," Eleanor said softly. "Not I."

Sebastién nodded, frowning. He studied his mother for a moment, started to speak, and then stopped himself. Rachael reached out and clasped his hand, and his gaze quickly returned to his mother. "Why did you abandon me?" he blurted.

"Hugh never stopped blaming me for Henri's death. I was sick with grief and left alone with two babies in a hostile household in a foreign land."

As she struggled to frame a reply, Hugh drew a chair aside and sat down stiffly. The gold braid trim of his coat caught the weak light as it filtered through an adjacent window, molding him in a pale outline.

"I decided to take my children and return home to England. It was a plan made in secret with the aid of Jeanette, one of the maids who had befriended me."

"They conspired to steal my grandsons from me!" Hugh accused.

"How was it that you left France with only Jacques?" Sebastién asked.

"You were taken from me," Eleanor said.

"*Non*, you were rescued!" Hugh amended.

"Allow her to tell it," Sebastién said curtly.

Hugh reacted as though his grandson had struck

him. His mouth worked, but no sound escaped.

"We fled one night after everyone had gone to bed. Jeanette's husband, Paul, had arranged for a small boat. Jeanette carried you and I carried Jacques. We left minutes apart. I reached the boat with Jacques, and waited for Jeanette to bring you.

"Suddenly, I heard Jeanette screaming as she came running toward me with you in her arms. Hugh followed her on horseback, lashing out at her with his riding crop. I will never forget the sight of Jeanette trying to protect my child from a whip wielded by his own grandfather."

"I would not have harmed my grandson," Hugh said diffidently. "Not so his mother, or her conspirators."

The look that passed between Hugh and Eleanor left no doubt in Rachael's mind that Eleanor had risked her life that night.

"When Jeanette fell, she rolled to protect you from the hooves of the horse. I watched as Hugh snatched you up like some prize from the hunt. He was laughing.

"Hugh rode toward us brandishing that terrible whip. I fought Paul as he lifted me into the boat. I vowed I would not leave without you. We struggled, and I fell and struck my head." She pushed back her soft gray hair, revealing a small scar. "I do not remember the voyage, or even being removed from the boat in England."

"How long was it before you remembered me? Was I struck from your memory as well?"

"You were all I thought about!" Eleanor protested. "As

soon as we arrived in England, I asked a friend in France to look for you. Your grandfather was clever and powerful, and there were too many places to hide you. You were in Marseilles, then Bordeaux, then Montpellier, then Paris, then Toulon," Eleanor recalled. "As soon as I learned where to find you, Hugh moved you again. I was always a step behind."

A look of comprehension crossed Sebastién's face and was swiftly replaced by anger.

"Summer in Saint Brieuc, spring in Saint Quentin, fall in Foix, winter in Wassy. You used to make a game of it, eh, *Grand-père*? I saw more of France in my childhood than most adults see in a lifetime. Was I the doted-upon grandson or the pawn in your game of revenge?"

Rachael pictured him as a child, shuttled from one region of France to another as Hugh plotted to keep him out of Eleanor's reach. He grew up believing his mother had abandoned him. The man who had raised him was cold and demanding, and she was the only person with whom he shared a relationship of any depth.

"I traveled throughout France until I was eight years of age, and then I stopped traveling," Sebastién said carefully. "Grandfather summoned me home to Marseilles. I remained in Marseilles until I was sixteen."

His tormented expression clearly asked his mother, *Where were you during all that time?*

"She claims she could not find you!" Hugh chortled. Sebastién's jaw tightened in reaction to the taunt.

"Just before your seventh birthday, I received word

that you had died of a fever," Eleanor said. "The news came from the same man who had searched for you all those years and claimed he could not find you. I learned much later that he had been in your grandfather's employ. I was told your remains had been placed in the family vault, and that I was banned from the property. I would not be allowed to visit your grave."

She turned to Porter. "I was stunned to discover my son was alive, but even more shocked to learn of the crimes he had supposedly committed. I am the housekeeper," she confessed. "I deceived my son because I wanted to discover what sort of man he had become. I learned that he is a good man. I only wish I had been able to change the circumstances of his upbringing," she added, with a hate-filled glare directed at Hugh. "It saddens me to see where his grandfather's influence has led him."

"All families have bones to rattle within their closets," Porter said. "And England has privateers of all flags in her gaols. The concern I have is that your son may commit future crimes against England in the name of France, particularly now when there is tension between our two countries."

"You will execute him just because he is French!"

"Hugh, be quiet," Eleanor snapped.

"You will be silent, or I will have you removed," Porter warned Hugh ignoring his outraged glower. "If I am to consider leniency, I must be convinced that the accused is not a threat to England."

Chapter Twenty-Four

Rachael felt the brief snatch and slide of Sebastién's fingers on her gown as he tried to stop her from approaching Porter and failed.

"What if he were to become a loyal subject of Queen Anne?" she proposed. "He has already been punished for smuggling. His mother and brother are both English subjects."

When Porter seemed to consider the idea, Sebastién came to his feet amid a thunderous rattle of chain. "*Non*," he said emphatically. "*Non*, I could not. *Non*," he repeated, shaken by the proposal. His jaw had gone slack, and his eyes were wide with incredulity.

"There is no pain involved in the process," Jacques assured him. His expression hinted at a suppressed smile.

"*Non*," Sebastién persisted, horrified. He looked at Rachael in dismay.

"If I am willing to risk my reputation to spare your life and restore your freedom, then you must be willing to make some sacrifices, as well," Porter cautioned.

"You ask me to denounce . . . everything."

"No justice," Hugh shouted.

"I ask you to embrace a new country. Men before you have done it."

"Impossible," Sebastién insisted. "I was born a Frenchman. I will die one."

"That is my point, young man," Porter replied, exasperated. "As a known French privateer, you very likely *will* die one."

"I have been divided between France and England all my life," Sebastién told Porter. He indicated Hugh, Eleanor, and Jacques with a sweep of his hand. "They will bid me do their will until I have no will of my own."

He snaked his arm through the lengths of chain and grasped Rachael's hand. "This young English girl has given me the only acceptance I have ever known. You cannot imagine what she has endured for my sake, and yet she remains at my side. She is my country. I would not be parted from her, unless it is by death."

While Porter had admired the young Frenchman's poise throughout the trial, he now regretted his stubbornness. He had enjoyed the challenge of ferreting out the facts of the case, just as his friend Phillip Morgan had known he would.

Porter preferred justice to power plays. Evidence,

rather than influence, should vindicate an innocent man. He would not have absolved Falconer of guilt on the basis of a plea from Morgan; such indiscretions had toppled men from loftier positions than the one he held.

He had quietly threatened Jacques's bribed judge with exposure and then installed himself as the man's replacement. It was a move that went uncontested, given Porter's considerable wealth, his personal connections, and his blood ties to Queen Anne.

He did not regret the deception he had undertaken; the subterfuge had been necessary to get at the truth. He had approached Rachael in the guise of a priest because men of the cloth often had access to information judges did not.

It had been a high stakes gamble for him, and he had wagered on the Frenchman's integrity. Falconer could have fled England despite the risks, leaving him to explain his unorthodox handling of a reputedly dangerous prisoner.

He had placed Rachael at dead center of a dilemma. Other than an infant brother, she was left with no family, and Falconer had no country. She loved the Frenchman; that much was obvious. But Falconer was unwilling to accept the English side of his heritage, and his upbringing had made him an enemy of England. They would never find peace in England or France.

Porter smiled as a solution occurred to him.

"There is another option," he said.

Tarry had borrowed a strange contraption from the late Henry Winstanley's collection of inventions, a chair mounted upon a set of wheels. The vehicle allowed him to leave the confines of his sickbed, and he was amazed by the ease with which he navigated the gangplank of the ship.

He wheeled by Rachael with a cursory greeting and his eyes swept the deck, a look of determination on his face. Spying Sebastién, he began to work the wheels of the chair briskly, his movement across the timber of the weather deck aided by the gentle swell of the sea.

"We need to talk," he informed the Frenchman. When Sebastién moved to aid him with the chair, he held up his hands. "I am quite capable," he said as he gripped the wheels. Sebastién nodded and followed him into an area behind a bulkhead. "So, you've gone and gotten yourself transported," Tarry said gruffly.

Sebastién nodded and smiled slightly. "Better than hanging, wouldn't you agree?"

"Yes, I suppose so," Tarry admitted. He paused. "And you're taking Rachael with you."

"I'm not abducting her this time, if that's what you mean," Sebastién said. "You can ask her yourself."

Tarry's eyes strayed to where Rachael stood on deck, engrossed in conversation with Phillip and Eleanor. He glanced back at Sebastién, clearing his throat and impatiently knuckling the moisture from his eyes as the Frenchman suddenly took an undue interest in the construction of the bulkhead.

"I will take good care of her," Sebastién promised.

Tarry cleared his throat again. "See that you do," he said sternly.

The silence that followed was strained. Finally, he drew himself up proudly in the chair and faced Sebastién squarely.

"I guess the better man won, then," he said. When Sebastién looked puzzled, Tarry nodded his head in Rachael's direction. "We never really were rivals, were we?"

Sebastién placed his hand on Tarry's shoulder. "She loved you first. I could never compete with that."

"But she loves you now. And she never loved me the way she loves you."

"You have only yourself to blame," Sebastién said.

Tarry shook his head. "I don't understand."

"You saved my life at the lighthouse, and you and your father saved me from hanging. You've had more than one opportunity to rid yourself of a rival."

"You didn't skewer me on the beach. Humiliated me, yes, but allowed to me to live. I felt I owed you."

"You have been a worthy opponent, in all things," Sebastién said. His eyes swept over the chair and the young man who occupied it. "The better man did not prevail," Sebastién told him. "The luckier one did."

Tarry smiled. He leaned back in the chair and

dipped one thin arm into his coat pocket withdrawing a small case he handed to Sebastién.

"Open it."

The black velvet box popped open under the gentle pressure of Sebastién's thumb and forefinger. A deep purple amethyst ring mounted in white gold reposed in a circle of black satin.

"This is so sudden," Sebastién quipped, resorting to humor to conceal his surprise. "We hardly know each other."

"Amethyst is Rachael's birthstone," Tarry explained. "Under the circumstances, I doubted you'd had the opportunity to visit a jeweler."

"They don't usually bring their wares to the gaol," Sebastién agreed.

He looked at Sebastién sharply. "You do intend to marry her, don't you?"

"If she will have me."

"She damn sure will," Tarry said. "I told her that in no event would she undertake a journey to the colonies without the protection of a husband."

"Oh, you did, did you?" Sebastién grinned and glanced at Rachael. She was looking their way with great interest. "What did she say?"

"She said in that case, if you didn't ask her soon, she would marry the first seaman who proposed to her."

Sebastién tossed the ring into the air and caught it without missing a beat then startled Tarry by seizing his hand and shaking it vigorously.

"*Merci*," he shouted to Tarry over his shoulder as he crossed the deck toward Rachael with purposeful strides.

The motion of the ship was soothing as it rocked in harmony with the gentle swell of the sea. Rachael stood on deck, looking at the shore where those who had come to bid them farewell still stood, watching as the great craft made its way out to sea. The individual most easily distinguishable from this distance was The Dane, who stood waving vigorously.

She heard the tap of footsteps on the planks behind her and spun around, smiling as Sebastién made his way to her.

"James is sleeping . . . like a baby," he informed her.

She laughed. The sound transformed his face, causing his eyes to brighten and the faint lines around his mouth to ease. He stood beside her, waving at The Dane as the shore of England continued to recede from view.

"Did you all have code names?" she asked.

"What?"

"The Frenchman, The Dane . . ."

Sebastién's shoulders shook with laughter. "No member of my gang ever called me 'The Frenchman,' at least not to my face. That was your term for me when you were angry."

"What about The Dane? That must have been a code name."

He erupted into laughter again.

"What?" She was on the verge of laughing in response to the comical expression on his face.

"The truth may disappoint you, *ma chérie*, but the reason most of us called him The Dane was because we could not pronounce his real name."

"Oh." The disappointment in her voice prompted him to laugh again, and he hugged her as she waved toward the shore.

"What do you think America will be like?" she whispered.

"Unlike France or England, I would expect," he replied. "I have never been to the colonies. Most of the men I have known who ventured there did not return."

She pulled a face. "That is either very encouraging, or terrifying."

He chuckled. "I think it is a good sign," he said reassuringly, as he folded an arm around her and drew her against him. "Porter is a fair man."

Rachael nodded in agreement. Porter might have sentenced him to death or to long imprisonment, but instead he had offered him a new life. If he had simply freed him, there would be those who might suspect that Sebastién had informed on them to save himself, and he would face certain jeopardy.

The kindly judge had recognized his torn loyalties and had suggested a solution that promised to free him from the past as well as assure him of a future of his own design. Even Jacques Falconer had supported Porter's decision. Jacques had even recommended that Sebastién be put aboard a ship bound for the colonies as a free man rather than as a transported prisoner of England.

Hugh had been strongly opposed to the idea of transport, but had ceased opposition after Porter had warned that under no circumstances would his grandson be allowed to return to France.

"Will you miss France terribly?" she asked softly.

"No more than you will miss England."

"It is a pity that you could not stay to see your mother married to Phillip Morgan."

"I care only about my own wedding. It cannot come soon enough!" he added, with a warm glint in his eye. He took her hand and studied the deep purple of the amethyst ring she wore. "Morgan will be furious when he learns you refused my proposal."

"I did not refuse you! I only said I would not marry you in England. I can think of no better beginning for us than to be wed in the colonies, in our new home. We will be neither French, nor English there!"

Sebastién looked at her. "*Non,*" he said after a moment of contemplation. "You will always be my beautiful English girl."

Rachael turned once more to watch the coast of England as it faded from view. It slowly became no more than a distant spot upon the horizon, and with its gradual disappearance came the certainty that life with Sebastién Falconer held a promise of love and adventure.

Author's Note

The Great Storm of 1703

"No pen could describe it, nor tongue express it, nor thought conceive it unless by one in the extremity of it."
—Daniel Defoe

The southern part of Britain was devastated by the most catastrophic storm it had experienced in five-hundred years on November 26–27, 1703. Believed to be a revitalized Atlantic hurricane, the storm began as a series of gales earlier in November, and brought with it a prolonged period of unseasonably warm weather, and high seas.

A warm front from the hurricane moved from the West Indies, traveled along the coast of Florida, and swept into the Atlantic prior to reaching England. The warm front collided with cold air, creating wind speeds estimated at over 120 miles per hour, and establishing conditions for a tempest that would peak during a six- to eight-hour period beginning at midnight on November 26. Although very little rain was reported, strong winds and a North Sea surge elevated tides by nearly eight feet, causing severe flooding.

There was significant loss of life. On land in England and Wales alone, collapsing roofs and chimneys killed more than one-hundred and twenty people, and injured more than two-hundred. Eighty more were drowned in marshland cottages surrounding the Severn Estuary.

Those at sea during the storm fared even worse. It is estimated that between eight-thousand and fifteen-thousand people lost their lives along the coast and in over one-hundred reported shipwrecks at sea.

Britain was at war and three fleets were assembled to aid the King of Spain against the French. By dawn, the majority of the vessels were destroyed, and fifteen-hundred seamen had lost their lives. Twelve warships with thirteen-hundred men were lost while still within sight of land. On the Thames, hundreds of ships were driven into each other in the Pool, the section downstream from London Bridge.

The Eddystone Lighthouse, in the direct path of the storm when the hurricane was at its most powerful, was destroyed. Its designer and builder, Henry Winstanley, was working on the structure at the time, and he was swept away with his creation.

No segment of the population was untouched. It was reported that Queen Anne stood at a window and watched as the trees in St. James's Park were violently uprooted by the force of the wind. She was forced to take refuge in a cellar when falling chimney stacks and a partial roof collapse damaged St. James Palace. The bodies of the bishop of Bath and Wells and his sister were discovered amid the ruins of their palace.

Property losses estimated at £6 million exceeded the £4 million loss suffered as a result of the Great Fire of London in 1666. In and around London alone, two-thousand chimney stacks were blown down, and over a hundred church steeples in the capital were damaged.

The heavy lead lining on the roof of Westminster Abbey was lifted and tossed some distance from the building.

All over southern England, streets were covered with tiles and slates. Rural village causeways and paved London roads alike were buried in slates and tiles from demolished buildings; even on hard ground they amassed to a depth of as much as eight inches. More than eight-hundred houses were blown away or destroyed by the collapse of a central chimney stack. The majority of the houses left standing were partly or completely stripped of roof tiles.

Windmills, common structures at the time, were particularly vulnerable. More than four-hundred windmills were destroyed. Many burned to the ground after their cloth sails rotated at such speed that friction led to fire.

Millions of trees were uprooted or damaged. In the county of Kent, over a thousand barns and outhouses were destroyed. There were reports of men and animals being lifted into the air by the force of the wind. Tens of thousands of sheep and cattle were lost.

Restoration would prove to be slow and costly. The day following the storm, in one of the first recorded instances of price gouging, the price of tiles jumped from twenty-one shillings per thousand to one-hundred and twenty shillings per thousand. English merchants were hard-pressed to keep a ready supply on hand; many had suffered the loss of company ships whose cargo holds had been burgeoning with goods.

The storm would remain in the collective consciousness of the British people as "The Great Storm" for many years to come.

Be in the know on the latest
Medallion Press news by becoming a
Medallion Press Insider!
<u>As an Insider you'll receive:</u>

• Our FREE expanded monthly newsletter, giving you more insight into Medallion Press

• Advanced press releases and breaking news

• Greater access to all of your favorite Medallion authors

Joining is easy, just visit our Web site at
<u>www.medallionpress.com</u> and click on the Medallion
Press Insider tab.

Want to know what's going on with
your favorite author or what new releases
are coming from Medallion Press?

Now you can receive breaking news,
updates, and more from Medallion Press
straight to your cell phone, e-mail, instant messenger, or
Facebook!

Sign up now at <u>www.twitter.com/MedallionPress</u> to stay on
top of all the happenings in and
around Medallion Press.

For more information
about other great titles from
Medallion Press, visit

m e d a l l i o n p r e s s . c o m